MW01166082

Jill Piscitello

ISBN: 978-1-68046-985-1

Published by Satin Romance
An Imprint of Melange Books, LLC
White Bear Lake, MN 55110
www.satinromance.com

Published in the United States of America.

Cover Design by Ashley Redbird Designs

For Rob, Kaelie, and Anthony

CHAPTER 1

C ricket stifled an involuntary gag at the sight of the balled-up sheets in the corner. Visible stains made it clear that they were the source of the stench. Her eyes watered, and she wondered if she was supposed to do something with them, or if someone else would come and exchange them for new ones. The bed was completely bare—one bunk bed for three people. She and Max slept on the bottom bunk, and Ashling took the top.

Better than no bed, she supposed.

The kids hadn't said much since they had arrived a week ago. She assumed they were in shock. December had just begun, and this was the last place she wanted to be with her family as the Christmas season got underway. She couldn't envision a less festive place to spend the holidays than a homeless shelter.

No way to sugarcoat it, far as she could see: They'd be here for a while, so they better get used to it. Cricket figured it didn't make much sense to stand around staring at the depressing sight any more than necessary and herded everyone out to the dining hall with hopes of finding someone to help remedy the bedding situation.

Scanning the crowded tables, she wished they could grab trays and head back to their room, but that wasn't allowed. This meant

Max would eat absolutely nothing. She'd once again be forced to hide his sandwich and a cookie in her pocketbook and encourage him to eat it later. Her mop headed six-year-old picked at his food in the best circumstances. He was more than reluctant to try what they served here.

After sitting down in three recently vacated seats with their full trays, Cricket scooped a forkful of bland mashed potatoes into her mouth. Ashling nibbled at her meatloaf and green beans. Mature for her thirteen years, she knew better than to complain about the food on her plate.

Although the meal lacked taste, it was the thought of staying here that Cricket couldn't stomach. They hadn't left much behind, but it had been theirs.

They certainly hadn't been ousted from a palace. The freezer had housed a full-blown sanctuary of cockroaches, for crying out loud. However, the place had had a small kitchen, a living room where Cricket slept, a bedroom for Ashling, and another for Max (though it had technically been a closet). Despite its obvious shortcomings, it had been home. For years, they celebrated birthdays, holidays, and life in general in that apartment.

Cricket's appetite evaporated as her eyes scanned the packed room, and she reflected on her two choices: Allow herself to be swallowed up in despair or make do with what they had and try to move forward. She had been struggling to choose the moving forward option, but no one was looking to hire someone without references. The supermarket didn't want her. The convenience store didn't need any help. The local fast food restaurants didn't even want her cleaning their toilets. Hard not to take that personally.

She stared at her daughter's half eaten plate, willing her to finish up. The common room television beckoned. The same channel with family friendly programs seemed to be on every night, but Cricket couldn't care less. The kids were entertained, and she was spared from hearing the questions that were growing more and more impossible to answer.

The next morning greeted Cricket with a wave of exhaustion. Max had developed a high fever overnight. With substantial effort, she dragged herself out of bed and shuffled to the restroom. One glance in the mirror sufficiently quenched any curiosity regarding her appearance. A shadow of a woman who'd once been pretty stared back at her, with prominent cheekbones that had become angular. Once delicate features turned sharp due to weight loss. Her appetite always disappeared when stress took over. The dull, lank hair dusting her shoulders no longer held a hint of shine. She swept away the stringy pieces falling into her eyes.

Although she struggled to keep it together, panic set in as she joined Max on the bunk. He needed to be seen by a doctor. Cricket carried his scalding, lethargic body out of their room and surveyed the facility for help. As she considered the possibility of obtaining a voucher for a taxi, Cari Montgomery, one of the shelter volunteers, breezed through the front door unbuttoning her coat. Her skin glowed, scrubbed clean of any make-up. Her auburn hair had been pulled back off her face to reveal a flawless complexion. Jeans and a vibrant pink cheetah print cardigan complimented her figure. Although her smile was slightly crooked, it grew to a mile wide when she spotted Cricket. Unlike everyone else zipping around the dining room, Cari hadn't had a chance to dive into the breakfast routine yet.

More than a little quirky, and always sweet with a quick smile, Cari had quickly become one of Cricket's favorite people in this dreary place over the past week. It was well known that she had recently inherited a popular farm and orchard. Another person would have dodged Max with his endless questions about honeybees, but Cari encouraged his curiosity.

Cricket held her breath as she approached. Limitations often restricted what volunteers could do regarding expenses. As Cricket described Max's symptoms, Cari nervously tucked a stray strand of hair behind one ear, feebly attempting to reassure her by cracking a joke about kids making it their job to get sick.

Cricket didn't find the humor in that and ignored the effort to cheer her up. "Do you know if there are any transportation vouchers available?" she asked. "I've tried everything, but this fever won't break, and it's over one hundred and four."

"You don't need a voucher. I'll take you. Get what you need, and I'll find Ashling."

Cricket gathered up their few belongings and, within a half hour, they sat in the waiting room of a crowded emergency room. Germs floated through the room, almost palpable with the coughing, sneezing, and groaning filling it. Cricket wondered why gloves and masks weren't there for the taking in the same way boxes of tissues lined the magazine table. The ticking of the clock droned on as they waited for Max's name to be called. Cari chatted with Ashling while Cricket held her son on her lap.

The relief that had surged through her at hearing his name in the waiting room faded as she perched on the edge of a chair next to the hospital bed while he slept. By the time the doctor stepped behind the curtain, she was also half asleep. After a brief examination, the doctor diagnosed Max with the flu and a double ear infection. Dehydrated, he needed to be hooked up to intravenous fluids. The doctor wanted to keep him for a few hours of observation and expected he could go home later that afternoon if his fever was under control and the fluids did their job.

Go home. To a homeless shelter. Not ideal for a sick little boy. But this wasn't the doctor's problem, so Cricket swallowed her fear. She returned to the waiting room and shared the doctor's advice.

"I don't want to take up your entire day," she finished. "We'll be fine. I can't thank you enough for driving us here."

Cari's eyes flashed back and forth between Ashling and Cricket, clearly unsure as to what she should do next.

"I don't have anything going on today and had just planned on spending the afternoon at St. Agnes's," Cari finally said. "I'll stay here with you to make sure everything is okay."

"You don't have—" Cricket started, but Cari interrupted her.

"I know for a fact that none of you had anything for breakfast today. Ashling and I will go check out the cafeteria and bring back something to eat. You keep Max company."

Ashling's face lit up at that.

"My treat," Cari added, recognizing the source of Cricket's hesitation.

"That's really kind of you. Maybe just something for Ashling. I don't have much of an appetite." Her stomach twisted with nerves. "The nurses offered to bring something for Max when he's up to it."

Ashling reentered the exam room almost an hour later, fidgeting with an elastic in her hair. Her head of curls, growing more unruly by the day, had been tied up in a bun. Cricket paused to gaze at her daughter's lovely face that had been hidden for the past few days. Moving her eyes to Ashling's other hand, she saw that she had taken advantage of Cari's generosity. A cardboard tray laden with a cheeseburger, fries, soda, and an ice cream lay clutched in her palm. Cari rounded the corner and passed Cricket a chicken salad sandwich and a cup of coffee, "In case she changed her mind".

Hours later, Cricket stood in the waiting room, insisting that Cari go home, when the doctor emerged from behind swinging doors and said he'd determined that Max could be discharged with a prescription. They were to come back if his fever spiked again. Not ideal, considering his mother had no idea where their next ride would come from if they needed it. She stared wide eyed while he talked and watched him briskly walk off, assuming all was well with the world. *His* world maybe.

"I'll—I'll go after him. Maybe I can convince them to keep Max overnight." Visibly shaking and on the verge of tears, Cricket clasped her hands together trying to still them.

Cari spoke before her brain caught up with her words. "Cricket, wait. Would you consider coming home with me? I can't stand the thought of you taking Max back to the shelter while he's sick. Even if they keep him 'til tomorrow, how much better will he be?" She glanced at Ashling. "And Ashling shouldn't spend the night here. She'll be the next one sick."

Stunned and at a loss for words, she knew Cari must have interpreted her silence to mean she was afraid to bring her children into a stranger's house. That's where her mind should have gone. Instead she struggled to process whether she'd imagined what had been said. Had she misunderstood?

Spurred on by the expression on Ashling's face, Cari strode over to Cricket, pulled her into a nearby seat, and stared directly into her eyes. "I know it sounds like a crazy idea. You don't even really know me. But I promise I'm not some wacko psychopath. I live alone and have plenty of room. Please, just think about it."

Cricket stared down at her lap and shook her head trying to comprehend the insanity of the idea, then jerked her neck up. "What's there to think about? You have more to worry about than I do. For all you know, my daughter and I might rob you blind!" She smiled for the first time that day.

"I'll take my chances," Cari grinned back.

That was unexpected, but a blessing for sure. Not that Max getting sick was something to be grateful for, Cricket considered, but it led them to one heck of a house for the night. A more careful mother might have thought twice about the situation, but Cricket had always been too impulsive. Still, Max needed a comfortable place to spend the night. Pulling into a lengthy driveway lit with decorative lamp posts on either side, Cricket decided Cari's place looked more than comfortable.

The driveway resembled a private street, leading up to an expansive parking area with a magnificent, white gabled farmhouse. Acres of farmland fanned out in all directions. Lights twinkled on the trees scattered across the front lawn, where life-like reindeer wearing giant red bows simulated nibbling at leaves. Walking up clean-swept steps onto the wraparound porch, Cricket could see a Christmas tree lit up through the picture window. This home looked postcard perfect.

Double doors led into an impressive foyer with gleaming hardwood floors and a grand staircase as the focal point. The dining room sat to the left, a generous living room to the right, and a kitchen spanning the full width of the house stood directly ahead through a wide hallway. As she entered the foyer, the sweet smell of vanilla tickled Cricket's nose.

"Were you baking this morning?"

"No, why?"

"It smells wonderful in here!"

"Oh, that's the candles," Cari said with a laugh. "They're all over the place. Along with the house, I inherited two cats. I'm not used to having pets and am always worrying about the house smelling like a giant litter box. I'm glad to hear the candles are doing their job even when they're not lit!" She reached down and began to pull off her boots.

Cricket didn't miss a beat and removed her shoes as well, while giving her children a clear signal to do the same.

"Thanks," Cari smiled. "I have a thing about shoes in the house. Normally I don't ask company to leave them at the door, but since you'll be staying the night…" She trailed off as Ashling arranged the shoes neatly on the floor mat, then gestured up the stairs. "How about we take a look at where you'll be sleeping?"

Without waiting for an answer, she led them up to a suite with two bedrooms and a common area. The guest bathroom resembled a spa, featuring floor to ceiling marble, an elevated jetted tub that could pass for a piece of furniture, and a glass enclosed shower with two rain head fixtures. Cari cracked open the closet and vanity allowing them to see she kept both stocked with enough essentials to attend to the needs of ten houseguests.

"Please help yourself to whatever you need. Don't be shy."

"Thank you," Cricket said, scanning the shelves.

"Don't thank me. It was all my Uncle Otto. He loved having family and friends stay." Cari walked back into the common area and flung open the door to a closet. "You can hang your coats in here, freshen up, and meet me in the kitchen for something to eat."

Cricket didn't want to keep her waiting and quickly put the coats away. Kneeling to meet Max at eye level, she asked him if he felt well enough to go downstairs.

"You'll carry me?"

He was getting too big for her to carry, but she also felt uncomfortable leaving him alone so soon. One trip up that staircase had probably wiped him out. Kissing his warm cheek, she scooped him up.

Minutes later, they found Cari rinsing a pan. She had already whipped up a can of chicken noodle soup for the patient and tossed a ready to go casserole into the oven for the rest of them. The kitchen was a chef's dream, with white cabinets, quartz countertops, a farmhouse sink, rustic exposed beams and a matching wooden door to the pantry. An oversized island provided an additional sink and seating for four. The double oven and pot filler were added bonuses. Floor to ceiling windows overlooking the sweeping backyard surrounded three sides of a breakfast nook. Centered in the nook sat a large round table with a dainty chandelier overhead.

Desperately trying to appear unfazed by her surroundings, Cricket hustled her children to the table. Ashling helped herself to the cheese and cracker tray Cari set before them. Max didn't eat much and asked for a can of ginger ale. Although sick, this little treat excited him because he so rarely drank soda. Once she'd made him eat a bit, Cricket brought him upstairs, and he fell sound asleep by seven. He still had a fever but looked much better.

Making her way back to the family room, Cricket overheard Cari blabbing on about how they should make themselves at home. Cricket suspected she rambled to fill the air, because they were all speechless. Even Ashling, who never shut her mouth. Spotting her mother, she seized the opportunity to pick up the remote control and distract them all with some television. Cricket sank down on the couch next to her daughter and was beginning to feel more at ease when Cari handed her a glass of wine.

When Cricket hesitated, Cari said, "I know you probably won't drain the bottle because you want to be alert for Max, but a little bit won't hurt. I promise not to even have so much as a sip just in case we need to go back to the hospital."

Less than thirty minutes later and after several failed attempts at small talk, exhaustion set in.

"I'm really sorry," Cricket said. "I know this may be rude, but I can barely keep my eyes open."

"Don't apologize," Cari reassured her. "You get some rest. Ashling, the TV is all yours. I think I'll grab a snack and go up to my room and read."

"Ash, try not to drift off with the TV on."

"Okay," she replied, eyes still glued to the screen. "Night, Mom."

Cricket dragged herself upstairs and changed into an old t-shirt and pair of sweatpants of Cari's. Leaving the extra bedroom free for Ashling, she climbed into bed with Max and fell asleep before her head hit the pillow.

Disoriented when she first woke up, it took Cricket a moment to remember where she was and why her bed felt so comfortable. Gently slipping out from under the down comforter, she tiptoed over to the window.

What a simply gorgeous street, she thought.

The side with Cari's house lacked neighbors as far as Cricket could see. The farm stretched seemingly forever in both directions. Across the street were several other homes, none of them as large as the farmhouse, but they all possessed character befitting a storybook.

Movement at the house directly across the street caught her eye. She spotted an old woman slip-sliding her way down her driveway with trash cans in tow. Moving slowly and stopping several times to regain her footing, she wasn't getting anywhere very quickly. Cricket threw on her coat and sneakers and went downstairs to see if she could be of any help.

Jogging across the road, she waved to her and called, "Ma'am! Can I help you with that?"

The woman stopped for a moment, clearly trying to figure out who she was.

"I'm fine. Do it every week," she replied gruffly.

As Cricket reached her, she placed a hand on one of the barrels and smiled. "Let me take one. I wouldn't want you to fall."

"Don't you listen? I said I can do this." The volume of the woman's voice neared shouting.

Her front door opened and closed as a man with dark hair came bounding down the steps.

"Fiona, let me get those! You should have told me it was trash day."

"I should have told you no such thing!" she yelled. "You've been here three days, and I've been doing this every week for many years. I haven't needed your assistance in all that time, and I don't need it now." She turned to face Cricket. "And I don't even know who *you* are. Thank you, but no thank you."

"It's the least I can do while I'm staying here," he pleaded with her. With that handsome face tilted to the side and those big brown eyes staring down at her, her posture softened.

"Suit yourself," she said with a huff before trudging back to the house.

Cricket stared after the ill-tempered woman.

"I'm really sorry about that."

Distracted and wondering about the woman's behavior, it took her a moment to realize he was talking to her.

"Don't be. She looked like she needed help, so I came over. No harm done."

"Fiona's a feisty one," the man said with a grin. "She refuses to admit that some things are getting more difficult for her to do on her own." He grabbed the barrels and walked toward the end of the driveway. "I get it, she's growing older and doesn't want me thinking she can't manage on her own."

"Moms are used to doing for their children, not the other way around." Cricket then remembered the woman's age. "Oh, wait. She couldn't be your mother."

"Grandmother. But she raised me." He set the barrels at the curb. "I moved in when I was eight, after my parents passed away."

"I'm sorry." Scrunching up her face, Cricket asked, "She's your grandmother? Didn't I hear you call her Fiona? Why not Grandma or Nana or something?"

He cracked a smile at the question. "When I was born, she told my parents that she didn't feel old enough to be a grandmother and preferred to be called by her name instead."

"You're kidding!"

"I'm not. What's funnier is that I have cousins in Florida who have always called her Gram. They're all five to ten years younger than me, though. Maybe by the time they came around she was starting to feel her age."

Before Cricket could respond, a shrill voice rang out. "Mom!"

Ashling half hung out of the front door. "You gotta come in here! Cari and I made pancakes! From scratch!"

"I'll be right in!" Cricket hollered back. "She'll wake the rest of the neighbors for sure, if they're not already up," she said. "I better get in there before she starts shouting again."

Hearing him laughing as she left, Cricket wished they'd exchanged names, before reminding herself that there was probably no point to that.

CHAPTER 2

Boris had been walking downstairs after his shower when he'd heard raised voices. Recognizing one of them as his grandmother's, he followed the sound outside. There she was, practically wrestling another woman in the driveway over her barrels. A thin sheet of ice had glazed over the pavement during the night, impacting their balance. Fiona wasn't always steady on her feet in the best conditions.

After she'd given in and shuffled back inside, he focused on the good Samaritan who had tried to help. Wearing oversized sweatpants and a coat, with her hair in total disarray on top of her head, it was obvious she had just rolled out of bed. Still, she was beautiful, with porcelain skin and large, expressive eyes. Petite with errant strands of chestnut hair grazing her jawline and a warm smile showcasing countless, gleaming white teeth.

He believed it was those eyes that had sucked him in. They had to be the reason he'd begun sharing personal information mere seconds into their conversation. No wonder she took off at the first opportunity without asking his name.

Whoever she was wasn't important, anyway. He didn't have time to allow his attention to be diverted. Back in town for a reason, he and his partners at Glynn, Stone, and West were prepared to bid on Honeycomb Hills Farm. The land provided the perfect location for his real estate development company to build an upscale shopping center. Fiona would most likely vehemently disagree with that sentiment. She would not view an outdoor mall as an ideal neighbor. However, the time had come for her to move into something smaller and more manageable. He knew she'd initially disagree, but in time she'd see that a retirement community would be the best place for her at this stage of her life.

Boris couldn't deny that it would be a bittersweet end to an era. Though he still missed his parents deeply, Fiona had done her best to give him an idyllic childhood. He had only fond memories of his years spent here in Blue Cove and knew Fiona had always hoped that he'd decide to move back to Massachusetts. In fact, she dreamed that he'd settle down one day with Cari, that they'd take over the farm when Otto was ready to retire and become the town's local power couple. She had visions of great grandchildren growing up a stone's throw away. But although he and Cari had always been good friends, neither of them had ever felt that kind of connection.

It crossed his mind, not for the first time, that she may not be receptive to his company's offer. She may even resent it. He'd need to be careful with his approach.

Joining Cari in the spacious sunroom with two steaming cups of coffee in hand, Cricket instantly felt lighter as she took a seat and glanced up at the pitched, beadboard ceiling with two oversized skylights. Seeing the breathtaking view of the land, she surmised Otto had spared no expense when it came to maintaining the exterior of his property. With a sprawling lawn blanketed in several inches of untouched snow, littered with mature trees leading up to a freshwater stream, she could almost convince herself that she was vacationing in an elite resort.

"Tell me about the red barn," she said, looking through the window over Cari's head toward the structure.

"It's actually a carriage house. That thing's been vacant for as long as I can remember. It's still heated, and the plumbing is up to date, as far as I know. But there's nothing in there other than old castoff furniture from this house."

"It has charm."

They fell into a comfortable silence, while Cari scanned the news on her phone and Cricket flipped through a magazine. Ashling took a nap, while Max sat propped up in the living room with a fresh glass of ginger ale and cartoons.

Cricket eventually broke the quiet to thank Cari and insist she didn't want to impose any further. She was ready to head back, but Cari interrupted her.

"Can I ask you a personal question?"

"Sure."

"You told me once that you're a widow," Cari began. "But you must have family, whether it's yours, his, or both. Are you in contact with anyone?"

Cricket sighed. "I'm close with my mom, but I couldn't bring myself to burden her with my problems. She can barely make ends meet as it is." She took a sip of her coffee. "Wally's parents moved to South Carolina right after he graduated from high school. After his accident we kept in touch. It's hard with the distance, though."

"You wouldn't consider asking them for financial help?"

She shook her head. "They moved to take advantage of a cheaper cost of living. I don't think they're any better off than my mom."

Cari stared out the window in thought. "I know this is going to sound a bit unconventional, but how would you feel about staying a little longer?"

Cricket's heart started pounding. "I don't understand…"

"Well, you can see yourself that this house is far too big for one person." She paused, then took a deep breath. "I'm asking if you would be interested in spending a few more days."

Taken aback, Cricket swallowed, trying to find her voice. "Why would you do that for us? Are you looking for a charity project or something?" She took another sip of her coffee to stifle a nervous laugh and looked out at the grounds away from Cari.

"I—I don't really know. What I do know is that it makes me really sad to think of bringing you all back there. Just stay a bit longer, to give Max the time he needs to recover."

How she could say no to that? It might be days before Max fully recovered. Sleeping on bunk beds in a loud, drafty room shared with multiple families would not be restful for him. Unfamiliar with people being kind to her without an agenda didn't stop Cricket from readily accepting such a tempting offer.

After Cari excused herself to review some spreadsheets, Ashling plopped down in the vacant seat with a sigh.

"I think we should have gone back to St. Agnes's last night. It would have been easier than seeing this place and having to leave it."

"Well, you'd better get used to the idea," Cricket said, smile growing as she got ready to share the news. "It's only going to be harder to leave once we've been here a few days."

Ashling sat up quickly, scraping her chair across the wooden floor.

"A few days?"

Cricket told her about Cari's generous offer, watching Ashling's eyes widen.

"What about school?"

Cricket shrugged. "I hate to have you miss too many days, but I don't know what else to do. I don't have a car, and I don't want to ask Cari for anything else."

A frantic tone crept into Ashling's voice. "There has to be something we can do, or I'm going to have too much work to make up!"

Although first impressions of her suggested a street-smart kid with a razor-sharp tongue, the tough exterior concealed an academically gifted young woman. She set high expectations for herself that included graduating at the top of her class and continuing to college with scholarships. Despite the financial challenges that had affected her family over the years, she never doubted the attainability of her goals.

"Today is already a lost cause. I'll try to figure out something for tomorrow, and in the meantime, I'll see if I can get in touch with your guidance counselor to explain the situation."

Ashling pulled her feet up on the chair and hugged her knees to her chest as Cricket stood and arched her back in a stretch.

"I'm going to peek in on Max," Cricket said.

She found him asleep again, although he'd only recently moved to the living room couch. Soft footsteps sounded behind her. She turned and saw Cari waving her into the kitchen.

"Why don't you and Ashling go for a walk?" she suggested. "It's cold, but so beautiful here in the winter. I'll bring my laptop downstairs and keep an eye on Max." She spoke in a hushed voice to avoid waking him. Ashling managed to hear her from the adjoining sunroom and tiptoed in.

"Could we, Mom? Just a quick walk? It's like a storybook Christmas scene out there."

Cricket hesitated. "If you're sure, Cari. I'm not a fan of freezing, so we won't be long."

"Go," Cari said, waving her hand toward the front door. "There are some extra hats, mittens, and scarves in the coat closet."

Cricket glanced one more time at her sleeping son, then joined Ashling on the front porch. As she closed the front door, she turned to see Cari's handsome neighbor making his way across the street toward them. Her heart fluttered for a moment. Silently, she berated herself in irritation for allowing that to happen. As if she'd had a choice.

❄

The biting cold air hit him in the face as he walked outside. En route to the grocery store, he saw Cari's adorable houseguest step onto the porch and found himself walking past his car. The teenage girl from the window descended the stairs beside her. It struck him that they looked more like sisters than mother and daughter.

"Hey, we meet again," he called from the sidewalk.

"We do. Cari is inside, if you're looking for her."

"No, I just wanted to say thanks again for attempting to help my grandmother."

She flashed that blinding smile at him. "No thanks needed."

He closed the distance between them and stretched out his gloved hand. "I also wanted to properly introduce myself. I'm Boris Glynn."

"Cricket Williams. This is my daughter, Ashling."

Enchanted once again by those eyes, Boris held her hand a few beats too long before releasing it. He regarded Ashling quizzically. "No school today?" The look exchanged between mother and daughter told him he'd asked a question they did not feel comfortable answering.

"We're in from out of town visiting Cari for a few days," Cricket replied in a clipped tone intended to close the subject. "If you'll excuse us, we're going for a short walk."

"It's gorgeous here!" Ashling exclaimed. "I want to see the whole farm before we leave!"

Boris noted an anxious haze pass over Cricket's face as her daughter spoke and found himself wanting to ease whatever worried her.

"Do you mind if I join you?" he found himself asking. "I grew up playing and working on that farm. I know it inside and out, from the orchards to the land dedicated to growing vegetables, to the tree lot, to the apiary. Have you ever wondered where the bees go during the winter months?"

"I always thought they died," Ashling replied with noticeable excitement creeping into her voice. "And wait, what's an apiary?"

"To answer your first question, some species of bees do die off, but not honeybees. They hibernate and can survive freezing temperatures in the right conditions. To answer your second question, an apiary is a collection of hives."

"Can we see the apiary, Mom?" she asked excitedly. "That would be so fun!"

A gust of wind blew, causing the three of them to burrow deeper into their coats.

"We can't get up close and personal today, but I can show you the lay of the land. Maybe I could drive us up the road, so we don't freeze to death," Boris offered.

"Can you have us back in an hour?" Cricket asked. "My son is sleeping, and I don't want him to be a bother for Cari when he wakes up. She's trying to work."

With the orchards closed and the apiary off limits, they strolled through the tree lot. The most popular draw this time of year, an elaborate enchanted village glittered along the rows of trees, wreaths, and kissing balls.

The kissing balls sent Ashling into a fit of laughter. "What in the world are those? Are they supposed to be giant balls of mistletoe?"

"No," Boris chuckled. "Once upon a time they were hung in doorways to bring good luck to people who passed beneath them."

As they walked, Ashling peppered him with questions about bees. The potential impact of extinct bee colonies fascinated her.

"Cari's uncle was passionate about this topic," Boris explained. "In addition to running his organic farm, he traveled all over the country educating other farmers about the effects of pesticide use."

"Do you think Cari will continue his work?" Cricket asked through chattering teeth. He noted her beet red cheeks and nose.

"I couldn't say for sure. She was always more interested in the business end of things. How to increase sales and all that." Afraid that he'd kept them out in the cold for too long, he suggested they make their way over to Honeycomb Hills Market.

They trudged up to the door and stood outside banging the excess snow from their boots before going inside to warm up. The doorbell chimed as the door pushed open into a cozy shop with barn board walls and a vaulted ceiling showcasing exposed beams. The scent of cinnamon and pine needles permeated the air. Warm lighting illuminated the store with a soft glow.

A barrel of apples sat to the right of the door inviting customers to help themselves. Centered in the room, a produce display offered an extensive variety of fruits and vegetables. The front of the store shelved pies, muffins, turnovers, and cookies.

"Boris!" Pia shouted from behind the register. Once enveloped in a hug from his best friend's sister, he lifted the slight woman off the ground and spun her around. "Took you long enough to come by to say hello!"

"Pia, you know Fiona keeps me busy when I'm in town. In fact, I should have already been home from the supermarket!"

"What is all this commotion?" Lex Owens emerged from the door that connected to the adjoining warehouse nearly dropping a stack of boxes in his arms. "Hey, man! I heard you were in the neighborhood. I can't believe you came to see my sister before visiting me!"

A surge of happiness ran through him at the reunion. It had been almost a year since he'd last seen them.

"It wasn't intentional," he laughed. Remembering his manners, he gestured to his companions. "This is Cricket and her daughter Ashling. I offered to show them around while they're visiting Cari, and we came in here to warm up. In fact, I was just telling them about the hives. I'm surprised you weren't out there."

"You dragged these poor souls out to tour the farm on a day like today? Boris, what were you thinking?" Pia scolded him in jest, still clearly overjoyed by his visit.

"Allow me to introduce my oldest friends, Pia and Lex Owens," he told Cricket and Ashling. "Pia manages this store and Lex handles just about everything else out here. He's also the resident beekeeper."

Lex interrupted before he could go on. "Before Boris has the chance to make fun of me, you might be interested to know that I just made a pot of coffee. Let's get a cup in your hands so you can start thawing out!"

Neither of his friends had changed a bit in the last year. Pia still piled her flaming red hair on top of her head, revealing a pretty face smattered in freckles. Lex remained his tall, lumbering self, wearing his standard uniform of a flannel shirt and jeans. Boris couldn't stop grinning as Pia poured the coffee into white ceramic mugs and offered Ashling a cookie from the elaborate gingerbread house she stood admiring.

"You see a woman every day and she doesn't think to mention she has houseguests," Pia muttered. "That's typical Cari for you. Her mind is always going in ten different directions. The mundane things that matter to everyone else don't always register on her radar. I would have invited the bunch of you over for dinner."

Once again, Boris noticed a subtle wave of emotion pass over Cricket's face. He instinctively wanted to offer protection from whatever unnerved her and steered the direction of conversation toward Pia herself, which was always one of her favorite topics.

"Pia manages the market. You will never find another store on this earth as efficiently run." He shook his head. "That was probably an understatement. She cares for this place as if it's an extension of herself."

"Not entirely true at the moment," she interrupted. "Olivia is moving to New Hampshire. She reduced her hours to allow for more time to pack. This place has been in shambles ever since. I don't know what I'm going to do without her."

"'Shambles' is a bit extreme, Pia," interjected Lex.

"Sorry, Lex." She placed a hand on his arm. "Lex has been a lifesaver, trying to fill in for her whenever he can. That's why you didn't find him outside today."

Boris turned to Cricket to fill her in. "Lex was Otto's right-hand man. He's been running everything outside these walls since his passing."

"Do you know as much about bees as he did?" Ashling asked.

"Not even close, but I try," he said good naturedly. "He taught me everything I know. You must have learned about pollination and all that good stuff in school."

"I learned more today than I have in all the years of school combined," Ashling replied. "I'd like to get some books about them at the library."

"Look at that, Boris!" Pia roared with laughter. "The big real estate tycoon from New York inspiring young minds!" Hearing the door chime, she then stood up and gave a quick squeeze to his shoulder.

It felt like he'd been punched in the stomach. Not for the first time, he worried about how the sale of this farm would impact Pia and Lex. They were both intelligent and had skills that would be an asset to any employer. Still, he knew working here was more than a job to them. The farm had been their second home for most of their lives. On more than one occasion, they'd expressed how blessed they were to be able to earn a living doing something they genuinely loved. Yet here he was planning to pull the rug right out from under them. When Cricket suggested they head home, he jumped at the chance to leave.

"So soon?" Pia pouted.

"My son is getting over a nasty bug, and I don't want to burden Cari with him for too long," Cricket explained.

"I won't take it personally then." Pia smiled as she raised her eyes to Boris. "But I'm expecting you to bring both kids back to see the secret operation that goes into this place."

With heartfelt promises to do so, they were on their way. One hour had turned into two.

CHAPTER 3

Cricket climbed out of Boris's car and thought back to the conversation with Pia and Lex, trying to determine if she'd missed something. For someone so animated, Boris had clammed up on the drive home. She tried to shake it off. His change in mood could not have been caused by anything she'd said or done.

Ashling prattled on endlessly about honeybees before planting herself in front of the television. Max woke up briefly but preferred to continue sleeping after being coaxed to drink more fluids. Although he still refused food, his fever had dropped to 101, bringing Cricket some relief.

The phone call to Ashling's guidance counselor also brought peace of mind. More than understanding of their situation, she assured Cricket that Ashling could make up missed assignments over the winter break if needed. Fortunately, she had the reputation of being an excellent student, and Ms. Snow insisted they would make any accommodations necessary. After hanging up, she gave Ashling the good news.

Cricket stood in the family room staring blankly at the television, having no idea what to do with herself next. She didn't want to look like a lazy slob sacked out in front of the TV while Cari worked, so she chose to busy herself with cleaning all five bathrooms, washing the floors, and laundering the few items of clothing they'd brought with them. Surprised to find it therapeutic for her overactive mind, she said as much to Cari when she found her scrubbing a bathtub and Cari asked her to stop.

By the time they sat down to a dinner of frozen pizza, she savored a sense of accomplishment. As she'd worked, it became obvious right away that Cari did not prioritize cleaning and hadn't yet hired anyone to do it for her. Cricket gave herself a silent pat on the back for discovering a small way to show her appreciation.

"I can't believe this place, Cricket! I'm embarrassed to admit that I haven't done much around here since first moving in. I'm used to having a one bedroom, one-bathroom condo to take care of. This place is overwhelming."

"Did your uncle have a maid service that you could use?"

"Oh, no," she shook her head. "He never would have allowed strangers to go through his things. I couldn't care less about that if someone recommended the person to me, but I haven't made the time to think about it yet."

"Wow, so he cleaned this place by himself all those years?"

"Yes, he did. Every Saturday morning, he'd cover all three floors. Even when I lived here with my mom, he didn't want us touching anything other than the bathrooms and the laundry. Like you, he oddly enjoyed it," she laughed and took a bite.

Ashling snorted at that. Like most teenage girls, wielding a mop was not at the top of her must-do list. "He and my mom would have been a perfect match. Nothing excites her more than washing and folding laundry!"

"Stop!" Cari shouted, smacking the table with her hand. "Really?"

"It's true. There are few things in life more enjoyable for me than removing what should have been a permanent stain on a piece of clothing," Cricket said with a smile.

Ashling and Cari howled with laughter and Max came padding into the dining room wanting to know what was so funny. Despite still rosy cheeks and glassy eyes, he asked for a slice of pizza.

Cricket, ignoring the other two, pulled him onto her lap and hugged him to her.

"I hope this means your appetite is coming back, mister," she said, smoothing his hair and kissing his cheek.

Although he took only a few bites, it was a start. As Cricket tucked him into bed an hour later, she felt that the worst was over. Restless, she joined Cari and Ashling in the living room. The room was dim, and the fireplace crackled in a blaze. Instead of allowing herself to sink into the comfort of one of the luxurious couches, she sat tense on the edge of a Queen Anne chair while Ashling rambled on about seeing the farm.

"And to think, all of it's yours," she finished in wonder.

Cari slouched at her words. "It's all mine, but you can't begin to imagine the work that goes into this place. I'm beginning to wonder if I'm cut out for it, and this isn't even our busiest season."

"When's that?" Ashling asked.

"It starts in July and runs through fall. We grow twenty-six varieties of vegetables, blueberries, and raspberries. There are twenty-two varieties of apples in an orchard of over one thousand trees. There's not much to see during winter, but the market is open year-round."

"Boris said something about taking us back to see the inner workings," Cricket said, "whatever that means."

"Take him up on it. The kids will love it."

They settled on a movie to watch, but Cricket quickly lost focus of the storyline. Instead, her mind drifted back to her morning with Boris. So unlike anyone she'd ever met, he piqued her curiosity. She could still feel his hand in hers from when he'd formally introduced himself.

She tried and failed to find any semblance of similarity between Boris and Wally. As much as she'd loved her husband, he was always a wildcard. With an impulsive nature similar to her own, he shared her penchant for making mistakes. Nothing was ever dull with him around, but it sure wasn't steady either. She always felt like her life could change on a whim, for better or worse. By contrast, Boris exuded confidence and methodical consideration of each step taken. She doubted he'd ever make the smallest move without thinking it through first.

Cricket chastised herself for allowing her mind to wander down a ridiculous road of 'what if'. Her thoughts shifted to what would happen next. Their time in this house was coming to an end. Every hour spent here would make it more difficult for the kids to say goodbye. Not only goodbye to Cari, but to the stability she'd provided to them these few days.

The following morning's newscast announced a major blizzard about to roll in. The original prediction of three to five inches of snow had increased to expectations of at least a foot. Cari invited her guests to spend the day hunkered down in front of a fire, watching movies and eating popcorn. Thankfully, Max's fever had broken. His temperature still hovered slightly over one hundred, but he looked and felt more like himself.

After a delicious spaghetti dinner, they planted themselves back in front of the fire in Cari's family room. Cricket stretched out on a couch and stared up at the cathedral ceiling with its wooden beams spanning the width of the room, making it appear larger than it already was. Allowing the crackling heat of the flames to drift over her, she easily could have closed her eyes and fell asleep for the night.

"Game time!" called Cari, entering the room with an armful of boardgames and a deck of cards in her hand. With that announcement, the lights went out.

"Game over!" laughed Ashling, sweeping her long dark curls up into a ponytail in the red light of the flames.

"Very funny! The light from the fire is good, but we're going to need more if we're going to play."

Cari lit the candles and turned on one of the lanterns that she had brought up from the basement that afternoon just in case.

Cricket had never been much for games and would have been ashamed to admit that she rarely played them with her children. Allowing herself to get sucked into everyone else's enthusiasm, though, she began to enjoy herself and realized it had been a long time since she or her kids had laughed so hard.

Tucking Max into bed early, the rest of them continued to play past midnight and woke up to a winter wonderland the following morning. Cricket stared out the window, wondering how they'd shovel the snow that had piled high against the door overnight.

She turned toward the sound of footsteps on the stairs. "I'm glad to not be alone here for my first snowstorm!" Cari joined her at the front door. "Condo living was easy because I didn't need to worry about shoveling, and there were plenty of neighbors close by if the power went out."

"If you have some extra boots and an extra shovel, we can tackle this after some coffee."

"Sounds like a plan to me."

Ashling came down the stairs and offered to help as well.

"I'm not comfortable leaving Max in here alone while all three of us are outside. Maybe you can just pitch in if one of us needs a break."

After a hearty breakfast of sausage and eggs, they exited through the garage. With all her years of apartment living, Cricket had shoveled as infrequently as Cari. Who knew it was such backbreaking work? One hour in and she felt like a human popsicle. With snow up her sleeves and down her boots, her skin burned with cold and her arms throbbed in pain.

"How's it going over there?" called a male voice.

She stood up straight in recognition.

"How does it look like it's going?" Cari hollered back.

"You two have made a dent. Maybe you can work your magic over here when you're finished!"

"Guess again Boris!" she called, laughing.

He plodded through the snow into Cari's yard.

"I figured as much. How about you two join me and Fiona for

some spiked cocoa later? We're all going to need something to thaw out our bones by the time this snow has been cleared."

"Tempting, but I have some work to catch up on after this." She looked over at Cricket. "I won't be offended if you two go ahead without me."

Boris lifted one eyebrow at Cricket. "Works for me."

Cricket's mouth hung open for a second or two. "I—I'd love to, but my son is still sick. It's not a great time for me to make any plans."

"Another time then," he smiled. "I'm going to hold you both to it."

By the time they finished and tramped back inside, power had been restored. Both women craved a hot shower followed by a seat in front of the fireplace again. After shaking off the snow and leaving her boots in the garage, Cricket walked to the window and watched Boris finish up. Resting her forehead against the cold glass, she instantly regretted turning down his invitation for hot chocolate. What harm could have come from it?

Silly question. She knew the answer to that.

CHAPTER 4

Stomping off his boots and entering the mudroom, Boris heard Fiona bustling around the kitchen. The power must have come back on. He closed his eyes, inhaling the scent of freshly baked brownies, and entered the kitchen to find his grandmother pouring two steaming cups of tea.

"Just what the doctor ordered," he said, kissing her on the cheek.

"I already added the milk and sugar."

"Ah! And these are still warm." He grabbed two brownies off the dish on the table and sat down with a thud.

"Do you have any idea how grateful I am that you were here for this storm? I would have been housebound for a week!"

"No, you wouldn't. Cari or someone else would have come over to help." He took a bite, savoring the chocolate chips that added a gooey consistency.

"I suppose. But there would have been some wait time while they dug themselves out." She took a seat at the table with him. "So, who was that woman out there with Cari? Is that the same one who tried to take my garbage cans away from me?"

"Her name is Cricket. She's a friend of Cari's, and she was only trying to help you."

She sniffed. "That must be her daughter I've seen coming and going."

"Yeah. She has a son as well, but he's been sick, so I haven't met him."

"They've been there a few nights," Fiona mused, still sounding suspicious. "Do you know where they're from?"

"No. It doesn't sound like they'll be here long. I'd imagine they have family to get back to before the holiday."

The subject was dropped as he drank his tea and Fiona busied herself with emptying the dishwasher. After a hot shower, he opened his laptop to seventy-three emails that had arrived while he was shoveling. He tried to sift through the important versus the less important, a simple task made difficult with his mind circling back to Cricket.

Skittish. That's the best word to describe her. Beautiful, but skittish. She was hiding something, afraid of something, or both. He reminded himself that he had plenty of work to focus on that didn't involve the personal life of a woman he'd just met.

A new email popped up on his screen. This one included an attachment to the final draft of the offer he planned to present to Cari. There had been several prior to this that he'd rejected. Satisfied after carefully reading it through, he determined it was fair to Cari while still being a fantastic investment for his company.

A spark of excitement replaced the nagging uncertainty of the deal. He pulled up the plans for what would put tiny, unheard of Blue Cove on the map. In addition to the upscale retail options offered at his other properties, he had insisted that some moderately priced stores be included at this new location. Shoppers who didn't typically browse high end designers would feel like they were on Rodeo Drive.

In his opinion, the biggest draw would be the entertainment venues, with a vast selection of restaurants, a comedy club, a movie theater, and a game house offering bowling and pool tables. An image of a jazz bar manifested in his mind. Live bands played every night while dinner and drinks were served. People enjoyed having a reason to get dressed up for a nice meal, music and dancing. Even residents in a quaint town would appreciate a great night out.

Completely engrossed in his screen, he didn't hear Fiona behind him.

"Doesn't that look elaborate!"

Not ready for her to know about his proposal, he jumped at the sound of her voice.

"Sorry, I didn't mean to startle you," she apologized.

"No, it's fine. I didn't hear you come in."

"So, tell me all about that," she said, gesturing toward the screen. "Looks like quite a fancy undertaking."

"It's just shopping and food. We've put up two of these venues so far, and they've done well. We're considering a potential third location."

"Nearby? We could use something like that around here." She corrected herself. "Well, not right in Blue Cove, of course. It's such a quiet town, and people want to keep it that way. But, just outside maybe?"

"We're looking in the area," he said evasively. "Nothing's been finalized yet."

Closing his laptop, he realized he'd worked up an appetite today that had not been satiated by those two brownies earlier. He also wanted to put an end to this conversation. Once Fiona started asking questions, it could be difficult to get her off topic.

"I'm famished. Time to raid the kitchen, Fi!"

"You go. I want to catch up on some reading."

She patted his shoulder and went to find her book, leaving him to question himself once again. All this time, he'd been worried about how she and Cari would react to the idea of building a shopping complex in place of the farm. He hadn't given much thought to the residents of Blue Cove and assumed they'd love having a new destination in town.

But Fiona had made a good point. People chose to buy houses in Blue Cove because they wanted to live in a small town. There was a reason big businesses weren't sprouting up on every street corner. This was a place where the cobblestoned main street was home to mom and pop shops that had been in families for generations. It was a town where children could ride their bikes from one end to the other without traffic buzzing around them. People often favored walking over driving when the weather permitted.

Although the farm was vast with its orchards and apiaries, the business remained unobtrusive to the rest of the town. An outdoor shopping and dining attraction would bring an onslaught of traffic to the area. It occurred to him that the residents here were as likely to fight the development plan as they may be to embrace it.

Cricket borrowed a laptop from Cari to search for jobs. She knew it would be more difficult to find something on her own than it had been when Sandy had assisted her. She used to joke about the social worker with sandy hair that matched her name. The woman had beamed sunny rays of positivity, serving to remind them of how little she really understood their situation. Her with her beautiful clothes, decent car, and college education. Cricket envied those advantages, yet knew she'd genuinely wanted to help Cricket's family. And she had.

The last time Cricket had found herself in dire straits, Sandy found her a job as a nurse's aide at Shady Oaks Rehabilitation Hospital. Her feet ached at the end of each shift and many tasks turned her stomach. But it was local, and she gained some confidence working with the patients. Ever the caretaker, she would go out of her way to try and make someone feel better. Some elderly patients loved an extended hot shower with the reassurance of not falling in the tub at home. Others radiated excitement when presented with the extra orange sherbet cups she'd smuggle to them after the single one served with dinner.

Dreams of going to nursing school grew stronger as the months passed. Things had been looking up, until she'd been fired. Not laid off, fired.

She had become friendly with a wonderful old lady of ninety-two. A feisty little thing, Helen brightened up Cricket's days. Cricket must have made her days just as pleasant because when Helen finally got her exit slip to go home, she handed her a crisp $100 bill.

At first, Cricket had genuinely tried to refuse it. But Helen had insisted, knowing Cricket had two kids to support. "Take it!" she'd nearly hollered while trying to stuff the money into her hand. "You have been so good to me. I wish there was something more I could do for you."

Cricket could still picture her pleading eyes and hear that ever so sweet and creaky voice. Helen had only wanted to find a way to thank someone who had been doing her job with a smile on her face. Cricket had made the mistake of giving in.

Somehow, someone told. Cricket suspected it was the woman sharing the room with Helen. She'd probably viewed it as another case of someone trying to take advantage of a loopy little old lady. She hadn't been there long enough to know that Helen was sharper than the two of them put together. As expected, taking money from patients for any reason was a no-no.

After that, it hadn't taken long before she couldn't keep up with the bills. Without any other options, she'd taken the kids back to St. Agnes's, hoping to find Sandy. Adding to Cricket's misfortune, Sandy no longer worked there. In her place was the new director, Eleanor Pace, who'd made her feel like a nuisance. Sandy might have been a little too upbeat, but at least she'd cared.

Cricket strained to bring her mind back to the present moment. Ruminating on the past would not help matters. She managed to apply to eleven jobs over the next two hours. If no one checked references or her address, she might have a chance at being hired for one of them. Submitting the last application, her stomach rumbled. She was ravenous and ready for leftovers from the previous night.

Max tumbled out of bed the following morning with renewed energy. Fever free for a full day, he ate his breakfast with a restored appetite and pleaded to be allowed to play outside in the snow.

It was Thursday. They'd been there for four nights. Cricket tried to discreetly explain to him that they needed to return to St. Agnes's. Her heart cracked at the sight of the tears spilling freely from his eyes.

"I don't want to go back there, Mama!"

How do you explain something like that to a six-year-old? She couldn't even promise that it would only be for a short time.

Cari overheard them and knocked at the door.

"Just wanted to tell you there's no rush." She shrugged at Cricket's expression. "Hey, if we get another snowstorm, I'd like to have the extra set of hands."

She moved on down the hall, leaving Cricket unsure as to what to do or say next. She took Max to sit with Ashling at the piano in the library and went off to find Cari. As she reached the top of the stairs, she could hear her clacking away on a keyboard in her office.

Cricket knocked on the partly open door and poked her head in.

"Can I interrupt you for a minute?"

Closing her laptop at the sound of Cricket's voice, she turned. "Sure. Have a seat," she said, gesturing to the antique wingback chair in the corner next to her.

"I'm really grateful that you'd suggest we could stay longer," Cricket began, "but I don't want to wear out our welcome. Max is back to himself, so it's time we return to St. Agnes's and figure out our next step."

In a soft voice, Cari asked. "Any idea what that will be?"

"Not at all. I just don't want to let the kids get too comfortable here, and there's no reason for us to continue invading your privacy at this point," Cricket explained.

"Cricket, I've been working on something I'd like to show you. You're going to need to keep an open mind," she said, opening her laptop back up to display a spreadsheet.

"What's that?"

"It's a—a contract of sorts. I've been wracking my brain and losing sleep the last few nights trying to find a way to help you. The thought of bringing the three of you back to the shelter is—" She paused, searching for the right word. "Well, it's excruciating to even contemplate. I may be overstepping boundaries here, but I'm going to tell you what I'm thinking, and if you don't like it, I won't be offended." She pointed at the screen. "This is a set of rules, or maybe 'expectations' is a better term. If you are willing to adhere to them, I'd be willing to have you move in on a trial basis."

"Move in?" Cricket repeated incredulously. "I'm sorry, I don't think I'm following what you're saying."

"You and the kids can continue staying here if we can reach an agreement. This page lists the do's and don'ts. It's a draft, so we can go through the items one by one, and I want you to feel free to let me know if anything stands out as a deal breaker. This tab," she went on with a click, "details what would be your salary, savings, and expenses. It's basically a breakdown of your budget."

"I'd have to find a job." She held out her hands with palms open. "How can you assume what my salary might be?"

"I need more help at the market. You need a job. It's a winning scenario for both of us."

Cricket shook her head slowly back and forth. "This budget though? I know how to manage money."

"I'm sure you do," Cari said gently. "It's just that you'd need to start building up your savings if you're going to be able to get a place of your own down the road. It shouldn't take too long really. You just need a little bit of help getting started. I'll take thirty percent for room and board, and I'll put away twenty-five percent of your paycheck into a savings account. The rest is for you to spend as you like."

Cricket stood and moved closer to the screen, her eyes scanning the lines of numbers. Spreadsheets had never been her thing, but these figures didn't add up. "You're not taking the amount you'd actually need to feed and house a family of three."

"True. But, if you'd be willing to keep this place presentable and cook the occasional meal, we could call it even."

"Seriously?"

"Yeah, seriously. Wait, I hope you're not offended by that," she said with concern.

Cricket stepped back and sat once again, hoping to steady her racing thoughts. "No, I'm not offended at all! I'm just surprised you'd be willing to consider that compensation."

"Well, if you didn't stay, I'd need to hire someone else anyways. If you are staying, you'd essentially be cleaning up after yourself and cooking for yourself. I don't make too much of a mess, and I'm not a huge eater."

"I guess that makes sense." Cricket clasped her hands in her lap and stared down at them. "What job are you hiring for?"

"Nothing glamorous, just cashier. One of my employees is getting married and moving in February. If you start now, she'll have just enough time to train you before she leaves. Pia Owens also works in the store and is the manager. I can't expect her to do it solo. It's not much more than minimum wage, but it's a job. Pia's pretty flexible. We decrease the store's open hours January through March. You could most likely work while the kids are at school. I'm sure Ashling would be willing to help out with Max if you needed her to."

If it meant staying here, she definitely would! Cricket thought, but she kept that to herself.

She raised her eyes to meet Cari's. "I've met Pia, and she's wonderful."

"Better than wonderful. Don't let her appearance deceive you. That mass of flaming untamed curls might have given the impression of someone who is frazzled. Disorganized." She laughed at that. "Let me tell you, nothing could be further from the truth. That woman is meticulous almost to a fault. Never an 'i' not dotted or a 't' not crossed."

"That should make my job easier. Sounds like I won't have any trouble finding my way around."

"Oh, no. Pia thrives on organization. She plans, sorts, and labels for the sheer enjoyment of it. Few things give her more of a thrill than physically checking items off a handwritten to-do list."

Cricket chuckled. "I'm sold. Do you have time now to go over the stuff on your computer?"

"I do," she smiled. "This is really unconventional, but if you are comfortable with it and agree to it, we can see how it goes."

Cricket would need to agree to a laundry list of rules, or they'd be out. She understood and appreciated Cari's professional manner when walking her through the items. Without any better options, she only worried about forgetting what was expected of them. Or not expected. Never having been a troublemaker, she figured she'd learn as she went and hope for the best. Cricket wasn't worried about herself or Max. More concerning was Ashling, who had never been much of a rule follower.

"So, what do you think?" Cari asked after going over the spreadsheets.

Cricket shook her head in wonder. "I think we're not your responsibility, and I can't wrap my head around why you'd even consider doing this for us."

"No, you're not my responsibility. And, I don't want you to feel belittled or pitied by my offer."

"But it is pity," she replied. "Of course you pity us. You have more than you could ever ask for and have to look at me, who can't even afford to properly care for her kid when he's sick."

"I'm looking at you and hoping you aren't too proud to accept some help."

Then Cari told her the rest of the truth. She felt uncomfortable living alone in such a large home. She missed small spaces and lots of neighbors coming and going. There was also a larger force driving her invitation. As a child, Cari had watched her mother struggle trying to keep a roof over their heads and food on the table. It took only one person reaching out a hand to lift them up to change the course of their lives. Cari could be that person for Cricket and her kids.

Once again, how could she say no? Cari was clearly someone who thought outside the box, and Cricket surmised that was something they had in common. Although part of her resented the pity, she didn't fault Cari. Her intentions were good, and they were in desperate need of a place to stay. The thought of bouncing across motel rooms and shelters indefinitely was far worse than being pitied.

CHAPTER 5

"Boris," Fiona called walking into the kitchen. "I just got off the phone with Cari. Could you run across the street and borrow some cream? She'll be expecting you."

"We have enough cream for coffee in the morning. I'll go to the store tomorrow and pick up a container."

"It can't wait. I was thinking maybe you could whip up a batch of your pasta with chicken and sundried tomatoes for dinner tonight. We don't have nearly enough creamer for that recipe and breakfast tomorrow."

Boris had just finished two heaping turkey club sandwiches and couldn't even think about dinner. Patting his stomach, he said as much to Fiona.

"Well, some of us haven't stuffed ourselves yet today," she said crossly. "You know how I love that dish. A few hours from now and you know you'll be looking to eat again."

He couldn't argue with that logic. Minutes later he found himself standing on Cari's porch with Cricket opening the door, hair still damp from a recent shower and wearing black leggings and an oversized pink hoodie. She smelled of soap and shampoo.

"Hi, Cricket. I'm told you and Cari are kind enough to spare some cream this afternoon."

"Come on in. Cari's upstairs working, but she did mention you'd be stopping by. I'll be right back."

She didn't invite him to take his coat or boots off, which disappointingly meant she wasn't asking him to stay. He stood on the mat feeling like an awkward teenager trying to get up the nerve to invite a girl to a dance. The smile on her face when she returned put him at ease.

"Enjoy your coffee!" she said when she handed him the container.

"This isn't for coffee. I'm apparently making one of my grandmother's favorite dishes for dinner tonight. She just sprung the news on me!"

"Ooh, what are you making?" she asked excitedly. "Anything that involves cream must be delicious."

"It's a pasta dish. I know your son isn't feeling well, but if anything changes, I'd love it if you joined us."

"Sounds tempting, but it's really just not an option today. He's getting over a high fever."

He knew he might be pushing yet couldn't stop himself from asking. She was still smiling, after all. "That's too bad. Poor kid. How about I bring a meal to you? I'll eat with Fiona, of course, but I'd love to have you try it. It's one of my specialties."

He held his breath waiting for another rejection.

"I'd be a fool to turn down someone's signature dish," she said, after a pause that seemed to take forever.

"I've never been one for name calling, but it would definitely be a regrettable mistake."

They both laughed. Cricket wrapped her arms around herself, rubbing one of her arms.

"I swear I still haven't lost the chill from shoveling yesterday. I'm going to go and join my kids in front of the fire. What time should I expect you?"

"How about seven? And save your appetite."

"Will do." She grinned, closing the door behind him.

He'd need to make a huge batch of food tonight. Fiona

wouldn't take kindly to having her leftovers brought to someone else if she didn't have enough for her lunch tomorrow.

Cricket had to admit that she enjoyed Boris's persistence. Handsome, thoughtful, and from the sounds of it, a great cook, and he clearly doted on his grandmother. She found herself looking forward to his return more and more as the hours passed. The only distraction was her earlier conversation with Cari repeating itself in her head. It sounded too good to be true. She pinched her herself once to make sure she wasn't dreaming.

Cari had been working at her great uncle Otto's store since she was fifteen years old. As a child, she adored visiting his beautiful home and traipsing across his farm. No matter the season, there was endless adventure to be found on the land. When she graduated with a business degree, Otto asked her to take over his store full time so that he could focus on his farm and efforts to sustain the bee population. This wasn't the glamorous job she'd imagined herself in, but it had meant so much to him that she'd decided that a few years of managing the store would be relevant experience to list on her resume.

A few years turned into seven as she found herself enjoying finding new ways to increase sales. The Honeycomb Market grew from a small general store to a thriving year-round business, shipping products all over the world. Her organic lip balms and lotions made from beeswax and honey were the most popular. In addition to Cari's marketing strategies, word of mouth spread across the internet and all media channels.

Despite Cari's innovative ideas leading to an influx of customers, she was blindsided to learn that Uncle Otto had willed his entire estate to her. Yes, Cari loved the farm. Yes, Cari believed in what her uncle was working for. That didn't mean she knew the first thing about running a farm. Lex Owens had served as Otto's right-hand man for the last ten years and had promised to help her every step of the way. This didn't do much to assuage her nerves, and she continued to find herself struggling to learn every aspect of the business.

A white gabled farmhouse sounds quaint. Charming. However, quaint and charming are more appropriate adjectives for Fiona's rambling cape situated across the street. Cari confessed she still hadn't picked up a cozy vibe in the five thousand square feet of living space, encompassing eight bedrooms, four and a half bathrooms, a dining room fit for a banquet, and a library that felt larger than the entire footprint of her old condo. Three floors of fourteen-foot ceilings overwhelmed her. The unfinished basement with its dirt floor surrounded by stone appeared untouched since the home was built over one hundred years ago. She claimed her skin prickled with every solo trip to the bottom of those stairs. Despite the company of Uncle Otto's Siamese cats, Arthur and Guinevere, she had been feeling like a ghost in someone else's home.

As Cricket tried to embrace the idea that her circumstances were finally changing for the better, a flash of Cari closing the discussion popped into her head. She implied that it would be disastrous if anyone learned the truth behind their living arrangements. They must ensure that everyone stuck to the same story of Cricket, an old friend, moving to Blue Cove. She would tell anyone who asked that she was staying with Cari only until she found somewhere else to live. It wasn't that far off from the truth. Hopefully this would keep the kids from raising too many questions if asked about the arrangement.

Boris valued punctuality and arrived precisely at seven. Ashling greeted him at the door. She let him in, saying her mother was upstairs putting Max to bed. They were starting school soon, and she wanted him to get in a good night of sleep to kick the flu to the curb once and for all. She took the still-hot bowl of pasta, allowing him to remove his coat and wet boots. As he followed her to the dining room, the warmth of the house settled into his bones. He welcomed the heat even after the short walk in the frigid air.

"I hope you'll be joining us. I brought enough for everyone," he said as she placed the bowl on the table.

"I already ate, but I do want to try a little before I go upstairs."

"You are in for a real treat. A little bit might turn into a heaping plate once you taste this masterpiece."

"Someone's confident in his culinary skills!" He turned at the sound of Cricket's now-familiar voice.

She had changed her clothes since this afternoon and was wearing jeans and a fitted red sweater. Her hair had been pulled halfway back, with pieces slipping out to frame her face. He couldn't help but wonder—no, hope—if she had dressed for him.

"I hope you don't mind my saying, red does you justice."

"Thank you."

"Oh, please," Ashling chimed in. "Every color is my mom's color! You must have noticed by now that she's gorgeous!"

Boris glanced at Cricket and saw her cheeks flaming. She tried to cover it by shaking her head to brush off the compliment and peeked under the tinfoil at the contents in the bowl.

"This was worth waiting for!" She inhaled deeply. "What did you put in this?"

"Make yourself a plate and see if you can figure it out."

"You won't have to ask me twice. Ash, pass Boris a plate please."

"No thanks. I didn't want Fiona to eat alone. This is all for you."

She stared at him in disbelief. "How much do I look like I eat?"

He held up his hands in mock protest. "I tried to bring enough for everyone. Tell me you didn't eat earlier."

"I didn't. Everyone else did, though. We never imagined you'd bring over so much food."

"It's barely enough for each of you to eat as a side dish." He grabbed a serving spoon, piled some pasta on a plate, and handed it to her. "You'd better dig in before it gets cold."

Ashling left and returned with three glasses of water. He watched them as they ate with unbridled enthusiasm, praising him in between bites. Cricket stood and reached for seconds as Ashling thanked him and excused herself.

Cricket sat back down with her dish. "You weren't exaggerating! You do know your way around a kitchen. Who taught you to cook?"

"My grandfather. Fiona did her best to avoid turning on the stove at all costs," he said with a chuckle. "She was fortunate to have a husband who prided himself on feeding his family well. He used to say that he cooked only because he liked to eat. The truth was, he enjoyed watching everyone else eat what he'd whipped up."

"Your grandmother is a lucky woman."

"Luckier because he had me working in the kitchen with him as soon as I moved in. He wanted to make sure that someone in the family would be able to make her favorite meals long after he was gone. Some of my best memories of him were the times we'd try out some new recipes together and host cook offs." A smile came to his face at the memory. "These would be major events. People begged for invitations to serve as judges, and we'd end up with a houseful of novice food critics participating."

"Did they know who'd prepared each dish?"

"No way! We'd each come up with some crazy name for ourselves. One of us might be Chef Chop and the other Chef Suey. They'd have no idea who was who. Not even Fiona."

"Sounds like some good times." She took another bite and then quickly covered her mouth with one hand and waved at him with the other. "Mm-mm!"

"What?"

She chewed quickly and swallowed. "I have an idea! How would you feel about another cook off? I mean, I know it won't be the same, but it could still be so much fun."

"What do you mean?"

"This may come as a shock to you, but I happen to be known for having some talent in the kitchen myself."

"You want to compete against me?" he asked, raising both eyebrows.

She lifted her chin. "You doubt I have what it takes?"

"I didn't say that. But you must be pretty sure of yourself to challenge me after eating this."

"Scared?" She twitched her shoulders flirtatiously.

He grinned. "Intrigued. You're on."

This was something to look forward to. They weren't able to settle on a date or a place just yet, but they sat for a long time talking through the logistics of how it would happen and who should attend to play food critic. He smiled at her enthusiasm and struggled to reconcile this vibrant, animated woman with the one who spent most of her time shying away from him. She was a puzzle he intended to solve.

CHAPTER 6

Everything should always start on a Monday, at least according to Cricket. Especially when it came to a new diet or exercise program. Cricket woke up at five thirty in the morning to squeeze in a half hour on the treadmill before anyone else woke up. Her first official workout since high school required solitude. Throwing on some leggings, a sweatshirt, and sneakers she headed downstairs.

Buoyed by the fact that she had already accomplished getting herself up so early to exercise, she told herself that she could make this part of her daily routine. She expected to find running on the treadmill easier than running on a track because the machine propels you along. Dismayed to learn that there was nothing easy about it, she also determined that it was not even the tiniest bit humane to get on that thing without coffee first.

Distracting herself with Cari's strict set of rules didn't help. After a mere fifteen minutes, she dropped to a fast-paced walk and tried to run through the plan in her mind while wishing she had the paper she'd printed in front of her.

Guests would not be permitted during what was referred to as a mandatory blackout period of one month. Despite welcoming Cricket into her home, Cari wanted to learn more about her and refused to open her doors to additional strangers, with the exception of meeting Cricket's mom in the near future. Cricket didn't view the blackout period as a deal breaker. At this point in her life, her mother was the only one she wanted to include on this new path.

A budget would be set up to account for living expenses, entertainment, and savings. She would be religious about birth control, willing to submit to random drug testing, and maintain good hygiene. Cari took things a little farther than the stipulations set at St. Agnes's, but this was her home, for crying out loud.

During the discussion, Cari reminded her to regard the list as a set of expectations. It sounded friendlier, while conveying a similar meaning. Her intentions did not include laying down these laws as if she was some sort of queen. This entire plan teetered on the pinnacle of both her and Cricket's impulsive natures.

When asked again why she would consider doing something like this, Cari shared that she didn't grow up with much herself. Raised by a single mother from the age of two, Cari watched her mother Nadine work two jobs to support them while barely getting by. Their electricity was often shut off due to outstanding bills. As a pre-teen, Cari frequently refused to give her phone number out to boys because she feared they'd call and hear a recording stating her phone had been disconnected. Most nights, they scraped together what shouldn't really pass for dinner. The worst was plain white bread smothered in gravy. She gagged at the mere memory. Some say you'll eat anything if you're starving, but that was not true for Cari. Those nights, she went to bed with her stomach rumbling.

She described vivid memories of the people they knew in those days. There were some unsavory characters to be sure, but she could tell you firsthand that being poor does not equal being a bad person. Or a lazy person. Or someone to be feared. Many people in that situation could use some help getting on their feet and getting a good life started. The people in Cari's circle now would have thought there was something inherently wrong with her mother. Otherwise, how could she have ended up in that situation? They'd never understand that she didn't deserve her lot in life. She tried to crawl higher and just couldn't catch a break. Well, until they moved to Blue Cove.

Although they had visited Uncle Otto for years, Nadine had been too proud to share her financial troubles with him. When his wife passed away, the truth came out. Not wanting to impose on him by staying in his home during his grief, Nadine insisted they would sleep at the Blue Cove Inn. It never crossed her mind that he'd be lonely and call the inn asking to be connected to their room only to be told that no one by the name Nadine Montgomery had checked in. Despite the late hour, he was restless and went for a drive. As he drove, he grew concerned for their whereabouts and decided to pass by the inn to look for their car. Perhaps the receptionist had made a mistake.

Nadine hadn't lied to her uncle. They were in fact staying at the inn. Not in a room, but in the parking lot. Spotting their car and pulling in next to it, Cari imagined his world crumbled a little bit at the sight of his two beloved nieces asleep in the backseat. Although it was mortifying for Nadine to be taken back to the farmhouse and coaxed into spilling her tale of woe, Cari believed that moment was the best thing that ever happened to her. They moved into the carriage house and a friend of Uncle Otto's promptly hired Nadine. This generosity profoundly affected both of their futures.

After walking for a few minutes to cool down, Cricket turned the treadmill off and started stretching. This also no longer came as easily to her as it had when she was seventeen years old. By the time she finished up, she heard someone up and about in the kitchen. Hoping she hadn't woken whoever it was, Cricket rounded the corner to find Boris filling a glass.

He turned and smiled. "Thought you could use this."

"Thank you," she said taking the glass. "I don't mean to be rude, but what are you doing here?"

He shook his head laughing at himself for a moment as he

poured another glass. "I'm so sorry! You were probably wondering if an intruder had broken in! An intruder who likes iced tea!" He chuckled at himself again and took a quick sip from his own glass. "Cari asked me to take a look at the garbage disposal and left a key under the doormat."

"Oh, so you're a plumber in addition to dabbling in real estate." She spoke while trying in vain to casually comb her fingers through her mess of a ponytail, knowing she looked a fright. He wasn't particularly well groomed himself this morning, wearing a hoodie and track pants. Cricket found something oddly appealing about that.

"Sometimes. I'm pretty good with miscellaneous home repairs."

Not knowing what else to say to him and feeling herself turning pink, she zeroed in on the dishes in the sink. "Well, thank you. I should get this stuff washed up." Turning the water on, she asked, "Safe to assume everything is fixed?"

"Yeah, it's all set for now. I'll need to get a part and come back though."

"Okay. I'll just take care of these in the meantime."

"You never mentioned that you were such an early riser." He walked over and leaned against the counter so that he could face her while she rinsed.

"Once the day starts, I never seem to find another opportunity to get in a workout. So, it's now or never."

"Do you walk or run on the treadmill?"

"Run. Well, to be honest, I haven't been at this very long and am still trying to build up my stamina."

"Oh, I hear that! I've been out of commission for a month and need to ramp up too."

"Injury?"

"Work. Poor excuse, but it is what it is."

"A month is nothing," she laughed. "I'm back at it for the first time since running track in high school!"

He lifted one eyebrow and grinned. "I'm going to be staying with my grandmother through Christmas. There's an indoor track at the Blue Cove Country Club. I don't let my membership lapse even when I'm not in town for an extended time. If you're interested, you can join me as my guest. I need to start getting myself back in shape, and rumor has it that working out with a partner keeps you motivated."

Cricket paused, wavering on her response. Even though they'd had such a good time last night, she didn't want to lead him on.

"Maybe." Drying her hands and swallowing, she decided to gracefully excuse herself without committing to an answer. "It was nice to see you. I need to take care of a few things before my kids get up. Thanks for stopping by."

"My pleasure. I'm looking forward to that cook off you promised me. Let's get together soon and nail down some of the details."

Smiling, she brushed past him and headed upstairs. Making plans for that was probably not such a hot idea either.

Boris wondered what made Cricket so anxious. Once again, she couldn't get away from him fast enough after their odd conversation. She sort of agreed to go to the country club with him, though. It would be interesting to see if he could make that happen.

Where did she come from anyways? He thought he knew all of Cari's friends and would have at least remembered her mentioning someone with a name like 'Cricket'. It also occurred to him that Cari hadn't said a word about her or her kids when she asked him to look at the sink. He'd thought about asking how she knew them, but figured she'd volunteer information on her own when the time was right. He didn't view this as a case of Cari being absent minded. She was deliberately keeping something to herself.

Again with the distractions! He wasn't in town to pursue the backstory of some stranger or to find a gym date, or any date all.

He still hadn't found a way to broach the subject of his real estate proposal with Cari. That was where his head should be at. Thinking about Cricket was just a way to avoid focusing on his task. The time had come to put it out there. Maybe Cari would welcome the opportunity to sell. As far as he knew, it had never been her dream to manage every facet of the farm. Still, if it was going to be such an easy endeavor, he wouldn't be procrastinating this much. Cari adored her uncle and believed in his mission. It would be a hard sell to get her to give up on it.

Lex and Pia continued to lurk as potential problems in his mind as well. He'd dodged several of Lex's phone calls and Pia's invitation to dinner. She had left a few messages saying how nice it would be if he brought Cricket over. Packing up his tools and double checking the disposal once more, he admitted to himself that under other circumstances he would have loved to get together with them. But to sit down at Pia's table over a meal she'd prepared for him and then to look her in the eye making friendly conversation while he was essentially plotting to oust her and her brother from their jobs? He couldn't do it. Resolving to ignore the guilt that relentlessly gnawed at him, he let himself out and returned to Fiona's.

Standing in front of the double vanity with its marble countertops, Cricket stared at her surroundings through the mirror and acknowledged once more how far removed this place was from the cockroach-infested project they had been evicted from. If she tried, she could still smell the stench of urine that had permeated those halls. It would literally hit you in the face when you entered the stairwell. And that was even a step up from the fleabag motel they spent almost a year in.

She grew up in a well-worn triple decker with parents who loved her in their own way. Most people plod through some sort of dysfunction in their childhood, so there was nothing special about that. Dysfunction was a fancy word, but her life was far from fancy. Her dad rarely came around and eventually left. At least she'd had a dad for a while and knew she didn't need to be missing him, unlike so many of her friends who'd never even met their fathers. Who was she to complain? Some had it much worse. She'd heard enough stories through the grapevine to know that she had it better than many other people.

Wally had entered her world as her senior year in high school was coming to an end. After what could only be described as the happiest summer of her life up to that point, she didn't hesitate when he proposed. It hadn't mattered that they'd only been together for three months. It hadn't mattered that they were both only eighteen years old. They'd intended to start a new life together. A life filled with promise and hope. Always an excellent student, Cricket had painted a picture of college in her future as well.

Despite the best intentions, her dreams were put on hold when she'd become pregnant with Ashling. That had almost immediately raised questions as to whether the pregnancy had been the reason behind the wedding. Although Wally had worked toward building what was becoming a thriving landscaping business, they hadn't had the means to pay for college or childcare. Ever optimistic, Cricket hadn't batted an eye at putting her plans on hold. She was young. It wouldn't matter if it took extra time to reach her goals.

There had been no denying it. That baby had been a true blessing. Corny as it sounded, she had shined a new light into their little home. Every day had brought something new. Enthralled with Ashling and experiencing the world through her eyes, five years had passed with little thought given to the college plans temporarily shelved. Although they hadn't had much in the way of luxuries, Cricket had been grateful to be able to take care of her child full time. As she prepared to enroll Ashling in kindergarten, the glimmer of new possibilities had begun to enter Cricket's mind. Until, as luck would have it, she'd found herself pregnant again.

She'd turned twenty-five three days before Max was born. Though desperate to pursue a degree, her dreams crashed around her when Wally voiced concerns. He hadn't thought it would be fair to Max to place him in the care of someone else during the day. Ashling had enjoyed the benefit of a full-time mom, and he believed that Max deserved the same. Give him three years. That was all Wally wanted. Three years. By then, Max would be ready for preschool. Only a selfish mother would reject such a reasonable compromise.

It might have been reasonable. Except for the fact that Wally had fallen off a second story roof while trying to trim back some tree branches. He'd died two days later, leaving Cricket with a life insurance policy that had barely paid for the cost of his burial. The sale of his construction equipment had helped her little family get through the first few months while she'd searched for a full-time job and affordable childcare. Despite her best efforts, Cricket had found herself unable to pay the rent.

Not wanting to impose on her mother who faced her own struggles, Cricket had taken her children to St. Agnes's, a temporary place of refuge for the homeless. The people there had been kind, but they had seen so many cases like Cricket's that immunity had stolen the space in their hearts once reserved for empathy. She'd recognized a certain amount of compassion was necessary to work there and appreciated their efforts. Still, it hadn't helped her feel less alone or terrified. Less than desirable accommodations had been the cherry on top of a bad situation turned worse.

The following morning, they'd all woken up exhausted. The kids had tossed restlessly all night, and Cricket had been too afraid to sleep. In hindsight, they'd hit the jackpot because luck had brought them there the same day as Sandy. The social worker had proved to be invaluable. At the time, the best she could do had been to move the little family to a motel. Not ideal, but better than nothing, and it had laid the foundation of a collaborative relationship.

Their new home had included one room, two double beds, a mini fridge, and a mini microwave. She'd tried to present it to her children as an adventure or a vacation. But Ashling had been smart enough to know that even people taking fantastic trips eventually looked forward to going home at some point, sleeping in their own bed, using their own things. Their vacation would not come to an end anytime soon, and no one would have described it as a happy one.

Eventually, Sandy had found them that vermin haven of a project to live in, with the promise of government assistance checks to help somewhat. Sandy, Cricket's new best friend, had promised that she would also help Cricket find work somewhere. Getting a job hadn't been as easy as she had implied. Childcare had posed a problem, and Cricket also had only qualified for minimum wage employment. She'd needed enough money to keep her new apartment after a preset date and had learned how to manage her money after getting a job at Shady Oaks.

Today, Cricket owned all her mistakes, and there had been plenty of them. But taking that $100 from Helen crowned the top of the list. She'd failed Sandy. She'd failed her kids. She would never let it happen again.

Pressing the fast forward button to the present, she moved to gaze out the window. She had never lived on a tree-lined street before. The other homes weren't what people imagined when hearing the word mansion, but there was some comfortable living going on there.

Yes, Cari owned a gorgeous home. Yes, they were moving in. These facts did little to ease her worry. How long could they possibly last there? They didn't fit. Just listening to Cari speak sometimes made her feel stupid. Could Cricket find a way to make this work, or would she blow it like she had so many other things in her life?

She needed to call her mother. She'd never gone this long

without talking to her. Hopefully her mom wasn't worried and had assumed that the phone bill hadn't been paid again. Not ready to tell her the truth, she was thankful when the voicemail clicked on. She kept it short and sweet, saying she didn't have a phone at the moment, all was well, and she'd be in touch again in a few weeks. That alone would make her mom wonder if something was wrong.

CHAPTER 7

Boris put his phone in his back pocket with a sigh. Dean Stone understandably wanted to know what the holdup was. He put him off by saying Cari hadn't had time to meet with him yet. His partners could be ruthless when pursuing properties they wanted to acquire. As much as he loved real estate development, his conscience always got the better of him when he knew a potential seller had an emotional attachment to a property. In this case, both the owner and her devoted employees concerned him.

Preparing to return to the farmhouse with the extra part for the disposal, he realized he was hoping to find Cricket still at home. That morning, she'd once again played her cat and mouse game. For reasons that escaped him, Boris still wanted to try to get to know her. He had to ask himself what he hoped to gain from the effort, but he didn't have an answer. At least, not one that made sense for his life. It would have been easier if he hadn't agreed to stay with his grandmother for another few weeks.

Fiona had made it clear that she expected him to stay through Christmas. The last few years, she'd visited his cousins in Florida for the month of December. This year, she was determined to enjoy the holiday in her own home with all the trimmings.

Venturing into the dusty, cobwebbed attic and dragging down

the boxes that held her favorite ornaments and decorations did not appeal to him. It was early in the month by his standards. Decorations could wait a few more days. With any luck, though, she'd be happily ensconced in her new senior housing complex by this time next year. At the very least, he could ensure this holiday met expectations with favorite traditions in her beloved home one last time.

Stomach grumbling, he put together two ham and cheese sandwiches and took a seat in the family room, hoping to catch the forecast. Through the front window, he spotted Fiona in Cari's driveway. Her stance told him that she wasn't happy. She hadn't lost her distaste for Cricket since the trash can incident, and he suspected that had something to do with her present demeanor. He'd heard her ranting on the phone that morning about the floozy across the street and knew she wasn't referring to Cari.

He'd apologize to Cari later. Right now, he needed to eat and get to work if he intended to find time left in the day to deal with that sink.

If Cricket had been hoping for a warm welcome from the neighbors, she should have looked elsewhere. Fiona's voice rattled the windows as she accosted Cari in the driveway as she was getting in her car. Cricket couldn't resist and cracked one open.

"Cari," she called in her distinctively shrill voice, marching her way toward the car.

Cari greeted her with a terse hello and deliberately hopped into her car, closing the door firmly. Opening the window to be polite, but turning the ignition to signal she needed to be brief, she said, "Hi Fiona, how are you?"

"Oh, I'm fine," she replied, placing her hands on her wide hips. Not a good sign. "I thought I'd stop by and see how you're holding up these days. I couldn't help but notice you have some houseguests. Family?"

"Friends."

"Ah. So, have you known them long?"

"Yes, they are old friends. I'm sorry Fiona, I really need to get going. It was nice of you to stop by."

"I understand," she said while not moving and clearly not understanding at all. "How long do you expect them to stay?"

"It's a big, empty house Fiona. As long as they want, I suppose." Putting the car in reverse, she added "I'll have to introduce you soon."

Cricket watched Fiona move aside, and Cari was finally able to leave.

Less than ninety minutes later, a loud knock sounded at the door. Cricket froze. The doorbell rang out the tune to Jingle Bells. She held her breath, heart racing, and attempted to reassure herself that the person behind the door would leave. Hearing a car pull into the driveway, she took a chance and peered out the front window. Cari had returned from the grocery store, only to be greeted by the woman turning away from the unanswered door. Cari had pointed out Tina and her husband Joe when they had been shoveling. She commented that they were rarely around and usually only seen with their baby coming and going. Too busy with their own lives to worry about the personal lives of everyone else on the street, they made perfect neighbors.

After hearing Fiona this morning, Cricket didn't want to know what Tina had to say, but curiosity got the better of her and she opened the window again to listen.

"Hey, Cari! Let me help you carry in those bundles," Tina said as she jogged over to the car and loaded up her arms. "I could use the arm workout!"

Cricket cringed. It looked like she'd be meeting her after all. Remembering Fiona's interrogation this morning, she decided introductions could wait until she felt ready and crept into the library.

Once they came inside and had everything loaded onto the kitchen island, Cricket heard Tina get right down to business. "So,

Fiona tells me you have some friends staying with you. That must be nice."

"It is." Short, detail-free answers seemed to be the way to go.

"Okay, so here's the thing," Tina stopped and took a deep breath. "So, actually, this is kind of uncomfortable. But Fiona is driving me absolutely crazy. She has herself all riled up. Normally, I'm inclined to mind my own business. I'm just here to shut her up."

"What are you talking about?"

"Well, you should hear her, 'They've been staying at that house for days on end. Talk about a gaggle of misfits! Where in the world did these people come from?' she says."

Cari laughed, and Cricket almost did as well. Her impersonation was flawless. There was no way Cricket would interrupt their conversation now.

"You think it's funny, but that woman's shrill voice could drive a nun to drink." She started unloading one of the bags.

An observer might say it was strange Tina had never met Cari's "old friend" Cricket before. It was not strange at all. What was strange was her hanging out in this kitchen as if she did it all the time. Nothing could be further from the truth. Cari moved in months ago and mentioned Tina had only been inside the house twice. Always friendly when seeing each other outside, one of them would inevitably start chit chatting a bit. Not for any length of time of course, but Cari claimed to honestly enjoy talking to her. Still, they weren't close.

She'd even let Tina keep the keys Otto had given her years ago. A fellow cat lover, Tina would check in on Arthur and Guinevere on the rare occasion he traveled, and he'd feed her cat Millie when she was on vacation. Cari said she would have loved to become better friends, but beyond being neighborly, Tina had never shown any interest in getting together socially. Cari didn't have the time to initiate such things, so they remained distant acquaintances despite living a stone's throw away from each other.

"I can't imagine what she's so worried about," Cari commented. "It's not like I asked her if my friends could move into her house."

"Oh, I hear you. And I'm sure she'll settle down once she has a chance to meet them."

"That should be sooner than later. I was planning to hold an open house style Christmas party soon."

"That sounds fun! When? Christmas is creeping up on us."

"I haven't hashed out all of the details yet. Let me look at the calendar on my phone." After a few moments, she said, "It's short notice, but Saturday looks good."

Cricket stifled a gasp. This wasn't supposed to happen so soon! She wasn't ready to meet people! She needed at least a few more weeks to acclimate herself to the new living arrangements.

Unaware of Cricket's distress, Cari continued, "I think it might be nice for Cricket's kids to meet a few people before starting school."

Nodding to herself behind the French doors, Cricket had to admit that was a pretty good idea. It wouldn't be easy for them to walk into a classroom midyear without a single familiar face.

"That would be so much fun!" Tina exclaimed. "I'll tell Joe tonight. I don't think he has anything planned that day for us." The monitor on her phone alerted them that the baby had stirred. "I'd better go. I only have a window of about ninety seconds before Lucie starts wailing to get out of her crib." Shoving her phone in one jacket pocket and pulling her house key out of another she called over her shoulder, "Text me what time and what we can bring!"

As the door clicked shut, Cari called out, "I know you're here, Cricket! It's safe to come out!"

"I am here," she said walking into the kitchen with a sheepish smile. "I was going to introduce myself, and then she started talking about me, and I kind of froze. I shouldn't have eavesdropped, but I couldn't help myself."

"Me too," came an unexpected third voice.

Boris, red faced, came through the door that led to the

basement. "I was downstairs checking out the water pipes and when I heard voices, I started up the stairs. But then I realized the conversation was about my grandmother, and she wasn't exactly being cast in a positive light, so it felt awkward to come barging in."

"No worries! Please don't pay too much attention to any of that." Now it was Cari's turn to be embarrassed. She started putting groceries away to avoid looking at them.

"Hey, Fiona has never been one to shy away from speaking her mind," Boris said. "It's not always going to leave a warm and fuzzy feeling for people."

Being the center of the conversation in question, Cricket's cheeks turned pink.

"Cricket, if anyone should ignore what was just said, it's you," Boris continued. "Fiona is harmless. She adores Cari and is probably just looking out for her. She'll come around as she gets to know you better."

Boris gathered up his tools and assured Cari that her sink issues should be completely resolved. He asked Cricket to see him out, claiming to need help opening the door with his arms full.

Pausing at the door, he adjusted the weight in his hands and looked at her with his mouth set in a thin line. "I'm really sorry about what Fiona said. Please don't take it to heart."

How could she not? Of course, that wasn't the appropriate response.

"I have a thick skin." No truer words have been spoken. "Don't worry about it."

"Did I understand correctly?" he asked, changing the subject. "Did Cari say that your kids would be starting school here in Blue Cove on Monday?"

"She did. They will." She was stammering. "Um, we liked the town so much that we decided to stay."

"You recently decided this? That seems kinda sudden."

"Well it wasn't actually. It—it was the reason we came to visit in the first place. I'd been thinking of making the move for a while and brought the kids to visit so I could be sure. And, I'm sure." She cringed at the unnatural high pitch creeping into her voice. "Unfortunately, we haven't found a place to stay yet. Cari said we could keep her company while I'm house hunting."

She could tell by his expression that he wasn't buying what she was selling but was gracious enough to not push too hard.

His expression turned serious. "I'm looking forward to seeing you again at the party. We never did have that spiked cocoa."

"Me too," she replied as she moved to close the door behind him. Surprised to realize that she meant it, she tried to push the thought out of her mind. Nothing good could come from getting involved with Boris.

She found Cari in front of the fireplace. At the sound of Cricket's footsteps, she began berating herself.

"Why did I do this to myself?" she moaned. "Tina's one thing. But Cricket, you don't know Vera and Tess. They live at the end of the street and are their own little clique. Oh, sure, they are friendly enough one on one. It's when they team up that there's a problem. Together they have the ability to make other women feel like an uncool twelve-year-old being whispered about by the popular girls."

"If the truth gets out about me, the whole street will think you've single handedly destroyed their neighborhood."

Cari sank to the stone hearth. "On the flipside, if they buy the story and take the time to get to know you and the kids, everything will be okay. It's not like you're a bunch of criminals, for crying out loud!"

"Not that you know of," Cricket giggled.

"Not even a little bit funny, Cricket," she said, laughing anyways.

CHAPTER 8

Boris walked into an empty house and spotted a note on the foyer table saying Fiona had gone to a Christmas bazaar with a friend and would be home for dinner. It also not-so-subtly hinted that she hoped he'd have a meal ready when she returned. He worried she was growing dependent on his cooking, but he poked through the kitchen cabinets and the refrigerator anyway, finding what was needed to make chicken fried steak, gravy, mashed potatoes, and baked asparagus. She may as well eat like a queen while the opportunity presented itself.

He had hours before he'd need to begin cooking, and he needed to work. Cricket had the right idea, squeezing in a workout first thing in the morning. As usual, he had a list of tasks waiting for him on his laptop.

The time had come for Boris to be honest with himself. His grandmother's new neighbor was becoming more than a distraction. He wanted to spend time with her, to get to know her better. There wasn't any good reason for this, just some sort of a pull. He sensed a new calm about her today, despite the fact that Fiona had said such awful things. The nervous energy that typically consumed their interactions had dissipated.

The upcoming open house would give Cricket and Fiona a

chance to get to know each other better. Not that he could say he knew Cricket well. He didn't know her at all. But, unlike his grandmother, he read people fairly well. From the few times he'd met Cricket, he'd caught glimpses of a caring woman compelled to rush out in her pajamas to assist a stranger, a mother her children were excited to share their pancake joy with, and a friend willing to shovel feet of snow past the point of exhaustion.

Boris had to wonder if she'd fallen on hard times. Why else would she move into her friend's home in the middle of the school year? There had to be more to the story—not that it was any of his business. He'd been so quick to share personal information with her the first time they'd met, while she had made it clear from the start that she wasn't an open book. It would be interesting to see if she'd let her guard down at the party and allow him to get to know her.

Turning his attention back to work, he reviewed the numbers on a Boston apartment building his company was in the process of selling. If everything went according to plan, it would prove to have been a fabulous investment. Each unit in the waterfront property had been renovated and the building now included an onsite gym and an underground parking garage.

It occurred to him that it may be more lucrative to convert the units into condominiums and sell each off individually. Checking his partners' calendars, he sent a meeting invitation for a mutually available time slot. While he awaited confirmation, he prepared a spreadsheet detailing the potential profit. This new venture might buy him some extra time to figure out how to best handle his pitch to Cari.

"They're here!" hissed Cari, dragging Cricket away from the dishwasher the next morning. "I'm not dealing with these two alone."

"What two? What are you talking about?"

"I dropped invitations in Tess and Vera's mailboxes last night and now they're walking up the driveway."

"So?"

The doorbell rang.

"So?" Cari asked incredulously. "Those two always come as a pair. Never one without the other, from what I've seen. You need to come with me to answer the door, so it looks like I'm part of a team too."

"Okay, but you're being silly."

Pulling open the door, they were greeted with two smiles brighter than the sun itself.

"Cari!" they said in unison.

"Hi ladies, come on in," Cari replied in a sing-song voice that matched theirs. She ushered them into her foyer. "This is my friend Cricket. Cricket, this is Vera and Tess. They live just down the street, past Tina."

Cricket shook their hands, noting their appraising once-overs while completing a scan of her own. One of them wore a strong perfume with hints of jasmine that smelled more potent than unpleasant. She suspected it was Tess, who had painted on an exceptional amount of makeup and donned bright red talons for nails. Her champagne hair indicated a fresh blowout and a white coat draped around her in a way that suggested she was off to the symphony, not her neighbor's home. Vera was much more subdued in a gray puffer jacket and jeans. While her golden hair also appeared to be freshly styled, her makeup had been applied with a gentler hand.

"It's so nice to meet you," said Tess. She twirled around for a moment and sighed. "This place is beyond stunning, Cari. Your uncle was a sweet man, but a woman's touch has done wonders."

"We won't keep you," piped in Vera. "We just stopped in to personally thank you for your invitation. Such a fantastic idea. Roger and the kids love a good party. You have to tell me what we can bring."

"Oh, I haven't thought that far in advance." Cari considered.

"Actually, just bring yourselves. I'm not cooking, so neither should you."

"Oh, which caterer are you using?" asked Tess.

"Reynolds. They've done a few events for my mom, and she's always been happy with them."

"I have an idea!" Vera chimed in. "In lieu of hostess gifts, you should ask guests to bring gifts for the Community Toy Drive."

"I love that idea!" Cari's eyes lit up. "I'll send everyone an email or a text letting them know."

"Well, I can't wait," said Tess with a toss of her shimmering head. "I was just saying to Scott that we should plan a block party for this summer. Be more neighborly, you know. But you beat me to it!"

Vera didn't waste any time stating what clearly sat at the forefront of her brain. "So Cricket, Tina tells us you're living here as well."

"Yes, me and my two kids. My daughter is in middle school, and my son is in the first grade."

"Wonderful!" Vera clapped her hands together and rolled up on her toes in a slight hop. "Your daughter will have to meet my twins and Tess's daughter. All close in age! Isn't it fantastic?"

"It really is," Cricket said sincerely. "I'm glad Ashling will have a chance to chat with a few people before starting school on Monday."

"There aren't any little ones on this street, other than Tina's baby Lucie. But the next street over does have a ton of kids in elementary school."

"That's good to hear. Though to tell the truth, I'm not as worried about my son making friends. He's a bit more social than my daughter. She always has her head in a book, while he's the life of every party."

Vera laughed out loud. "Sounds like my twins. Polar opposites."

"We'll let you get back to whatever it was you were doing before we popped in," said Tess. "I'm sure you have lots to tackle over the next few days. Please don't hesitate to reach out if we can help you with anything."

"Sounds great. Thank you both for stopping by," replied Cari.

They whirled out as quickly as they'd fluttered in.

Cricket couldn't hold her tongue. "I'm sorry Cari, I have to admit it. I think I liked them."

"Me too!" she sputtered, wide eyed. "I think I was just worried that they saw me as someone who'd had everything handed to her on a silver platter. That I haven't technically earned the right to live on this street."

"I'm not one to throw stones. Let's just be glad that they were so genuinely friendly and excited about your party."

An invisible weight had been lifted. Prior to that visit, an unspoken question loomed as to whether Vera and Tess would come with their families. It had been entirely possible that they wouldn't want to be bothered with one more thing to do during the holiday season. Now, knowing that people were actually looking forward to the event breathed new life into the planning of it.

Trying to squeeze in some online shopping before work, Boris groaned. He was having the worst time trying to find gifts. He'd love to go with gift cards, but Fiona always complained that they were impersonal. In his opinion, impersonal was a better option than nothing at all.

He needed to get away from his laptop for a while. Closing the screen and standing up, he decided to divert himself with a trip across the street to see how the party plans were going. He hadn't offered to help or to bring anything yet. That was as good a reason as any for an impromptu visit.

As he rang the doorbell, he began to second guess himself. Why had he come over here? Was he procrastinating? Was he honestly there to be a helpful neighbor? Or was he looking for an excuse to see Cricket? He feared the truth hid behind door number three.

"Who is it?" called a small voice.

"It's Boris," he called back.

"We don't know any florists!"

"Boris. Not florist."

Footsteps were followed by, "Max, who are you hollering to?"

"The florist, Mama."

"What?" Cricket pulled open the door a crack.

"I think he couldn't hear me well," Boris, said, smiling apologetically. "I told him it was Boris."

"Well, that makes sense," she said, pulling the door fully open. "Come in. You should have brought flowers!"

"Next time I will be sure to do that," he laughed. "I just thought I'd see if I could do anything to help with the party."

"That's Cari's realm. She's running the circus. I just do what she tells me."

He half smiled, taken aback by her playfulness. Where was the woman with her shield held high?

"Is she home?"

"Not at the moment. She took Ashling out to shop for supplies, even though I can't imagine what else she might need."

"I was just trying to get some shopping done myself," he admitted. "I said 'Self, this'll be the year you're not shopping on the day of Christmas Eve for once.'" He threw his hands up in mock desperation. "I got nowhere! I'm having a mental block when it comes to gift giving."

"Maybe I could help."

"Maybe you could. Are you doing anything right now?"

"Now?"

This was much too spontaneous for him, but he didn't want to turn back. "Yeah. If I don't get this done today, it won't cross my mind again until December 24th. Take a trip over to the mall with me. You and the little guy here. I'll buy you lunch after as a thank you."

"Well, don't thank me yet. What if you don't like my suggestions?"

"Is that a yes?"

"What do you think Max?" she asked the little boy. "Do you feel up to a trip to the mall?"

"Will Santa be there?" he asked excitedly.

Boris seized at the opportunity to close the deal. "Absolutely! We'll stop to see him first and get a picture taken."

"I'll get my coat and sneakers!" he yelled, tearing up the stairs.

"You sure know the way to a little boy's heart in December," Cricket said, smiling. "He just got over the flu though, so we really shouldn't stay out long. It may not be a great idea to have him in a crowd for too long. If at all."

"Not a problem. We'll see Santa, hit two stores at most, and then get lunch. We can even bring lunch back here, if that would be better. Your call."

Once they were pulling out of the driveway with carols playing on the radio, he asked if she'd done any shopping herself yet. He couldn't see her face but sensed a hint of sadness when she said she hadn't had a chance.

"Will you be seeing family?" he asked.

"Probably just my mom at some point. We haven't made plans yet."

"If things don't work out for some reason, you're welcome to join me and Fiona. It's going to be quiet this year. She usually goes to Florida, and I stay in New York. It would feel more festive having you guys around."

"Thanks. We might take you up on it."

It made zero sense for him to extend an invitation like that. He'd be leaving the day after Christmas. He felt selfish wanting to spend the holiday with her. Or any day at all. It wasn't fair to either of them to start down a road they couldn't see to the end.

CHAPTER 9

Walking into her favorite department store, Cricket suppressed the urge to close her eyes as she inhaled the scent of newness everywhere. It had been so long since she'd gone shopping for anything. Even the kids' clothes were all secondhand donations. She could have some fun today, though, since she was spending someone else's money.

As promised, they went to see Santa Claus first. It hurt her heart to think about what Max might ask for, because he would not likely receive it. After his picture was taken, Boris asked about his wish list. She could have cried when he said he wanted school supplies for his new class. He'd be happy with a box of crayons, some pencils, a few glue sticks, and something to carry it all in other than a plastic bag from the supermarket. She would have crawled under a clothing rack when he'd added that last detail if she hadn't been too busy trying to keep her tears in check. Stunned by Max's lack of greed, Boris didn't notice her emotional reaction.

"Something tells me Santa can manage that list with one hand tied behind his back."

Hah! If he only knew! She didn't have the money for an eight pack of crayons, never mind a backpack. She watched Boris crouch down on one knee and reach out to ruffle Max's hair. Then, she took in the stare Max gave him. It was one of disbelief. Not in the way other children his age found magic in Christmas. It had never been a holiday that bestowed luxurious gifts upon him. He looked at Boris with the eyes of a child who had seen and experienced enough to suspect that magic just might not exist, even when it came to things others might view as basic needs.

The scent of peppermint filled the air, music played through speakers overhead, and children squealed while waiting in line. Cricket felt her heart crack a little bit more. Boris remained oblivious and stood, suggesting that they shop for Fiona first. If he could find something for her, he had zero shame purchasing gift cards for everyone else on his list. Pulling off his jacket, he led the way.

Three stores later, they remained empty handed.

"If you want to call it a day, I understand," Boris said, sounding defeated.

Sensing a cloud of despair hovering around him, Cricket suggested they find somewhere to eat. Maybe some food would rejuvenate him. It turned out that she had been of little help thus far. She didn't know the first thing about Fiona. If her own grandson couldn't figure out what to get for her, how was she supposed to know what he should buy?

As they waited for their burgers at a pub next to the food court, Cricket tried to pick his brain. "Name something you've given her in the past that you know for a fact she absolutely loved."

Playing with the straw in his soda, he pondered her question before answering. "It was a blanket."

"A blanket? Then she's a woman of simple tastes. This should be easy."

"It wasn't just any blanket." He fidgeted some more and looked up at her. "I took pictures of all of the places she'd traveled to over the years and had them printed on a blanket. When she curls up in front of the TV, she has her memories to keep her company."

"What are the pictures of?"

"The usual vacation destinations. The Eiffel Tower, the moors in Ireland, glaciers in Alaska, the New York skyline at night." He trailed off. "I don't even know anymore. There's ten to twelve pictures on that thing. My grandfather took her anywhere and everywhere she wanted to go. I think, in truth, she chose every place she wanted me to see. If I couldn't have my parents, she wanted to give me the world."

Despite his best efforts to maintain a flat expression, his gratitude for the life they'd provided for him filled his face with emotion. She instinctively reached out and placed her hands over his.

"That is one of the most beautiful things I've ever heard."

"The blanket holds images of the most exotic places on earth, but her favorite is the photo of her cottage on Martha's Vineyard. Mine too." He grinned. "It didn't matter what the grand travel plans were for any given year, that place was our home away from home. Long weekends, spring break, weeks and weeks every summer. It never got old. Some of my best memories were made there."

"Does she still own the house?" Cricket asked.

"Yeah, but it's been years since we've made the trip. This summer I should make it a priority to see what condition it's in."

Their food arrived. Starving, they ate in silence for a few minutes, while Cricket thought over what she'd heard. Pictures made Fiona happy. Memories brought her joy. Why not stick with that theme? Cricket glanced at Max, enthralled with both his burger and his picture with Santa. He couldn't even stop staring at the photo long enough to complete the connect the dots puzzle on his place mat. An idea flashed before her eyes.

"You've done travel destinations, but what about people?"

Boris started at her in confusion.

"Pictures of people," she explained. "Could you discreetly pull out some of her favorite photos of family members and have them matted into a nice frame?"

Chewing and swallowing, he nodded. "So, like a blanket for her wall."

"Yes, but not a blanket. It should be a showcase. Something she will love to look at and enjoy showing off to visitors. Her beautiful family, and all that good stuff."

"I love it!"

"You do?"

"I absolutely love it! There's a custom frame store in town. Some day when she's out, I'll go through her albums. She has a bunch of favorites that she never looks at because they're buried in those archaic books. I can have them enlarged." He smacked both palms on the table making her and Max jump. "Cricket, this is a fantastic idea! I could kiss you!"

That statement could have made things awkward. Especially once Max started giggling. But a rush of electricity ran through her, and she chose to make light of it and laughed as well. Now she needed to brainstorm gift ideas for the people on her own list.

The towels were just about folded, and Cricket was anxious to get upstairs to prepare dinner. They'd be having baked spareribs tonight, and they never took less than two hours from start to finish.

Lex surprised her by walking downstairs into the laundry room. One of the kids must have let him in.

"Hey, Cricket, I came across these books and remembered Ashling saying she'd like to do some reading about bees."

"Aw, thanks, Lex. You didn't have to do that!"

"I don't mind. Gives me an excuse to get outside for a half hour and get some vitamin D. And she is going to love this book in particular, so it's worth the trip," he said, holding up one with vivid photographs of honeybees and their hives.

She took the stack and hugged the books to her.

"By the time she finishes, she'll feel like she'll move mountains to save them!" He took the book on top from her and started pointing out some of his favorite chapters, phrases, and notes he'd made in the margins. Wrapped up in hearing about the value of bees, Cricket didn't hear Boris come in.

"You two look like you're hard at work studying," he said from behind them.

Cricket turned and smiled, wondering why it always felt like she'd received a punch to the stomach when she looked at that man.

"We are," replied Lex. "Ashling will be able to teach us all a thing or two when she finishes reading these."

"This was so thoughtful of you," Cricket said earnestly. "Thank you so much."

"Any time. I'll swing by again if I come across any more books that look interesting." He gave Boris an odd look. "In the meantime, how about that dinner we'd all talked about? I know for a fact Pia's itching to have you over to get to know you better." He gave Boris another meaningful glance, making Cricket wonder what was not being said. "I know everyone's busy, but all work and no play makes Boris a dull boy."

"We wouldn't want that!" said Cricket.

"Har har," Boris laughed humorlessly. "Name the day and I'll be there, if Cricket here will agree to accompany me."

"I'd love to go. Just tell us when and we'll be there."

As she said it, she wished she could rephrase her words. Not the agreement to go, but she'd said it in a way that made them sound like a couple.

"Pass the invite on to Cari," Lex added. "She brightens up any table."

After a few minutes of small talk, Lex received a text and excused himself, saying he needed to get back to the farm. Boris and Cricket were left standing in a moment of awkward silence.

"So, do you two have something going on?" he asked leaning back against the counter.

"Me and Lex?" She was floored. She had only met the man once and didn't have the slightest bit of interest in him aside from being friendly. "I... No. Not at all."

"Okay. It's just you two looked pretty cozy together when I walked in."

"Well..." Why was it suddenly hard to swallow? Why was her heart racing at the thought of Boris seeming bothered by the idea? "Well, he was just pointing out a few parts he thought Ash would like."

He laughed and shook his head, "I think he wants to show you more than his books." His laughter wasn't genuine. No, his facial muscles constricted setting his jaw in a firm line.

"And, what if he does?" She asked this suspecting she knew the answer.

He held her gaze for what felt like an eternity. Finally, Cricket walked over to him. Standing so close unnerved her to say the least. She wanted to be the cool girl and come up with a coy remark. But her breath caught in her throat as she looked up into his eyes. "Would that be a problem?" she asked in a whisper.

Daring him to kiss her, her head swam. Struggling to form a coherent thought, she eventually managed to remember that this wasn't a good idea. She didn't remember why. Only that she shouldn't be doing it. Pulling away with both hands covering her face as if she were praying for a moment, she attempted to regain her composure.

"I'm sorry, we shouldn't."

The front door slammed, and several voices provided enough distraction to cause Boris to back away as well. Ashling and Max barreled down into the laundry room in the middle of a full-blown argument, letting Boris know exactly why he should turn and run away from her as fast and as far as his feet would carry him.

✳

He knew he'd overreacted. He felt his cheeks flame in embarrassment at the memory. What right did he have to get upset if Lex was interested in Cricket? Boris had spent some time with her, but it wasn't as if they were dating. Still, something had come over him when he saw them standing close with their heads together. Pure jealousy had surged through his veins. Even knowing that nothing was going on between them, his blood boiled at the thought of them together.

This wasn't him. He'd never been the jealous type, and he didn't want to start now.

Cricket had detected the energy within him. It was as if she heard his heart about to beat out of his chest. And yet, she incited further emotions by calling him on it. He felt certain that she enjoyed seeing him like that. She'd pulled away, but he knew she'd wanted him to kiss her. He needed to find out what was holding her back. She didn't strike him as the kind of woman who toyed with people.

Jolted when she said 'we'll be there' in reference to Pia's dinner, he'd savored the sound of it more than he wanted to. Lex passive aggressively called him out on blowing him and Pia off last week, and he couldn't blame him. If he put them off any longer, behavior dismissed due to work overload would quickly become viewed as rudeness. As Pia's text popped up on his phone suggesting Sunday night for dinner, he responded immediately with a yes and noted they should run it by Cricket the following day.

He still wasn't sure what to make of this open house or Cricket's story about moving here. A visit from an old friend had evolved into an old friend moving in permanently. It didn't make sense. Maybe if she had shown up during the summer months to check things out and then wanted to enroll the kids in school at the start of the year, her explanation might have rung true. But to arrive in December, seemingly out of the blue, with the kids missing what seemed like an excessive amount of school days while she made up her mind sounded as if she was spinning a tale out of desperation.

He doubted Cari would tell him what was really going on. She'd been unusually closed lipped about Cricket and her kids. She had always been eccentric, but this fell more in the arena of covertness. What were the two of them covering up?

CHAPTER 10

The week blew by in a blur. Getting the kids registered in a new school consumed every minute of free time. They'd only be able to attend for a little more than a week of classes before winter break, but perhaps it would ease the transition in January.

In addition to that, Cricket and the kids spent hours each day helping Cari prepare for the party. The woman may as well be Miss Christmas herself! She'd added more decorations to her already festive house, hired a caterer, and chose the menu. A bartender was booked in addition to the waitstaff hired to serve and clean up after the party. With no expense spared, Cricket expressed guilt over the effort and money poured into the event. Cari swept away her concerns insisting she wanted the party for herself. This would be her first Christmas in her new home.

Adrenaline surged through her veins before the party started. Today, Cricket would have a chance to meet everyone in the neighborhood. Cari had loaned her a form fitting, cream sweater dress that accentuated her figure perfectly. Her dark chestnut hair grazed her chin in subtle, sleek waves as she strode down the holly-trimmed staircase into the foyer, which was decorated in white and silver from floor to ceiling.

Enchanted, she turned in a slow circle, trying to absorb every extraordinary detail before guests arrived. A massive silver sleigh had arrived that morning and would be used to hold the presents being donated for children in need in lieu of hostess gifts. The great room's fire blazed, and the tree in front of the window towered more beautifully than the night she arrived. That first night, she had thought she'd never in her life seen a home as gloriously decorated for Christmas as this one. Nothing prepared her for what Cari added once she'd decided to throw the party.

The doorbell chimed, and guests arrived continuously for the next hour. At one point, a woman with a baby on her hip made a beeline for Cricket.

"You must be Cricket! I'm Tina, from just across the street. Cari told me all about you!"

Now she could match the voice with a face. Tina hadn't made much effort dressing for the party. Mousy hair pulled back in a ponytail exposed a face that might have once been pretty. Tonight, dark circles under the eyes and a sallow complexion conveyed exhaustion. She wore an oversized tunic over leggings in what appeared to be an attempt to conceal baby weight that she hadn't yet fully lost. She needn't have worried, with her baby stealing the spotlight. In her arms sat Lucie, with cheeks so pudgy they swallowed her eyes when she smiled.

"Nice to meet—"

"This. Place. Is. Stunning!" shrieked Vera, walking toward her with arms outstretched, Tess and several kids right behind her. Perfectly manicured hands gripped Cricket as air kisses breezed on either side of her face. "These are my children. Zane, stand up straight please, and Liz."

"And this is Bernadette," interjected Tess. "Our husbands were right behind us, but they must have gone off in another direction," she said, scanning the room.

Ashling pounced over like a kitten when she saw her mother greeting Vera and her children. She had also gotten herself all dolled up for the party. Her long, dark hair twirled down her back, wild with shimmering curls. Clear blue eyes glittered in a face that looked as if it had been chiseled by an artist.

Tess's daughter Bernadette wore a look of boredom combined with annoyance. But, once Liz started talking, Ashling relaxed her shoulders. Liz, a tiny little thing, vastly different in appearance from her mother and brother with their dark hair and dark features, made up for Bernadette's ice queen attitude.

Zane stood tall and wiry with a bone structure almost too delicate for a boy. He was, in a way, prettier than his sister. Liz did not have a traditionally beautiful face. With everything just a little bit "too", her features were striking. Azure eyes blazed too big for her tiny, snow white face. Her upturned nose and mouth were too small. With her flowing, pale blonde hair and wispy bangs, she resembled the little dolls found in gift stores. Liz, the same age as Ashling, looked more like a young child.

Leaving the kids to their own conversation, Cricket excused herself and walked into the foyer. Although Cari had hired a small waitstaff for tonight, noticing an empty tray of champagne flutes, she picked it up. Thankfully, the tray was bare because she nearly dropped it when Boris and Fiona stepped through the front door.

Until tonight, she'd only seen him dressed casually. Here he stood in a pair of dress pants and a white button-down shirt with his hair combed back.

He caught Cricket's eye, and she bolted for the kitchen, praying that he hadn't noticed her staring. Moments later, as she busied herself pouring champagne, he joined her in the kitchen.

"I'm pretty sure Cari hired people to do that. Why aren't you out there mingling?"

"Oh, I'm on my way. I just hate to see an empty tray."

Grabbing two freshly filled glasses, he handed one to her and held his up.

"To Christmas and new friends," he said.

"Absolutely," she replied clinking glasses and taking a sip. Not knowing what to say, she took another.

"So, I'd like to know more about you, Cricket," he started as they walked back into the great room. "What do you do for work?"

She stiffened at the thought of a question-and-answer session, before resigning herself to the fact that such things couldn't be avoided forever.

"I'm going to be starting a new job on Monday. In sales." She laughed at herself.

"What's so funny?"

"Nothing, I just made it sound a bit more glamorous than it actually is. I'll be working at the Honeycomb Hills Market."

"With Pia?"

"As luck would have it. You seem to know her well." She grabbed a few canapes off another tray that passed by on the hand of a waiter, realizing she'd better get something into her stomach before having more champagne.

"Small town. One gets to know everyone fairly well." He grinned. "So, where are you from?"

And there it was. The first of what was sure to be many inquiries into her past.

"The city. This is all very rural for me, but I love it." In an attempt to divert the attention away from her background, she inquired if it was Christmas that brought him back to Blue Cove.

"That was part of it," he responded. "I also had some business to take care of in the area. I expect to be headed back before New Year's Eve."

She knew there was no good reason for that to niggle at her, but it did. She tried to shake off the thought, reminding herself that it was for the best.

"Do you take any time off during the holidays?"

"I had hoped to, but it's been insanely busy. I'm glad I can work remotely."

"Fiona must love having you around."

"Yeah." His eyes drifted down to the bubbles in his glass. "I need to start making more of an effort to check in on her, though. She's always been fiercely independent, but I can tell she's slowing down a bit. This visit has been a real eye opener. I wish I didn't live so far away."

"She must have been very good to you as a child."

"The best." He gave a sheepish smile. "It's probably difficult for you to picture her as the sweet, gentle granny of storybooks."

Cricket admitted to herself that it sounded pretty far-fetched, but she believed him. "Maybe, but I have a hunch you're telling the truth."

"Oh? I strike you as the honest sort then?" He laughed and feigned a bow.

She giggled. "I suppose you do!"

Max bounded through, interrupting their light moment. She had always told her children that lying was a terrible thing to do. Yet here she stood, praying her six-year-old would remember the tall tale he'd been taught to rattle off if necessary. She needn't have worried, though.

"Mama, the entry is being served! The entry is being served!"

"The what?"

"The entry! All the rest of the food!" he called, tugging at her hand.

"The entree!" she corrected, laughing.

"Bring your friend! Wait 'til you see it. There's food everywhere!"

Bring her friend. Boris would probably make a good friend. He'll even fix your sink if it's not working. She had a feeling he'd make more than a good friend.

Once she had a plate filled for herself and one for Max, she glanced around the room looking for Ashling. Moving toward the library, she spotted her with a plate of food on her lap sitting with Liz and Zane. All three were laughing at something. The sight of her daughter having such a wonderful time made her pause. She couldn't pull herself away and wanted to freeze this moment in time. It had been so long since Ashling had smiled like that.

"Penny for your thoughts," Boris whispered in her ear.

Turning, she smiled up at him. "My thought is that Ashling

would be mortified to see her mother spying on her with her new friends."

"Your instinct is probably right. There are some seats open in the dining room and one hungry looking little boy waiting for you."

"Max! I thought he was with me when I went looking for Ashling. The poor kid! He chose everything on this plate," she said, lifting the one in her right hand. "I hope it's not cold."

Cricket's mouth fell open in astonishment at finding him in the dining room chatting away with Fiona. She said a silent prayer that he'd not given away any of their secrets. Setting his plate in front of him, she apologized for making him wait. "I was checking to see if Ashling wanted to eat with us."

"Oh, Mama! She probably wants to sit with Liz and Lane."

"Liz and Zane," she corrected him.

"Yeah! That's what I said. Liz and Lane," he replied as he took a forkful of lasagna.

Fiona found that hysterical and laughed out loud.

"He's a character!" she said. "He's told me all about starting a new school on Monday. Something tells me he'll have no trouble making new friends for himself."

Conversation while they ate was smooth. Fiona didn't say too much to Cricket, too busy thoroughly enjoying Max's company. Neither of them took notice when Boris asked Cricket to join him outside for some fresh air.

The brisk chill felt good as they walked along the sidewalk. Boris hadn't put on a jacket.

"I won't keep you out here long," he said. "Was it me or was it getting hot in there?"

"Maybe a little. I have to admit that this was a good idea. It's refreshing."

"Your son appears to have charmed the pants off of Fiona!"

"Yeah, he has that effect on people." She pulled her scarf tighter around her neck and nestled into it. "I wish I could say the same about Ashling, but they're nothing alike. Don't get me wrong—she has a beautiful heart and would move mountains for someone she loves. It just takes her a while to let people in. She's not as trusting and keeps her guard up when she meets new people."

"Teenagers can be a strange. Did you have a chance to talk to Pia yet?"

"No, I feel incredibly rude. Every time I ventured over to say hello, I was pulled in another direction. I have to make sure that I see her as soon as we go back inside."

"We both should. She asked if tomorrow night worked for dinner. I'm free, but I didn't want to commit you to it without your approval."

"Yeah, it's fine. I'll ask Ashling to watch Max for a few hours."

He grinned at her with one eyebrow lifted. "I have a proposition for you."

"Do tell."

"How about we bring the dinner to Pia? We'll have three judges at the table. Unless it's too short of notice for you to come up with something to make."

"Don't be cute," she said, poking him in the arm with her elbow. "I knew what I was going to make the day I challenged you to this thing."

"Excellent!" He grinned. "So, Miss Cricket, what brought you to Blue Cove? I don't want to pry, but is there a father for Ashling and Max in the picture?"

Cricket's stomach turned over at the sudden change in topic. She had rehearsed various scenarios similar to this one with faceless bodies. Yet, she remained unprepared to answer him. After a few moments, he began to apologize for asking but she stopped him.

"It's okay. Ashling and Max did have a father. His name was Wally and he was my first, my only, great love. We were just starting what was turning into a wonderful life together with two gorgeous children when I lost him."

His face clouded. "I'm so sorry. For all of you. I know all too well what it's like to lose a parent as a child. Has there been anyone since?"

She shook her head, "No, it was five years ago. I lost myself for a while. Things have turned around since Cari suggested we move out here and have a fresh start. That woman is kindness incarnate." There. She'd done it. Nothing she'd said wasn't true. She may be evasive or withholding of information, but she was not a liar.

"That woman has always led with her heart. How long have you known her?"

Innocent question. Vague answer. "Oh, a while." Pretending to shiver she suggested that it was time for her to get back inside.

CHAPTER 11

Lying in bed after the party, Boris acknowledged to himself that he had made some progress. Only when he'd asked Cricket about her friendship with Cari had she become jumpy. Until that moment, they'd been walking and talking companionably. The information about her husband was naturally a difficult topic. But something else troubled him. There had to be more to her story and the reason she ended up in Blue Cove. He'd known Cari most of his life and couldn't understand how this friend of hers had slipped past him all these years. It didn't make sense.

The sound of his watch ticking away on his nightstand kept him awake. Sleep wasn't in the cards at the moment, so he got out of bed and took the watch downstairs. Sitting on the sofa, he flipped the TV on and scrolled through channels. He shivered at biting cold air in the room, belatedly remembering Fiona set the temperature to drop at night, but he refused to grab a blanket or anything else. Maybe by the time he went back to bed, the comfort of climbing under the covers would lull him to sleep.

Settling on a sports station, he leaned back and tried to zone out while his mind continued to run in overdrive. Like Fiona, he found Max to be irresistible. Ashling wasn't as openly welcoming, but that could be chalked up to her age. Cricket radiated self-preservation. With the screen flashing at him in the darkened room, it was her face that he saw. Her expressions swung from happy, to playful, to near panic, depending on the topic of conversation. It would be interesting to see which Cricket joined him for dinner Sunday night.

Tina knocked on the door the following morning.

"Imagine my unpleasant surprise finding Fiona waiting on my front porch as I arrived home last night," she said when Cricket answered, breezing into the foyer. Throwing a hand on her hip, she seemed to channel Fiona.

"She 'couldn't help but notice' how much time I spent over here last night. Apparently, Vera and Tess left the house laughing like flipping hyenas. Fiona's worried we'll have a gaggle of grown women traipsing up and down this street in next to nothing, making spectacles of themselves!" She continued to rant as she headed for the kitchen and plopped down on a stool at the island.

Cricket laughed. "Can I get you something to drink? Coffee or tea?"

"No, thank you. Well, tea maybe, if it's not a bother. I've got an hour before I have to get back so Joe can leave for work. Is Cari home?"

"Just me."

Tina continued talking, apparently not caring who was there to listen as long as she had a set of ears. "I really enjoyed myself at the party and was *not* in the mood for her. I tried to tell her we'd catch up today because Joe was waiting for me." Spooning some honey into her tea, she continued. "Cricket, I'm telling you, it was as if I hadn't spoken."

"Sounds like my presence has rocked her world."

"She started by saying maybe she's passing judgement too quickly, but there's quite a lot to be said for first impressions, in her humble opinion. And, she went on ad nauseum about her keen eye for people." Tina postured imperiously, mimicking Fiona. "She can size anyone up in seconds flat and tell you if they are or are not the respectable type you'd like to see moving in. And according to Fiona, the self-proclaimed queen of our neighborhood, you are not a good fit for Lamplight Lane."

Cricket rested her elbows on the island. "I'm sorry she dumped all that on you."

Her mouth fell open. "That's not why I'm telling you this. You have nothing to apologize for. I only wanted you to have a heads up on what she's thinking. And who knows what she's said to the other people on this street."

Cricket sighed and shrugged. "I can't allow myself to worry about that."

"I hope you don't. I like having you around. Oh, on the upside, she admitted to quite enjoying Max's company." Her face scrunched up. "She said Cari is entitled to some odd behavior given the loss of her uncle and taking on so much responsibility, but not if it's going to impact *her*. She claimed the time had come for her to speak with Cari and that it caused her grief just thinking about it. Supposedly, she loathes confrontation! Pu-lease!" Tina's eyes rolled back in her head. "That woman thrives on drama!"

Tina added that everyone on Lamplight Lane knows enough to nod while Fiona rants, and eventually she'll move on to someone else to complain to or about. Most of the time Tina didn't hear a word she said, but this time she did pay a bit more attention. She admitted wanting to dislike Cricket when her husband commented on Cari's 'cute friend'. "But, you're so genuinely friendly! I almost felt bad for you moving into the lion's den ruled by Tess, Vera, and Fiona."

Confessing that she couldn't imagine being the new kid in town and going to a party knowing no one other than the hostess, Tina admitted to routinely freezing up in a crowd.

"I swear, half the time I hardly know what to say to people I've known for years! Not real friends of course, but certainly people I'd consider myself to be friendly with. My anxiety skyrockets while I scan the room trying to find someone to talk to."

"I'd never guess that about you," Cricket said with her head tilted.

"Cricket! Your friendliness when I arrived yesterday saved me. And you mentioned something about noticing how I bundle up Lucie for short walks, and to be sure to come knocking if I ever feel like company. I always feel like company! Now Fiona wants to drive you out of the neighborhood. Well, I simply won't have it, and I want you to know that."

"Thanks, Tina. Don't worry about it." Cricket straightened up. "She'll get used to me being around. It's not like she's going to have much of a choice."

"I suppose. But you don't know her. This is her neighborhood as far as she's concerned, and we're all allowed to live in it. If she can find a way to convince you to leave, she will."

"The advanced notice is appreciated and will be taken under advisement." She plastered on a smile, knowing it didn't reach her eyes. "I have a question for you. So, I originally wondered if Tess and Vera came to the party out of sheer nosiness. I'm surprised to admit that I found myself liking them despite that. Do you think they share Fiona's sentiment?"

"I couldn't say for sure, but I don't think so. They seemed to genuinely love the idea of neighbors being... neighborly."

A glimmer of relief passed over Cricket. Even though she envied Vera and Tess's ignorance of the multitude of challenges faced by those less fortunate, Cricket found that she genuinely enjoyed their company.

For years, this had apparently been a very quiet street with little social interaction between neighbors. As the conversation easily flowed, they came to realize that each of them had been dreaming of living in a neighborhood that socialized together. Everyone's perception of the others being too busy kept them from finding time to get together. Cari's open house had been the spark they needed. A summer block party had been mentioned multiple times.

Tess had volunteered to initiate a plan and had offered her stately, hip roof colonial as the prime location for the festivities. She had been quick to point out that her jam-packed schedule would require strategic time management for the block party to live up to expectations. Vera assured her that they'd make it happen. Cricket's tongue still ached from biting it. She knew they had things to do, but she had once been a stay at home mom and knew firsthand the lifestyle didn't compare to that of a single, working mom.

Pulling up to Pia's adorable yellow Cape Cod style home with white trim, Boris caught Cricket smiling to herself.

"Penny for your thoughts."

"Pia's house looks like it fell out of a storybook!"

"Sometimes I wonder if Pia herself fell out of a fairytale, so I suppose that's fitting."

"Like Cinderella?"

"More like Tinker Bell. She's as tiny as a bird, always fluttering around sprinkling her fairy dust to make everything beautiful, and she's fiercely devoted to people she cares about."

Cricket's smile grew. "I can't wait to get to know her better."

Pia flung open the door before they'd reached the top step and steered them into the dining room to deposit their pans. Removing their coats, the heat from the wood stove seeped into their bones as she wrapped each of them in enthusiastic hugs.

Pia reached for their coats. "I'll put these away while you two set up in here."

Once she'd scurried out, Boris and Cricket got to work dividing a serving table in half. When they'd finished, one side held a pan of oyster dressing, a dish of seasoned fingerling potatoes, and a platter of chateaubriand. The other end of the table offered a tray of duck leg confit, honey glazed brussels sprouts, and roasted parmesan green beans.

"Let's not keep them waiting," Boris grinned, sweeping an arm in the direction of the living room.

Their audience hopped up with enthusiasm as they entered.

"Let's get this party started!" Lex rubbed his stomach and linked his arms through Boris's and Cricket's as he led them into the dining room. "To say that I'm hungry would be a gross understatement."

Clinking his wine glass to get everyone's attention, Boris stated the rules of the cook off between Chef Donner and Chef Blitzen. Their true identities would not be revealed until all votes had been cast. Each chef had the potential to win in three areas: presentation, creativity, and of course, taste. Judges would take two plates, being careful to not mix up dishes from either side of the table. They could choose to eat one whole meal or alternate between dishes as long as they filled out the corresponding tickets for each entry as they ate.

"Let the games begin!" Boris declared in an authoritative, booming voice.

Pia and Lex had been under strict orders to refrain from serving appetizers of any kind. Staring at the spread before them, both voiced their thanks for that rule.

In the spirit of the competition, Cari had agreed to spend the afternoon at Honeycomb Market so that she wouldn't see or even smell what Cricket cooked up.

"Good thing I stayed away from home today. I never would have been able to keep my nose out of the kitchen if I walked in while either of these meals was being prepared," she said. "Who gets to go first?"

"Hm, how did you used to do it, Boris?" asked Cricket.

"It was buffet style. People took turns helping themselves."

Cari picked up her first plate and started scooping up the oyster dressing. "No time like the present. I'm not too shy to dig in first!"

Cricket whispered to Boris that the room had grown disturbingly quiet while everyone ate.

He pulled her closer and whispered, "I'm too busy scrutinizing their faces to eat anything. How about we have our dinner after a winner is announced?"

She nodded and tried to hush her giggle. "Their sound effects are too much while they chew."

With the last mouthful eaten and the final vote turned in, they tallied the numbers. Chef Donner had won for presentation and creativity, but Chef Blitzen earned the best taste accolades.

"Hah!" Cricket yelled. "It's the taste that matters. That counts as winning the whole shebang!"

"I don't recall reading that anywhere in the bylaws. Two is greater than one. Donner is the clear winner."

"What bylaws? Show them to me."

Cari clapped her hands. "I'd say you both win."

"There can't be two winners," Boris argued. "I challenge you to a rematch!"

She sauntered up to him. "Done. Name the time and the place, but you'd better bring your A-game."

He rubbed his stomach. "Will do, but right now, this man needs some sustenance! Let me at that oyster dressing. Something tells me that pan is the reason you won for best overall taste."

He placed a forkful into his mouth and instantly knew he'd never been more right about anything else. It was hands down the most amazing food he'd ever tasted. Inhaling another bite, he tried to express as much and failed, shaking his head with his eyes closed. The sight of him sent Cari into a fit of laughter.

"Hey Boris, do you want us to leave you alone with that?"

"No! Especially you, Cricket. You're not getting out of here tonight without telling me how you made this. It's insanely good. Addictive!" He shoveled another bite into his open mouth. "I can't stop eating! I think I could have it for breakfast!"

"I might be willing to share my secrets if you admit that I'm the winner of tonight's cook off."

Incapable of arguing with her, he scarfed down another bite. The oysters encrusted in breading and seasonings exploding with flavor were impossible to resist. He stood up and gallantly bowed in her direction.

"I concede! I concede! Cricket Williams is without question the winner tonight and every other night in perpetuity as long as she serves these oysters!"

"Thank you kindly for acknowledging that, dear Boris." She tried to curtsy and stumbled into him. Catching her in a bear hug, his arms wrapped around her tighter than was necessary in a rocking motion. Her arms instinctively wrapped around his waist in response.

As usual, lacking in common social graces, Cari spoke without a filter. "I don't know about the rest of you, but I'm getting the feeling I'm intruding on something here."

Cricket stepped back abruptly. "Don't be silly. I just tripped over myself."

Cari's eyes bulged out of her head. "You tripped into a pair of well-toned arms!"

Seeing the tell-tale pink creep up Cricket's neck and over her cheeks, Boris drew the attention to himself and announced his plans to open a jazz club in the area. He carefully dodged location-related questions and kept the conversation centered around the food and entertainment provided.

The unexpected sharing of information threw everyone off balance, and they fell quiet processing what he said.

Pia spoke first. "So, wait. You're opening up a restaurant? When is this happening?"

"It's early stages. There's a lot to work through before I can think about finalizing a timeline."

"Are you a silent investor or would you move back here to run it?"

"I actually already have two in New York that are doing well. This would be an expansion. With the model we use in place, I can do my part from anywhere as long as I visit the site from time to time. It would be more often than not, if I had my way. When the place is packed and I see an enormous crowd having an amazing time, the thrill is all-consuming. It's exhilarating to be a part of creating that atmosphere."

"Sounds like you missed your calling," Pia commented. "Maybe you belong in the nightclub business."

"That's just it. It's not some cheesy nightclub full of people who barely reached the legal drinking age cavorting around in ripped jeans and tube tops. It's classy. Our clientele is made up of men and women with careers and families who are looking for a place to get a good meal, a few drinks, and the option of dancing to a live band. They aren't there to get inebriated or to partake in all the shenanigans that come with the club scene. I'm not talking black tie, but everyone makes an effort to get dressed up to some degree."

The more he talked, the more excited he grew at the prospect of making this happen here. He could see that his enthusiasm was contagious. Maybe it could all work out. Maybe Lex and Pia would want to come on board and work for him. That was an option he hadn't previously considered. It was a long shot for Lex. He'd been someone who needed to be outside expending his energy on manual labor since they were kids. But Pia would be happy anywhere as long as she was allowed to organize stock and schedules to her heart's content.

A few more laughs and memories were shared before Cricket apologized for being the party pooper of the group. She wanted to get home to make sure Ashling went to bed at a decent time. Her first day of school was tomorrow, and it would be hard enough to fall asleep without adding a late bedtime. Clean up ended quickly with Pia shooing everyone out the door and insisting she could have everything back in order in fifteen minutes if they'd all get out of her kitchen. Hugs and cheek kisses were exchanged as coats were put on, and they left the warmth of her home.

The car ride was peppered with pleas for more details about the jazz club. Cricket listened to him talk, fascinated by the idea and saying it sounded like a speakeasy from the roaring twenties. It was high time to bring back some of the glamour from that time period. As far as she was concerned, the efforts people made to dress down would be better spent putting themselves together. Everyone felt good when they looked good.

Parking the car, he walked her across the street.

"Tonight was the most fun I've had in a long time," he said as they approached the porch.

"It was a fantastic night," she agreed. "Your friends are great company."

"True," he said pausing at the foot of the stairs and turning toward her. "But having you there, getting to see such a fun side to your personality, that was the best part for me."

He leaned down and kissed her softly. Not wanting to go too fast too soon, he forced himself to be the first to break away.

"I should let you get inside; it's freezing out here. I'm sure I'll see you at some point tomorrow, neighbor. I hope the kids have a great first day."

"Thank you. You'd better get inside yourself." She hopped up the stairs and entered the dimly lit foyer.

Leaving her driveway, he admitted to himself that this was turning into something more, and he didn't relish the idea of putting an end to it. He wanted her in his life however he could manage it. People had long distance relationships all the time. Why couldn't they make it work?

CHAPTER 12

"I'm so done with Bernadette! She'll be lucky if I don't decide to permanently straighten those stupid little blonde corkscrew curls of hers!" Ashling hurled her backpack onto the couch. "She thinks she's perfect, but that big butt of hers looked enormous in her little mini skirt. And, I'm not saying that because I'm jealous of her. It's true!"

"Ashling!" Everyone was walking in after their first day of school and work. Cricket gaped at her daughter. "Where is this coming from? You girls seemed to get along great over the weekend."

"Yeah, until she decided I'm some sort of loser. When I got to school, I saw her standing with some other girls I've obviously never met. I figured whatever. This would definitely work to my advantage, because if they're friends with her and think that I'm friends with her, maybe they'll want to get to know me too." She groaned and rolled her eyes. "I know I sound ten years old! But when I said hello, she completely ignored me! My first thought was that she may not have heard me. So, I said hi again, but she turned around without looking to see who called her name."

"So, maybe she genuinely didn't hear you."

"Oh, she heard me. I put myself in front of her so she couldn't

95

miss me. I said hi again, but this time right in her face. Do you know what she did? She turned away from me *again*. It's like she knew it was me and didn't want to say hello. Or worse. She didn't want her friends to see her saying hello to me." Ashling shook her head and began to pace. "This is my first day. She doesn't know anything about me. Not to mention, what gives her the right to ignore me? What makes her think she's so great?"

Cricket's blood boiled. Her forehead creased as she searched for words to console her daughter.

"And to make my morning even better, there was Zane, walking toward me from across the lawn. So, I panicked and went inside. I don't even want to know if he saw what happened. I couldn't live with anymore embarrassment today."

"I'm really sorry things didn't get off to such a great start," Cricket began.

"Oh, wait. It gets better. I also ate alone at lunch. It was so embarrassing. I thought I was prepared, after barely talking to a few other kids about super interesting topics that included borrowing a pencil sharpener and asking someone to point me in the right direction for gym. But you can't really prepare yourself for that level of humiliation."

"It must have been awful."

"I just sat down at an empty table and pulled my sandwich out with my assigned reading book. I'd already read it, but it gave me something to look at other than everyone around me hugging it out with their besties in some sort of weirdo Monday euphoria."

Cricket sighed and sat on the edge of the couch. "Are Liz and Zane assigned to a different lunch period?"

"Oh, that's the best part! Zane snuck up from behind and covered my eyes with his hands." She slouched over and dropped onto the couch next to Cricket. "I pretended to not know who it was."

"Why?"

She shrugged. "I didn't have a good reason, I just thought it would be more humiliating if I recognized him after only hanging out with him once. If that was even possible. He took away his hands and sat down next to me and was like 'Seriously?' So, I had to admit that, yeah, I had some idea. It's not like I know a ton of people here who would sneak up and grab me from behind. Of course he wanted to know why I was eating alone. My mouth opened, Mom, but I had absolutely nothing to say to that."

"You must have said something!"

"Nope. But I could literally feel my cheeks flaming red."

"You always turn red at the drop of a dime."

"He said he was sorry and not trying to be a jerk," Ashling admitted. "He just meant I was new and it's not unusual to not know many people in the cafeteria yet."

"He's right!"

"Yeah. Nothing odd at all about this being halfway through the day, and I haven't managed to meet one single person to sit with in there."

"You've never been the timid kind. What's going on?"

"I'm not shy," she said with conviction. "It's just, I somehow went too long not knowing how to start a conversation or introduce myself that it snowballed. I'm stuck now. Everyone probably thinks I'm a mute."

Cricket laughed at that. "One thing I can promise is that no one is thinking about you at all! No offense, but you're not even on their radar yet. I mean that in the best possible way. Most people are too focused on what's going on with themselves to notice what's going on around them."

"Maybe. I think I just miss my old friends."

Cricket knew this wasn't entirely true. Ashling never had what she'd call besties. She was her own best friend and thoroughly enjoyed her own company above anyone else's. Cricket wished she believed that was acceptable, but she'd always hoped Ashling would find the lifelong friendships that chick flicks are made of. But how was that supposed to happen when you didn't know where you'd be living month to month?

Max brightened the mood, interjecting with positive tidbits

about his day. Fortunately, he did as well in school as she'd expected. He spoke well of his teacher and how she'd introduced him to some boys to play with at recess. They'd welcomed him with open arms, and one had invited him over for a playdate later in the week. Now that he'd shared the highlights of his day and Ashling had finished venting, he wanted to hear all about Cricket's time at the store.

Cricket yawned, drop dead tired at four o'clock in the afternoon. She wanted to spend the little energy she had left making dinner and tried to appease him by saying she and Pia got along great.

"Why don't you have more to say about the store?" he asked.

"I do not have one good reason for that. I think that learning can sometimes be as tiring as doing."

"Oh, I know what you mean, Mama! Sometimes, at the end of reading a book, I want to take a nap!"

"It's worth it though. We both have a job to get smarter," she said, hugging him.

The truth was she felt drained from trying to find ambiguous answers to questions about her past every time a regular customer came in and saw a new face at the register. Where was she from? What did she do before this? Was she married? How does she know Cari? Did she live in the area? It was endless. Now, Cricket wanted to immerse herself in cooking dinner, watch some mindless T.V., and pass out. With any luck, her interrogation would be over in a day or two, and she'd be able to start focusing on her job.

Ashling returned to the family room with a glass of water, a banana, and a request to go to St. Agnes's the following afternoon with Cari. She also apologized for ranting earlier.

"Sorry if I sounded like a brat. I know there are worse things to complain about than girls like Bernadette."

"Everyone has something to complain about. We're all coming from unique perspectives with our own hurdles to jump. Don't beat yourself up over it."

"I want to go. Other kids go for community service hours, so I won't seem out of place. I don't want to start a great new life if it means forgetting the old one. There are so many kids in there that can use a tutor. That'll be my first stop."

Cricket didn't love the idea, but couldn't think of a valid reason to say no. There were many, but she was too exhausted to think of them.

Standing up to stretch at his desk, Boris recalled seeing Cricket and her kids walking onto the front porch of the farmhouse and letting themselves inside. He'd stifled an urge to walk over and say hello. He was due for a break but didn't want to intrude on the heels of everyone arriving home from what he suspected had been a long day. Earlier that afternoon, he'd also resisted the temptation of dropping by the Honeycomb Market.

He could have played it innocent enough and pretended to need a pie or a wreath, but Cricket would have seen right through whatever excuse he came up with. He wanted to see her. He wanted to know how her first day at the market was going. Tomorrow or even the next day would be better. The last thing he wanted to do was fluster her on the job. Perhaps he was getting ahead of himself, making assumptions that she'd be easily flustered at all.

Needing to stretch his legs, he threw on his coat and hat and walked outside. The temperature had significantly dropped since earlier that afternoon, and the sky had darkened early on the moonless night. He'd have to stick to a quick pace to stay warm. As he reached the recently plowed sidewalk, Cricket came out the front door of the farmhouse. She saw him right away and looked for a moment as if she might turn around and go back inside. He waved and called to her before she had the chance.

"Hey, Cricket! I'm taking a short walk. Care to join me?"

It crossed his mind that she might be too polite to refuse, but he pushed the thought away and gave silent thanks as she agreed.

"I really shouldn't even be out here," she said as they began walking. "It's cold, I'm tired, I have ten zillion things to do tonight…" She shook her head. "Sorry, I don't mean to be such a downer."

"What brought you outside?" he asked, hoping that maybe it was him.

"I love the cold air at night in winter. And I'm embarrassed to admit that I haven't been back on the treadmill since that day I bumped into you in the kitchen and thought you were a prowler."

He laughed at that. "No judgement here. I haven't exactly been running laps myself since then."

"The cold makes me walk faster, so I tell myself I'm getting in some cardio, however little it may be." She gazed at Cari's pristine, snow cloaked land to their right. "This gorgeous view is an incentive, even in the dark. Almost makes you forget the cold."

"Almost," he said. Burrowing into the collar of his down jacket, he asked, "How was your first day at the market?"

"Great. Everyone who came in was so friendly. They're all excited about the holidays and looking for the perfect gifts and desserts. The atmosphere is beyond festive, and Pia had the patience of a saint while training me. Not that it's rocket science, but they have such a large inventory that I was struggling to help customers find what they were looking for."

"It'll get easier. You know how it is starting something new."

"Absolutely!" She looked up at him as they came to the end of the street and turned back toward home. "Tell me about your work, Boris. What exactly is it that you do?"

Now it was his turn to hesitate before responding as she had done so many times before this. "I own a real estate development company. My partners and I buy property, convert it into something lucrative, and sell it."

"Sounds like Monopoly."

"Not quite," he laughed, pulling his hat down over his ears.

"Do you enjoy it?"

"I used to. In the beginning, we started out buying run down properties, renovating, and then would sell them for a profit. It was exhilarating to take these eyesores and create something beautiful. The business and our ambition took off. Now though..." He trailed off, unsure of how to continue. "Now, I'm not sure. I've always been a driven person. My goal was to take something and make it better. To create something that would benefit other people in some way."

He shoved his hands in his jacket pockets. "My partners once shared that vision with me, but I'm afraid that greed has taken over. When they set their sights on something, they will stop at nothing to acquire it. I'm embarrassed to say that sometimes our recent projects haven't done anything to improve the location for the majority of people. They tend to cater development now to a much higher clientele."

There he went again, sharing too much information. He couldn't help himself. This was the first time he'd been put on the spot and had to acknowledge what was going on with Glynn, Stone, and West. Boris went into business with them because he wanted to do something that mattered and had believed his partners shared his vision. Too much had changed, but he didn't know how to fix it.

CHAPTER 13

The house had taken on a life of its own. Cricket knew her kids filled up every breathable space. Not that Cari would complain. Cricket made a point to tackle everything that needed or would need to be done so they didn't create more work for her. But she knew that getting used to their comings and goings, the ever-present lull of voices, must take some getting used to for Cari, who was accustomed to living alone.

Although she counted her blessings daily, Cricket didn't feel at home yet. The rules Cari had imposed still had her walking on eggshells, and the feeling had yet to evaporate. At least the nervous energy went both ways. Cari had asked her once if she'd imposed too many stipulations, and did everyone think she was a complete witch? To allay her concerns, Cricket feared she overcompensated with an excessively and totally unnatural positive attitude.

Jolted from her thoughts, Cricket's stomach dropped as Cari frantically caught up with her in the hallway and asked her to remain out of sight. Although Cari had seen her mother several times since Cricket and the kids had moved in, she had conveniently forgotten to mention them in conversation and managed to keep her away by saying she needed a change of scenery and wanted to get out of the house.

No such luck today. She'd missed her mom's call when in the shower and came out to a message stating that she was stopping by with a great book she'd just finished. Cari had tried in vain to call her back. Unable to reach her, she'd gone into a panic at the realization that her mother would be stepping onto her porch any minute.

The kids were upstairs, but it would be impossible to hide the evidence of their existence in this house. Cari gripped Cricket's wrists with eyes widening at the light knocking followed by the sound of a door opening and closing.

"I'm so sorry to do this to you," she whispered. "My mother is not someone who appreciates surprises. She'll want to have heard about you before she meets you."

"It's fine."

"You clearly haven't met Nadine. There is nothing fine about this."

Wanting to put off the inevitable for as long as possible, a minute passed while Cari seemed to brace herself. She then took a deep breath and walked out to the empty foyer. Cricket couldn't help herself, so she tiptoed out into the hallway and peered around the corner.

Nadine, a chic older woman sporting a sleek silver bob and a black wrap coat over a fuchsia dress, stood gaping at a mess that could only be left by children. Sweatshirts were strewn about near the couches and the Lego set that had been dug out for Max was littered all over the floor. He had been so engrossed in building his Lego ship that no one had the heart to make him put the pieces away. Cari had promised she'd find a place to keep it when completed.

"Cari?" Nadine's black patent heels clacked across the hardwood floor. "Are these donations for the shelter, or have you been playing with toys?"

"Hi Mom... Um, I have some friends staying with me."

"What friends?" she asked in a clipped, high pitched voice. "You haven't mentioned anything, and from the looks of things in here, your friends have been staying more than a few days."

"More like a few weeks. You should sit, it's kind of a long story."

While she tried to explain, Nadine sat rigid with her mouth hanging open, wide eyed, gently shaking her perfectly coiffed head.

"I can tell by the way you're looking at me that you think I've completely lost my mind."

"That's an understatement."

"Mom, I..."

"Uh, no. Don't even try to spin this in a rational light. This is the very definition of insanity. This is not what anyone means when they talk about helping people in need. What this is, is dangerous!"

"Mom," she tried again.

"No. The only thing we're going to discuss is getting whoever these people are out of this house. It's not like they are renting from you, so there shouldn't be any legal hoops to jump through. We can start packing up their things, and when they come back, you'll politely tell them to leave." She stood, ready to begin. "If they refuse, we will call the police and say they are trespassing."

"We are not going to do any of those things. They are not breaking any laws. The only crime they've committed is accepting my invitation and hospitality."

"Hospitality?" Her voice grew shrill. "They have preyed on your vulnerability!"

"I know that's what it looks like. Hearing myself tell you about this, it sounds ridiculous even to my own ears. But I'm telling you these aren't con artists. It's just a mom and her kids who have fallen on hard times. Well, harder times. I get the sense nothing has ever been what you'd call easy for them."

Cricket leaned back against the wall and closed her eyes at the distress she heard creeping into Cari's voice.

"I have the sense that all of *your* common sense has been tossed out the window!"

"You are just going to have to trust me on this," Cari said patiently. "They're home. Stay and meet them."

"Home? So, this is home to them? They think this is their home after spending mere weeks with you?" Inhaling deeply with her head down and hands over her eyes, her body seemed to soften a bit as she focused on a controlled exhale. "Cari, I think you're lonely. It's not always easy living alone in such a large house. I promise, you will get used to it."

"Maybe, but for right now this is what I'm doing. Mom, I enjoy it. I like having them here. Just meet them. I love you and am grateful for your concern, but they are staying. So I'm going to need you to give them a chance." Her voice softened. "You, of all people, should be willing to do that."

Nadine conceded that she understood their struggle while arguing that her daughter's safety came first. Before Cari had a chance to form a response, Ashling and Max burst into the room full of excitement to tell Cari about their day. Cricket crept into the room after them, unnoticed. Nadine offered a chilled greeting. It took the wind out of their sails somewhat, but not enough to bring them down. Catching the cool vibe from Nadine, Ashling froze up matching the woman's iciness with her own brand of steel. That didn't help matters.

Ready or not, Cari was forced to make introductions. Cricket struggled to breathe and suspected that the smile she attempted to plaster on her face looked more like a grimace. The woman before her strayed far from the image she had drawn in her mind: An older version of Cari, full of joy and disarmingly ready to welcome anyone and everyone with open arms. That fantasy evaporated. Instead, Cricket met a hard, suspicious gaze. This woman had seen enough in her lifetime to withhold trust until it had been earned. She held herself with an almost palpable confidence in her intelligence and ability to succeed at any goal. A stab of fear pierced Cricket at the thought of Nadine's determination to get them out of this house.

"I need to get going," Nadine said to Cari. "We'll talk more later." With a perfunctory kiss on her daughter's cheek, she left.

Hearing her shoes click down the porch steps, Cari turned to them with her cheeks flaming in embarrassment. "I am really sorry about that!"

"She's just worried about you. I'm a mom. I can understand that."

"Still... Try to not to take it personally. My mother has never been what you'd call warm and fuzzy. She is a force of nature."

Before Cricket could respond, Cari changed the subject. "Speaking of moms, I know that we talked about a blackout period, and it hasn't seemed to bother you too much, but Christmas is coming. There must be someone you'd like to see."

"We always spend it with my mom."

"Invite her here. Lex is coming over. It would be so much more festive with you and the kids."

"If you're sure, I'll call her now."

"I'm positive. Now, if you'll excuse me, I've got to tie up some loose ends at work."

As soon as she left, Cricket reached for the phone and dialed her mother's number. When the voicemail came on, she left a message with the address and an invitation to join them there on Christmas Day. Hanging up, she realized she probably should have left the telephone number. As she considered calling her back, Cari re-entered the room.

"Hey, ask Ashling to babysit tonight. Vera, Tess, and Tina are going out, and they asked if we'd join them. I'd say after my mom's little fit we could use a good time."

She left without giving Cricket a chance to respond. The mention of Nadine opened a whole new can of worms in Cricket's mind. She had to assume Nadine would be there for Christmas dinner as well. That should make for quite the holiday gathering.

If it had been anyone else doing the asking, Boris would have turned down a night at Bar Hop, but Lex had insisted that he was going to lose his mind if he didn't talk to someone. Sitting on a stool, Boris scanned the dimly lit sports bar, not seeing anyone he knew despite the large crowd for a Tuesday night. Lex came through the front door in a gust of howling wind. Spotting Boris right away, he made his way through a cluster of people and sat down next to him at the bar.

"Hey, man," Boris said, "so what's the big emergency?"

Lex shrugged off his coat and turned around to hang it on the back of the stool with a growl.

"It's Cari," he said, sitting. "She's been giving me mixed signals. Just when I think I have an opening; she shuts me down."

"Wait. You and Cari have a thing going?"

"That's the problem. I'm not sure. I want it to be a thing, and sometimes I'm sure she does too, but then she holds me at arm's length. All business."

"Maybe that's the issue. You do work for her now."

"This started long before she inherited the farm." He took a sip of the beer Boris had ordered for him. "Sunday night at Pia's everything felt...right. I thought, finally, we're on the same wavelength. Then, this afternoon," he shook his head and took another sip, "I went to her house and asked her if she'd spend Christmas Day with me. You know what she said? She was all flustered and said we'll have to talk later because she's got too much on her mind."

"That wasn't exactly a no."

"It sure as heck wasn't a yes!"

Boris tried to be the voice of reason. Cari was known to get caught up in her own head at times and may not have been thinking too hard about her reaction to what Lex saw as a big question. "You know Cari. She was probably juggling ten plates in the air when you asked. I'd give it some time. Maybe mention it again another night when she's more relaxed."

"Should I bother?"

"I would."

"I don't know."

"Hey, you dragged me out and wanted my advice. Why bother doing that if you're not going to take it?"

Lex laughed. "You're right. I think I wanted you to give me the kick in the pants I needed to get up the nerve one more time."

The door swung open with a group of women rushing in to escape the cold. The ladies of Lamplight Lane. The lovely subject of their conversation led the charge, followed by Cricket. A hostess walked them over to a large table where they began shedding their coats and scarves. Boris and Lex watched them, unnoticed, from the other side of the room.

"No time like the present," said Boris, finishing his beer.

"I'm not going to rush over and intrude on her ladies' night out before it's even started."

"So, let's hang out here for a while longer, and then we'll both go over to say hello. I've got someone over there I'd like to talk to myself."

"Cricket?"

"That obvious?"

Lex smirked. "You'd have to be completely oblivious to miss the sparks flying between the two of you."

Boris snuck a glance toward her table. The way Cricket fidgeted with her glass, and sat quietly in comparison to her friends, had him wondering if she wanted to be there.

"Sometimes I see fireworks, and other times it feels like she's trying to put them out."

"Understandable. She probably doesn't want to get too involved anyways. Not with you heading back to New York soon." Lex considered. "But you know what? She's a good fit for you."

"I was thinking maybe we could take turns traveling back and forth. It's not like we'd be dependent on flying to see each other. It's a four hour drive, at most."

"Only four hours?" he asked sarcastically. "You do realize she has two kids?"

"They'd love New York."

"Be practical. And, she just moved here, so she's not likely to pick up and move again any time soon." He sighed. "I'm not trying to be negative. But if you think this is the real deal, you should start thinking about whether or not relocating is doable for you."

As impractical as it may be to expect Cricket to take time out of her busy week to travel to see him, it would be just as irrational for him to consider uprooting his life for someone he'd just met. There were too many unknowns at this early stage. Not to mention the countless times she'd dodged his advances and tried to squash his interest.

Pulling him out of his thoughts, Lex said something about Cari not relishing her new role. He diverted his attention away from Cricket's table and strained to catch up to what Lex was saying.

"I know she has what it takes to bring the entire business to a new level. She just doesn't see it! Sure, there's going to be a learning curve, and she's going to make some mistakes. She's just not looking at the big picture."

Boris looked up at the commercial playing on the flat screen T.V. hanging over the bar. Lex should be having this conversation with anybody other than him.

"Maybe she doesn't want to."

Lex shook his head. "No, she's just overwhelmed with everything being thrown at her. I don't think she can see beyond it. She's just trying to get through each day."

Tearing his gaze away from the game that had returned to the screen, he turned toward Lex. "Now you know why she didn't give you a straight answer about Christmas."

"Maybe, but I suspect there's more to that story." He drained his bottle and signaled the bartender.

Boris took this opportunity to pick his friend's brain.

"What do you see happening with the farm going forward?"

"Hard to say. Things might start to click, or they won't. She'll either put someone else in charge, or she'll pull the plug on the whole idea and sell it."

"Why doesn't she let you run it?"

"That was her original plan. But she said it would be irresponsible of her to not know every aspect of the business before doing that. Makes sense. Just as long as we make it to the other end of the rainbow."

His guilty conscience resurfaced, and Boris found it hard to look his friend in the eye. Instead of receiving a huge promotion six months from now, the man could be out of a job altogether after being stabbed in the back by his best friend.

Seeing Cricket leave her table, he excused himself to follow her and encouraged Lex to snag her now empty seat next to Cari.

CHAPTER 14

Cricket had tried to get out of going. First, she'd said it was a school night. But Cari had assured her they wouldn't leave until she tucked Max snugly into bed at seven and vowed to have her home by nine. Cricket had continued to protest, proclaiming herself a teetotaler. Cari had countered saying they didn't need to get sloshed. She'd insisted they'd both benefit from blowing off some steam.

Cari had refused to accept Cricket's complaints of fatigue and reminded her that she knew her schedule better than anyone. After an absurd amount of back and forth, Cricket had given in. She'd resigned herself to the fact that girls' night with Cari, Tina, Vera, and Tess would be unavoidable and asked to borrow something fabulous from Cari and get on with it.

Cari had tossed blouses and dresses at Cricket to try on as if she were a doll to dress up. Eventually, they'd settled on a shimmery pink halter top loosely tucked into a pair of jeans and ridiculously uncomfortable stilettos that made everything else look amazing. After a final once over, she'd grabbed a thin sweater and assured Ashling she'd check in over the next few hours.

Bar Hop welcomed them into its laid-back vibe. The atmosphere was nice enough to allow people to dress up or down according to preference. Vera and Tess both wore jeans and dressy tops with heels. Apart from Tina in her typical athleisure, the women appeared to have coordinated their outfits.

Cricket ordered a glass of wine. Vera, Tess, and Cari ordered drinks she'd never heard of. She wondered what "a twist" entailed. Too embarrassed to ask, her mouth remained shut. Tina, in her chronic ponytail, wavered on her order before settling on a glass of merlot. Cricket suspected she wasn't sure what the others ordered either and didn't want to take any chances getting tanked when she had a baby who'd probably wake her up at some point in the middle of the night. She had said as much earlier and was nice enough to offer to drive everyone tonight.

Vera and Tess made no secret they'd be taking full advantage of having a designated driver. With them getting louder by the minute, Cricket found them to be wildly entertaining with their stories of local gossip. She made the mistake of allowing them to order one of their fancy cocktails for her. Only her second drink, it hit hard. A few sips in, she stumbled off to the restroom to freshen up.

Cricket pushed open the door, already feeling better. Despite the freezing temperature outside, she congratulated herself for selecting a sleeveless top. An oppressive heat had emerged in the crowd. She ran a brush through her hair and glided on a touch of gloss, savoring a moment of peace. A boisterous trio of women plowed into the restroom, shattering the quiet. Zipping her purse, she smiled at their merriment and returned to the sweltering lounge.

"Hey beautiful, let's go get you a drink." A swaying giant of a man blocked her path as if he'd been lying in wait outside the restroom.

"Oh, no thank you," she replied with a smile, trying to slip past him.

"Aww, come on now. You're not even givin' a guy a chance." He grinned. "One drink won't kill ya."

"I'm cut off for the night. My friends are waiting, could you please move?"

"You know, using the word please don't make you sound more polite. I think *you* think that pretty face of yours is too good for me." A hand, larger than an oven mitt, reached out to smooth a piece of her hair. He grabbed her wrist in a vise as she moved to block his hand from touching her face.

Boris appeared, shoving his way in between them.

"I think she made it clear that she's not interested."

"Hey man, I didn't know she was here with someone. She kept that to herself. Maybe you two need to have a little chat about not giving out mixed signals to other people." He looked Cricket up and down with a small grin and walked away.

With a face of steel, Boris moved to go after him.

"Hey, what are you doing?" she asked, pulling him back.

His eyes blazed in fury. "I don't like the way that guy looked at you. It's disrespectful."

"You're right, but do you honestly think he's the first person to look at me like that? Do you think he'll be the last, regardless of who I am or am not with at the time?"

His jaw set in a firm line. "So you just let it go?"

"Look, I'm pretty good at handling myself, and sometimes that's the easiest thing to do." Another man headed for the restroom bumped into them. Cricket teetered forward into Boris. Solid arms wrapped around her, his hand resting on the small of her back. Using the distraction and the elimination of personal space to her advantage, she placed a palm in the center of his chest. The last thing she needed was to be part of some bar brawl. A classy act like that would surely rank high on Cari's list of don'ts.

"It's nice to have some back up though, when someone gets a little too aggressive," she conceded. "Let me buy you a drink to say thank you."

She could feel him slightly relax as the tension eased from his chest. "I should probably be the one buying you a drink," he said, cracking a wry smile. "To say thanks for putting up with such a hot head."

Cricket laughed but agreed to a soda. By the time Cari walked over to tell her everyone was leaving, Cricket searched for a reason not to like him more than she should. Considering she could have sat there all night, her thought process in the matter was blurred.

"I'm going to stop in the lady's room, and we can go. Back in a few!"

She couldn't have been any more obvious about giving them a moment alone before leaving.

"Can I have your number?" Boris asked. "I can text you to make plans for our run."

It took every ounce of restraint for her to refrain from groaning out loud. Who doesn't have a phone permanently attached to them these days? Cricket, that's who.

"My cell is on the fritz and I haven't gotten around to replacing it. Can you maybe call on Cari's house phone?"

"Sure."

Well, that was easy enough. She'd never been the lying type, but there was no other way around it. And, perhaps she should take her own advice so wisely bestowed upon Ashling whenever a conversation revolved around boys. It was never a bad idea to have a man put in a little extra effort.

After a restless night of little sleep, Boris sat up in his bed at the first sign of sunlight glinting through the window. He didn't want to wake Fiona but couldn't spend one more second lying there. Instead of tiptoeing downstairs to make a pot of the coffee that he so desperately needed, he decided to do some stretching until he heard her rustling around in the hallway.

He was tight! It had been too long since he'd properly worked out. Today was the day. After breakfast, he'd see if he could convince Cricket to join him at the gym. As he bent over for downward dog position, it hit him that he'd sought out opportunities to spend time with her every day since their first meeting over trash barrels. He tried to picture himself back in his New York City apartment not having a hope on the face of the earth of bumping into her. He had a full life there, with a successful career and a large circle of friends. Yet, he couldn't imagine picking up where he left off.

Maybe moving back to Blue Cove wasn't as far-fetched an idea as it appeared on the surface. If he had a laptop and an internet connection, he could work from anywhere. It wouldn't be out of the question to drive into the city from time to time in the same way he had considered handling a potential long-distance relationship. As it was, he and his partners flew all over the country scouting new properties to buy. They rarely trekked into the office on the same days.

Laying on his back and pulling his knees into his chest, an image of himself after flipping his first house flashed before his eyes. He could still feel a glimmer of the thrill that ran through him that day. It had been a long time since he'd experienced that. An exceptional amount of work had been required, but he'd enjoyed every minute of it. Their booming business today didn't allow time to enjoy success. The near constant travel and extensive hours were multiplying. Great for the bottom line, less so for having a personal life, settling down, and starting a family. At least, not in the way he'd prefer to do it.

He'd grown up without his parents and wanted to be involved in his children's lives. Starting a family wasn't imminent, but he'd like to be prepared when the time came. What if he returned to his roots? If his partners bought him out, he'd have a financial cushion and be able to start a business here. Would that be a step backwards in his career or a step forward in his happiness?

The bedroom grew brighter while Boris moved through a series of yoga poses. Nothing had to happen right away. There was plenty of time to see how things played out during the rest of his stay. Hearing Fiona's bedroom door open and her footsteps padding down the stairs, he headed for the shower, glad to get on with his day. After a quick breakfast, he'd take one more look at his offer for Cari and set up a meeting with her. She'd think it strange of him to go through such formal channels when he could just knock on her front door. That's not the way this could play out if he wanted her to seriously consider selling. If she engaged in negotiations, he'd deal with the ramifications with Lex and Pia later.

Cricket could hear something buzzing from a distance. Scrubbing at her eyes, the noise grew louder and rattled her nerves. The alarm. Ugh. She was not cut out for trips to places like Bar Hop on a weeknight. She resolved to remember this unfortunate fact the next time Cari tried to persuade her to join another little adventure. Cricket had two children to get up and out to school before taking herself to work. Every available second of beauty rest was necessary for a smooth morning.

Warmth spread over her remembering her conversation with Boris. She supposed that was worth the exhaustion she experienced now. She reminded herself that this wasn't the time to daydream about the next time she'd see him. Hauling herself out of bed, she padded off to wake Max and Ashling.

One hour later, both kids had boarded buses, lunchboxes in hand, and were on their way to their respective schools. She savored the last of her coffee and tried to shake off her first week on the job jitters. Visualizing herself zipping around the market six months from now brought a small measure of comfort. Overall, the work was far easier than what had been required of her at Shady Oaks. Cricket reminded herself that stocking shelves with honey and selling pies didn't require the same level of responsibility it took to care for a human being. She could do this.

The phone rang before nine o'clock, interrupting her thoughts.

"I'm hoping that after a late night out, you haven't hit the treadmill yet." Boris. He didn't waste any time calling. She smiled at that.

"I haven't," Cricket said, walking to the sink with her breakfast dish and mug.

"I was thinking of going over to the club around two. Do you want to join me?"

She'd have just enough time between work and the kids coming home from school. An hour or so wouldn't take up her whole day. "That sounds good."

"Great, I'll meet you this afternoon."

Hanging up, a touch of panic set in. What was she doing? She wasn't in a position to encourage anyone's advances right now. Especially considering her entire backstory had been fabricated. Boris knew that she had two kids and wasn't fazed by that, but it would be impossible to predict how he'd react to finding out how she ended up living across the street from his grandmother.

Was this a date? A gym date? Boris couldn't be sure, but he remained hopeful. She was warming up to him and making less of an effort to avoid him.

That afternoon's plan entailed using the track for their jog and then getting a late lunch or a smoothie. The jog shifted into a walk after the first few laps as they grew winded from talking too much.

"I'm sorry," she panted. "This is probably not what you had in mind for a workout. My heart is just not in it, worrying about Ashling. Max is easy. He's never walked into a room that didn't love him. Ashling usually walks in with a fortress around her. It's just a defense mechanism, though. She has a heart of gold."

"Hey, being the new kid isn't easy for most people at any age. She'll settle in. And don't worry about my workout. You're doing me a favor. Remember, I'm easing back into this after a hiatus."

"Still, you didn't come here to listen to my tale of woe."

Her tone told him embarrassment and maybe some regret had set in. It had probably been easier to talk freely while they walked. He suspected she had more on her mind than her daughter's first week jitters.

"It's my pleasure, Cricket. I mean that sincerely. What do you say to grabbing some food?"

"You must enjoy playing therapist," she laughed.

"That, and I'm famished!"

To his surprise, she agreed, saying she'd worked up quite the appetite venting.

With a cheeseburger in front of him and a grilled cheese placed before her, he decided to not overthink things and ask her out again.

"Have you taken your kids to see the light display at the Holiday Express Railroad?"

"I've heard about it, but we've never been."

"Would you be interested in going tonight?"

"All of us?" she asked taking a bite.

"Yes, all of you. Christmas is for kids. It wouldn't be the same if we didn't see it through their eyes."

He held his breath, waiting for her to finish chewing and answer. Was he moving too quickly by involving her children?

"I'm sure they'd love it."

"Great! My treat. Is seven good?"

"Can we say six? I don't want to keep Max out too late in the cold."

"Six it is." Realizing he could fully exhale now, he did so and took the first bite of his burger.

CHAPTER 15

There she went again, being impulsive as ever. Acting without thinking. Answering without processing the question being asked. Agreeing to take Ashling and Max out with Boris had to rank high on her list of "why did I do that?" moments. At the time, she had been enjoying herself and his company. She wanted to see him again. That was bad enough, considering he'd be leaving in a week. What was the point really? It would only be made worse by the fact that her kids would be in tow. Max might be enthralled by the lights, but Ashling could be unusually perceptive.

Cari met the news of Cricket's plans with a hoot. "I just knew it, pretty lady! That man has had his eye on you since day one!"

Blushing, Cricket futilely attempted nonchalance in her response. "Don't be silly. He's probably just trying to find a reason to get out of the house for a few hours. Maybe he's feeling nostalgic about Christmas in this town and doesn't want to go alone."

"Oh, honey. Save the act for someone else. He found a reason to see you twice in one day. If that doesn't spell serious interest, then I don't know what does."

Seizing the opportunity to take the attention off herself and get the dirt on Cari's personal life she shrugged. "Speaking of interest, you and Lex were looking pretty cozy last night. Do you two often hang out after hours, or is he looking for excuses to spend time with you outside of the farm?"

Now it was Cari's turn to be dismissive. "That was nothing more than a total coincidence. We just got talking."

"Oh. Well, he seems nice."

"He's been a lifesaver. I've asked myself more than once what I would have done without him."

Cricket watched in amusement as Cari grabbed a dishrag and began fussing around the counters, cleaning nonexistent dirt. Was it her imagination, or was Cari avoiding eye contact while going on the defensive?

"His dad worked with my uncle for over thirty years. Lex joined him part time during high school and when he was on summer breaks from college. No one expected him to come home permanently. He was supposed to go back to law school, and who knew where he'd end up from there."

"What brought him back?"

"Well, when his dad passed away, he offered to help Uncle Otto keep things running smoothly until he could find a replacement." She laughed at that. "Impossible task! The man was irreplaceable!"

"I'm guessing Lex was a close second though," Cricket said as she shooed both cats off the island and sat down. "I can see him helping out short term, but why did he stay? Did he feel guilty about leaving your uncle?"

Cari rinsed out the rag and busied herself with emptying the dishwasher.

"Not at all. It was like once he stepped into his dad's shoes, he didn't want to take them off. My uncle tried to convince him to go back to school, but he insisted law wasn't the path for him after all. He realized he could never be in an office all day."

The more Cari talked, the less Cricket believed the 'just friends' story and asked the obvious question.

"Any chance you were part of the reason he gave it up?"

"Oh, no! I've known Lex since I was a little girl, and he's never been interested in me. I had a gigantic crush on him all through school, but he was four years older than me, so I barely existed to him." She smiled over her shoulder. "Except for when I was making a fool of myself trying to get his attention, of course. I was nothing more than an annoying fly buzzing around him in my homemade clothes."

"Your mom made your clothes?"

"No, I made my clothes. And let me tell you, a seamstress and a designer I was not!" She shook her head and turned around. "There was an ancient sewing machine in my uncle's attic that I could just about thread. I knew my mom didn't have a lot of money and told her I wanted to make my own clothes because I had dreams of becoming a designer. The woman was so busy working herself to the bone that she didn't even notice how little talent I had." She plopped down on another stool at the island. "It's okay though. I probably wouldn't be the fashion plate I am today if that hadn't happened." She giggled gesturing over her white smocked peasant top, black leather pants, and red heels.

"You definitely have a flare all your own! Deny it all you want. Lex may not have noticed you when you were a child, but there's no way you've slipped under his radar as the beautiful woman you are today."

"If that's true, it'd be nice if he started sending some clear signals on the matter."

Cricket let it drop, knowing there was more going on, even if Cari wasn't ready to admit it to herself.

Just before dinner, Ashling pranced into the kitchen with a smile on her face, overjoyed that a more welcoming reception greeted her at school today. Liz moved her schedule around so that they would have the same lunch. She'd stopped by yesterday to say that Zane had filled her in on the solitary meals. Although mortified, pure gratitude had washed over Ashling when Liz had insisted she would have none of that. Not showing the slightest bit of self-consciousness, she'd shared that one of her classes had been too challenging this year, but, she hadn't wanted to disappoint her mom by moving down a level.

As luck would have it, report cards had come out last week and her mom had been the one who offered the suggestion. If she made the change now, she could still end the year with a passing grade. Arriving early that morning, she'd made a beeline for her guidance counselor's office and requested the change to her schedule, which affected her lunch period, much to Ashling's delight.

As Liz's friends had joined them, Ashling had been determined to push through the nerves creeping in. One by one, two by two, their table filled up quickly. Liz was more popular than Ashling had realized. Not in the same way Bernadette appeared to be popular, with her mean attitude and meaner friends. Liz simply, genuinely exuded likeability.

She beamed at her mother. "I don't expect to become a member of the group right away. But I have a place at the table. It's a start."

"I'm so happy for you Ashling," Cricket said with a smile. "I knew you needed to give it more time. I get where you're coming from. I'm the new kid at the Honeycomb Market. Everyone who comes in has known Pia for her entire life. Some of them look at me like I'm from Mars!"

"Mom, there's more. I think I have a date!"

"You're thirteen!"

"Mom!"

"Well, who with?"

Breathless with excitement, the story flew out of her mouth. "When I was leaving the cafeteria, I bumped into Zane again. It was embarrassing because I wasn't watching where I was going. But, we kinda laughed it off and he asked what I was doing after school tomorrow and did I want to hang out. Mom, I was about to hyperventilate! So, I just said sure and took off before asking him when or where."

Cricket chuckled. "If he wants to get together bad enough, I'm sure he'll catch up with you at some point to make plans."

"I guess," she replied, dumping her backpack on the table. "It's not like I have a phone like everyone else."

"Join the club."

"That's not what I mean. I don't expect you to get me a phone. I'm just saying he's going to have to find me in school or stop by or something."

"It's good for boys to show a little effort. It's a lost art these days, with texting and social media."

"Oh, Mom." She rolled her eyes, smiling as she began pulling homework out of her backpack.

"How did it go at St. Agnes's?"

"At first, it was awkward. Ms. Pace was her usual unfriendly self. I saw a few familiar faces though and could tell they were wondering what I was doing with Cari."

Cricket raised an eyebrow at the understatement and crossed her arms. "Would you go back?"

"Oh, I already asked Cari to take me again. At one point I looked up and counted twelve kids at my table. Every one of them needed help with math or reading."

"Who knows, maybe you'll be a teacher someday."

"Maybe, but I think I'd rather have Ms. Pace's job."

This kid never failed to surprise her.

Cricket waited until after dinner to tell them about their plans. Max was over the moon. Ashling showed little expression. Maybe she should cancel. She didn't want to cancel. Aside from wanting to see Boris again, Cricket also wanted her children to see the railroad. Places like that were always too far above her budget. It probably wasn't a great idea to take him up on his offer to pay, but this might be her only chance at going while her kids were young. It might also help to brighten up what had been a challenging week for Ashling.

The dishwasher had been loaded and the table wiped clean when a knock sounded at the door. Cricket opened it to find Lex standing there with his brilliant, toothy grin.

"Hi Cricket! Cari should be expecting me."

"Oh, she stepped out. You're welcome to come in and wait if you'd like."

"I'm early, but it didn't make sense to go all the way home and then come back. I don't mind waiting."

Joining Max in the family room, Cricket wondered to herself why Lex would be visiting after hours. After their night out at Bar Hop, she'd been wondering if his relationship with Cari was more than professional. The next forty-five minutes of conversation left her feeling like he might just be a good match for her quirky friend. A bookworm at heart, he shared several novel suggestions. When Cari arrived home, she thanked him for the book list and excused herself and Max to get ready for their night out.

Max gasped as they pulled into the parking lot. He could only see a glimpse of what lay beyond the walls and was already in awe of the lights. Boris couldn't wait to see his face when they passed through the gates. He understood what Cricket meant when she said that everyone loves that kid. It wasn't just momspeak. Max oozed enthusiasm for life. Ashling looked like she'd need more time to thaw out. She wasn't rude, but he could tell that she had her guard up. Once again, he found himself wondering what had brought them to Blue Cove.

Brilliant railroad lights and animated Christmas scenes illuminated every square inch of the property. Even Ashling couldn't conceal her admiration for the spectacular display as they rode the train. As the tour came to an end and they descended the train's steps, people dressed as elves greeted them with cups of hot chocolate. A red carpet led to Santa Claus beaming from atop a glittering red sleigh. Children waited anxiously in line and took turns climbing onto the sleigh to share their wish lists and to take a photo. The magical scene took their breath away.

Reaching the front of the line, Ashling helped Max onto the sleigh. Although he'd already met Santa Claus at the mall, he was over the moon to share the experience with his sister. Boris turned to see Cricket smiling up at them as if she were lit from within. He couldn't tear his eyes from her stunning face. Noticing him staring, she dropped her gaze to meet his.

"Thank you for suggesting this. Tonight has been perfect. And look." She smiled. "We're finally having that hot chocolate you kept talking about."

"Yep. And, it's better than I thought it would be." He blew on the top of his steaming cup. "Tell me more about how your new job is going."

"It's going. There's a learning curve, for sure. The honey piece of the business is a monster. Who knew there were so many varieties? First of all, there's dark honey and light honey. Then, there's the different flavors." She began to count off as many as she could remember on her fingers. "Raspberry, strawberry, blueberry, and even elderberry! Oh, and let's not forget the apple, lemon, and peach."

"I like to add the elderberry honey to my tea if I feel a cold coming on."

"I'll have to make a mental note of that the next time I'm sick."

She tugged her hat down over her ears and shivered. Boris's first instinct was to wrap his arms around her, but he restrained himself. A public display of affection in front of her children would not likely be well received. Instead, he put an end to their festive night by suggesting, with a twinge of regret, that the time had come for them to get out of the cold and go home.

CHAPTER 16

Marching into Honeycomb Market, Fiona made a direct path toward Cricket and invited her outside for a private word.

"I'm sure your busy, so I'll get straight to the point," she said, once they were alone. "From what I can gather and for reasons I can't figure, Cari Montgomery has taken a liking to you and appears to be bending over backwards to be of assistance to you. I would ask that you not seek similar favor from my grandson. He's always had a big heart and a soft spot for pretty faces. I do not want to see him get tangled up with you and your," she paused, searching for the right words, "your situation. Once he's ready, I know he'll find the right person to start a life with. And, it will not be a woman, such as yourself, who already has a daughter with a chip on her shoulder the size of a boulder. Max is a love, but you're a package deal. More probably, a baggage deal."

Cricket froze, not having the faintest idea how to respond. She was insulted. She was embarrassed. Yet, she could also understand Fiona's perspective—even if she was out of line.

Dredging up a strangled voice, Cricket forced herself to respond. "I'll take your opinion into consideration. If you'll excuse me." She didn't wait for a reply, turning on a heel and hurried away.

Fighting a gust of wind to pull open the door, she could feel Fiona's eyes on her. Once inside, she headed for the ladies' room to catch her breath and slow her heart rate. Gripping the sink, her mind swam with the stinging retorts Fiona deserved for accosting her in her place of work. That had to be calculated. She knew Cricket would never make a scene here. It was a much safer setting for her to say her piece than, say, bravely knocking on Cari's front door. She also knew there'd be little chance of Boris overhearing their conversation.

Fiona was not a woman who pulled punches. She left no room for interpretation of her feelings. Cricket attempted to look at that from a positive point of view. She didn't need to second guess herself or chalk suspicions regarding Fiona's opinions up to her imagination. Nope. She'd come right out with it today.

As much as Cricket wanted to go home to confront her, something held her back. She enjoyed spending time with Boris. She looked forward to seeing him more than she'd care to admit to anyone. And yet, it terrified her. Cricket did not move into Cari's house in hopes of meeting her prince charming. She knew better than anyone that it was dangerous to allow yourself to rely on a man.

Her singular goal was providing her children a safe and stable place to sleep every night. The kids finally had some security in their lives. Now, that one goal included finding a way to sustain that security without help from anyone. Cari had been beyond generous. But Cricket and her children were not Cari's responsibility. She had bestowed an incredible opportunity, and Cricket refused to let her down.

Would it be possible to find a way to balance that goal with having a personal life? She didn't know if she felt ready for any kind of a commitment and would need to prepare herself for the fact that she may not have a say in whether Boris stuck around to find out.

Boris knew Fiona wouldn't likely forgive him any time soon for this snafu. Yesterday morning, she had made him promise to bring down all her Christmas decorations. She wanted the house fully decorated before her Christmas Cookie Swap. Between meetings, going to the gym, and taking Cricket and her kids to the see the railroad lights, it had gone right out of his head. Guests were expected at twelve sharp. Other than hanging a wreath he'd picked up at Honeycomb Market, time had run out to do much else.

To make matters worse, she wanted him to spend some time at the swap to say hello to her friends. Spending an afternoon with a group of women discussing cookie dough recipes was not top on his list of fun at the moment, but he swallowed that thought and agreed to stay for a short time, knowing she couldn't wait to show off her grandson.

He envisioned himself politely nodding at her friends while plotting his escape route as she gushed about his big career in New York. Her guests would graciously smile at him as it took every ounce of effort for their eyes to not roll to the back of their heads.

After calling Cricket and pleading for her assistance, he laid a red tablecloth across the rectangular dining room table and brought up an additional six chairs. Christmas carols blared and Fiona sang along as she baked her last batch of snickerdoodles. The house smelled incredible. She could never stay mad at him and brought in a tin holding a variety of cookies to hide in his room before anyone arrived.

"I hope you don't mind, I told Cricket to stop over when she comes home from work. It was last minute, so she didn't have time to bake anything, but I know she'd love to continue to get to know the neighbors better."

She pursed her lips. "I wish you would have asked me first."

"What's one more? You're always left with more cookies than you can eat after the swap."

"The cookies aren't the problem."

"Then what is the problem?"

She sighed, placing her hands on her hips. "Never mind. It's not as if you could uninvite her." She stalked off to the kitchen, upset with him once more.

Cricket held her breath standing at the front door. After Fiona's recent harassment, avoiding her would have been the wisest choice. When Boris called saying he needed help gracefully exiting his grandmother's party, she made countless suggestions that he could have used. Yet, he insisted she come over. He needed a knock at the door to answer and exit through with a shouted good-bye and a wave before anyone could stop him or hold him further verbally hostage. Cricket finally gave in, with hopes that Fiona would be too preoccupied with her guests to notice who had arrived.

Standing on the porch, laughter and cheerful voices resonated through the door. Peering through the front window, she saw the dining room table laid with a silver tea set and a variety of finger sandwiches and desserts. Her heart skipped a beat when Tess turned and spotted her. Rushing to the door, she pulled Cricket inside with a rush of words and led her to the table of food.

"Grab a plate. We don't want leftovers, so eat up!"

"Thank you, but I'm not staying."

"Oh, you must though," she said with a pout. "Vera and I were just talking about the Christmas pageant at the community center. We could really use another set of hands if you have some spare time." She popped the remaining bite of a cookie in her mouth. "Besides, Fiona's cookies are to die for. She's been baking at Sprinkles for just about forever. There's nothing that woman can't do with flour and sugar."

One hour. Cricket had sincerely planned to adhere to that time frame but found herself having a decent time. Despite Boris's original intention of sneaking away, he seemed to have settled in to enjoy the company as well. Tina arrived next, and Pia walked in soon after her. Lost in conversation and food, almost two hours passed without her realizing it. When Boris alerted her to the time, her excitement deflated as they said their good-byes.

The music could still be heard from Cari's front porch. Boris and Cricket entered the house to Ashling and Max's voices drowning out the Christmas carols playing on the speaker in the kitchen. Joining them, they found the kids and Cari getting ready to bake.

"I think you're a bit behind schedule for the cookie swap," Cricket said.

"Oh, I mixed up my schedule. I thought I had meeting after meeting today and declined the invitation only to glance at my calendar this morning and find out my schedule was clear. Strangest thing!"

Max ran around the island in circles waving a spatula in the air. "We're making honey buns, Honey Bun." After repeating this chant several times, he dropped to the floor consumed with giggles.

Cari's phone chimed with a new text message. "Oh, no! How is this happening?" She typed frantically at her phone. Receiving an almost immediate response, she jerked her head up at them with her mouth agape. "There must have been a glitch in my calendar. There's a roomful of people waiting for me at the farm. I swear, if it's not one thing it's the other causing me to constantly drop the ball." She pulled her apron over her head and handed it to Boris.

"Looks like it's up to you to save the day. Do you still remember Uncle Otto's honey bun recipe?"

"It's etched in my brain for life."

"Good, be a love and take over for me. I'm so sorry, kids. I promise we'll make candles when you're on vacation."

Candles, Cricket mused. Just what every mother wants her six-year-old playing with.

Cari rushed out the door in a flash. Boris put on the apron and proceeded to teach Ashling and Max every step in the process of making Otto's secret recipe.

Max was suspicious. "If it's a secret, should you be sharing it?"

"We're allowed to share it only with the most special people. Arthur and Guinevere do the choosing, and from what I've heard, they've both taken quite a liking to you two."

Max jumped up and down. "They do love me. We take turns feeding them and they even sleep with us at night. On our heads!"

"That does it, we better get down to business."

Cricket glanced at Ashling expecting a doubtful expression but saw her smiling ear to ear.

The following morning, business was slow given the early hour. Cricket used the opportunity to familiarize herself with the online inventory program. Engrossed in the vast amount of information before her, she barely registered the front door chiming the arrival of a customer.

"I knew you were hiding something. I knew it all along," barked a voice behind her.

Turning around to face the counter, Cricket was confronted with Fiona's mouth twisted into an angry sneer. She knew something.

"Fiona," Cricket began with her heart about to beat out of her chest, "I'm not sure what you're talking about. But could we please discuss it later? I'm trying to work."

"Pia can spare you a few minutes. Not that you deserve my discretion, be thankful that I am actually trying to spare you the embarrassment of having this conversation in earshot of Boris or Cari. Perhaps, even your children."

Her children? That didn't make sense.

Stepping outside and walking toward the parking lot, Fiona refused to make eye contact.

"Does the name Eleanor ring a bell?"

"Eleanor who?" she asked, but her heart was pounding. How in the world did she know about St. Agnes's?

"As if you have no idea?" She stopped abruptly and turned to stare her directly in the eyes. "Eleanor Pace was at my party on Saturday. Do you remember her?"

Eleanor Pace. The new social worker at St. Agnes's. The one who never had even a hint of a smile on her face. Cricket absolutely did not see her Saturday.

"You're awful quiet, Cricket. Let me refresh your memory. She works at St. Agnes's. You're familiar with the place. Cari has volunteered there for years. Surely she's mentioned it." Tapping her chin with her finger as if deep in thought she added, "Oh, wait. That's where she met you, isn't it?"

Cricket's throat dried to sandpaper. She couldn't swallow. "I—I didn't see Eleanor Pace."

"Apparently not. I'm relieved to say she saw you. She came late and saw you walking across the street as you were leaving. She recognized you immediately and made a point to tell me."

"Being homeless doesn't make me a threat, Fiona."

"Perhaps not. Still, I wonder what caused you to end up in that predicament. You may have pulled the wool over Cari's eyes. The woman has a heart of gold. But, I'm not quite as naive as that."

There would be no convincing Fiona. She'd been looking for something to hold against her since day one.

"You look like you've just seen a ghost, my dear Cricket. Perhaps there are a few secrets between you and my grandson. I'm presuming he's blissfully unaware of your truth."

Her stomach turned over. "Please stop, Fiona. I get the point."

"I've been running through this in my head, and I have a proposition for you."

"What are you talking about?"

"As much as I genuinely like Cari, my grandson comes first. You break things off with him, and I'll keep this unfortunate news to myself. You and your children can continue to take advantage of Cari's generosity for as long as she is willing to bestow it upon you. Your new friends need not know either. Vera, Tess, and Tina can go on believing you're Cari's oldest and dearest friend."

This was another one of those moments where she'd be sure to come up with the perfect response hours from now. But, in the moment, her mind blanked.

"What am I supposed to say to him?" she asked.

"You'll think of something. By tomorrow morning, I want to be consoling my grandson." Fiona paused and studied Cricket's face. "Look, I'm sure things haven't been easy for you and I'm sorry about that. But it feels like you're using Boris as the answer to your problems."

She felt lightheaded. Sick. Moving to a nearby bench, she sat down. Ashling was having a hard enough time adjusting in school. The last thing she needed was for the neighborhood to be discussing their past. It would most certainly get back to Bernadette, and Cricket knew for certain that girl wouldn't keep such delicious gossip to herself.

Another problem came to her. The news spreading might be an embarrassment to Cari. Nothing short of a miracle had allowed them to last this long without her second guessing herself and driving them back to St. Agnes's. They'd be homeless again. She abhorred the thought of hurting Boris but could not jeopardize her current situation. She could not risk losing the small taste of stability they were growing accustomed to.

Cricket averted her eyes from Fiona, unable to continue meeting that condescending gaze. Furious and humiliated, Cricket also knew deep down that Fiona truly believed she was doing what was best for Boris. If she had been in her shoes, maybe she'd share that point of view.

"I'll talk to him tonight."

Fiona didn't respond. She nodded to herself, turned around, and strode away.

CHAPTER 17

Boris didn't know what to make of his grandmother's behavior. Was she upset that he left the cookie swap early? He had never agreed to stay for the duration of her party. Sure, she hadn't been receptive to hearing he'd invited Cricket, but everyone else had been happy to see her.

The source of her sour mood must be related to something or someone else. She'd been on and off the phone with her friend Eleanor since this morning. After each call, she'd march about the house with her lips in a thin line and her brow wrinkled.

Right now, he needed to finish answering some emails so he could get ready to take Cricket out. They were going to try a new Italian place that had opened the next town over. A surge of energy coursed through his veins. It wasn't the food that excited him. This would be the first time they'd be going on what could be considered an official date.

Relief flooded Cricket as her shift ended. She'd been distracted all day by Fiona's visit, worried about what she would say to Boris. With Christmas right around the corner, a steady stream of customers strolled in to shop. She grew more and more frazzled with each new question that she hadn't yet learned the answer to.

Right now, though, they were headed to help with the pageant. Cari and Ashling would catch up with her and Max at the community center. She still had reservations about her daughter continuing to go to St. Agnes's, but hadn't found the time to give the matter much thought. Cari raved about her dedication. She wished she felt the same.

Cricket did her best to refrain from expressing any emotion regarding how out of character it was for Ashling to agree to participate in the pageant. She knew Max would love being a part of the show, and a thrill ran through her at the prospect of Ashling showing interest in her new community. It surely had something to do with Liz and Zane's involvement.

Walking into the main hall, she saw some of the performers already gathering on the stage with Bernadette. Even from afar, it was easy to see that she was ordering everyone around.

"You're here!" came a voice from behind her.

Turning, she found Tess with an armful of decorations and pulled some items from the top of the heap.

"With bells on," she smiled. "Just tell me what you need, point me in the right direction, and I'll get to work."

"We have five days to get this place looking like a winter wonderland. With everyone's busy schedules this time of year, it's not going to be easy. The decorations are over there in boxes," she said pointing toward the far end of the room. "Just start pulling things out and putting them where you see fit. No guidelines. I trust your judgement. Just make it festive."

Ugh. Cricket felt uncomfortable with this. She would have preferred step by step instructions. Creativity was not her strength. Taking a deep breath, she began pulling items from a box on the floor. Garland, giant stars, animated characters, ornaments. There was no rhyme or reason to this stuff. She had to wonder who had packed these boxes last year. That person had a severe lack of organizational skills. What she lacked in skills related to holiday decor, she would make up for when it came time to put all of this away.

As she opened a second box, Max bounded over.

"Mama! Ashling is here for the recital!"

"The rehearsal, Max," called Ashling walking toward them.

"That's what I said. The recital!"

Cricket gave him a warm hug and a kiss on the cheek before sending him over to the stage with Ashling. She cringed at the sight of Bernadette strutting around with her hands on her hips in what appeared to be annoyance with the other kids. Good luck to Ashling dealing with her over the next few days.

Two and a half hours later, they called it quits for the day and prepared to go home. Boris was planning to pick her up, and she still hadn't worked out what she wanted to say to him. What right did Fiona have meddling with her personal life? Or his, grandson or not? Ashling interrupted her stream of irritated thoughts.

"That girl's about all I can stand. You know, I'm trying to tune her out and ignore her. But that only seems to make it worse. She gets to sing a few lines solo this year and thinks that makes her the star of the show."

"I could tell something was going on over there."

"She walks up and down that stage giving orders to everyone and criticizing everything we do. It's supposed to be fun, and she's making everyone completely miserable!"

"Maybe you should speak to the director."

"Oh, no. There's no way I'm going to be the one who does that." She held up both hands in protest. "I'll just sound like I'm jealous of her, and that's the last thing I want. I swear though, if she tells me I sound pitchy one more time, I can't be held responsible for my actions." She crossed her arms and jutted out her chin. "That girl has no idea who she's dealing with. I've handled far worse than her uppity attitude."

"You can and you will be held responsible," Cricket sighed and zipped her jacket. "Look Ash, I get where you're coming from, and I don't expect you to be a doormat for her or anyone else. Just promise me you'll find a way to talk to her without causing a scene. The last thing we want is trouble here."

"I know, Mom. It's the only reason I've held it together this long. She goes out of her way to start something every single day at school, and I keep trying to pretend it's not happening." She knelt to help Max with his coat. "Like when she and her lab partner sit behind me during science and make fun of me all through class. It's all I can do to not turn around and tip her lab table over on top of her!"

"I didn't realize this was going on. Do you want me to contact the principal? Or, I could say something to Tess."

"No way," she said, rising. "You'll just make it worse. Promise me you won't do that!"

"How about this, I'll promise not to say anything just yet. But, if this continues after winter break is over, I'm going to talk to the school and her mother."

Ashling didn't say anything for a moment. Finally, she agreed begrudgingly. It would take every ounce of self-control Cricket had to stay quiet. She knew it was vital for her daughter to learn how to handle things like this on her own. But the mama bear in her wanted to storm over to Bernadette's house and lay into that girl for being so mean to someone who only wanted to fit in and have a fresh start. She seethed.

The sight of Nadine shedding her coat as she walked into the room did nothing to improve Cricket's mood. A short list of options raced through her head. She could pretend she never saw her and leave. She could wait for Nadine to approach her first. Or, she could take a deep breath and force herself to go over and say hello. Not one of these sounded appealing.

No one would believe she didn't see the woman. If she waited for her to make the first move, it might never happen, in which case she'd be left wishing she'd made the effort. That left her with the difficult task of slapping a smile on her face and extending the first pleasantry. Walking over with trepidation, she caught Nadine's eye and gave a brief wave.

"Hi, Mrs. Montgomery. Nice to see you today."

Not even a hint of a smile was returned. Instead, she scanned the room. "Should I assume your children will be performing in the Christmas pageant?"

"Yes. They're really looking forward to it."

"Hmmm. Well, I know more hands are always needed getting the show up and running. I'll make a sweep of the place and see what I can help with."

Cricket reached a hand out to her arm. "Please wait." She froze for a moment, unsure of what to say next and wished she'd been ready for this encounter. Nothing like two awkward run ins to contend with in one day. "I—I want you to know that you have raised an incredible human being. I'm a mom and can understand why you might be concerned about your daughter inviting strangers to live in her home."

Nadine regarded her thoughtfully. "Cari is an intelligent woman, so I'm going to have to trust her judgement on this. She's given you the opportunity of a lifetime. Don't waste it."

Hearing the sincerity in her voice, Cricket smiled as they parted ways.

With little time remaining before he needed to leave to pick up Cricket, Boris sat down at the kitchen table intending to review his January calendar. Turning on his laptop, he heard a loud crash overhead. It sounded like someone had fallen through the ceiling. A flicker of panic passed over him. Above him was the master bathroom off Fiona's room.

He stood and went to holler up the stairs. "Hey Fi! Everything okay up there?" Not receiving a response, a pit in the middle of his stomach began to form as he took the stairs two at a time stopping just outside her room. "Fi! Is everything alright?"

Still not hearing anything, he opened the door and rushed to the bathroom. "Fi?" Heart racing, he turned the knob and poked his head inside. A part of him expected her to shout at him for barging in on her. Unprepared for the sight in front of him, his heart skipped a beat at the sight of his grandmother lying unconscious on the bathroom floor.

Digging his phone out of his pocket, dropping it once, he called 911.

"We need an ambulance at 27 Lamplight Lane. My grandmother fell in the bathroom, and she's not responsive." He stayed on the line with the dispatcher while throwing a towel over Fiona and trying to coax her awake to no avail.

"You need to open your front door," came the voice over line. "The paramedics will have no choice but to break it down if it's locked, and no one is there to answer it."

He flew down the stairs and flung the door open just as the ambulance and fire truck pulled up to the house. He had passed frantic minutes alone and screamed at the paramedics to move faster. Herding them upstairs, sickened by his helplessness, he watched them load her onto the stretcher and carry her outside.

"Sir, would you like to ride in back?" One of the paramedics asked. "You don't look like you should be behind the wheel."

Not waiting for an answer, she ushered him into the back of the ambulance and continued to talk. She spoke reassuring words, repeating that Fiona's vital signs were stable and she was beginning to stir. He missed most of what she said and fixated on every breath, every movement Fiona made on the trip to the hospital.

Arriving with sirens blaring, the paramedics rushed her inside, but told him he needed to remain in the waiting area in the emergency room. A nurse guided him to a seat, saying she'd be back once they had assessed Fiona's injuries. He wouldn't interfere in their work, but he'd never be able to stay seated and rose as soon as the nurse left. Pacing the lobby like a caged animal only increased his level of stress.

After what felt like an eternity, the same nurse returned to say Fiona was awake. She'd broken several bones. He needed to wait a while longer before he'd be allowed in to see her. Overall, it was good news. Bones healed. She was going to be okay. Taking what felt like his first breath in hours, he savored the air filling his lungs and exhaled slowly.

Cricket had every intention of ending things with Boris that night. She had it all worked out in her head and in a way, it made sense. She prepared to tell him that they'd been spending too much time together and she simply was not ready to get involved in a serious relationship. It would be better for both of them if they parted ways.

In truth, she knew it wouldn't be fair to string him along while she worked herself out and he could be meeting the woman of his dreams. Someone more ready to settle down. In many ways, it was probably something she should have put out there in the beginning. If she had stopped things in their tracks, she never would have been at that cookie swap, Eleanor Pace never would have seen her, and Fiona wouldn't have any ammunition to threaten her with.

Cricket ran through the imaginary conversation for the umpteenth time in her head and felt as ready as she'd ever be when the phone rang.

"Cricket?" Boris's voice croaked. Something was wrong.

"Are you okay?"

"I'm really sorry, but I'm going to need to cancel our plans for tonight. I'm at the hospital."

"What? Why?"

"My grandmother fell today. I'm not really sure what happened. I found her unconscious on the bathroom floor."

"Oh, my gosh! Is she going to be okay?" Fiona didn't rank on Cricket's favorite person list, but she didn't harbor bad wishes toward her.

"They have her stabilized. I don't have a lot of details right now," he said in a rattled voice. "I'm just waiting for the doctor to talk to me."

"I'll drive over. You shouldn't be sitting there alone."

"You don't have to do that, Cricket," he began.

"Ashling was already planning on babysitting. I'll leave now." She hung up without giving him a chance to argue.

Cricket arrived to find Boris pacing in the waiting room with no more information than he had when she'd disconnected their call. It was almost another half hour before the doctor came out.

Fiona had regained consciousness for a short time and had been able to explain that she'd fallen while trying to clip her toenails. Of all things! She'd had one foot on the floor and one on the toilet seat and lost her balance. She must have hit her head on something on her way down. She had a concussion, a broken ankle, and a broken wrist. But she was otherwise in good health and would make a full recovery. The doctor encouraged them to go home.

Looking up at his strained expression, Cricket wrapped her arms around Boris's waist and rested her head on his chest. He enveloped her in a bear hug. They stood in that position for several minutes until she felt some of his tension release. Without speaking, they put on their coats and walked hand in hand to the parking lot.

CHAPTER 18

Conflicted while climbing into Cari's car, Boris buckled his seatbelt and laid his head back with a sigh. He'd barely gotten any words out before Cricket had hung up the phone and left to keep him company at the hospital. It was just as well because he needed a ride home. The problem was that he wanted to stay with his grandmother. Both doctors treating Fiona advised him to go home and get some rest. It was almost eleven. She would be given a sedative and wouldn't know whether he was there or not.

That was irrelevant. *He'd* know.

Cricket read his mind. "She's going to be fine. Sore, but fine. You will be of no use to her if you're walking around like a zombie tomorrow when she needs you most."

"That's the logical point of view."

"I know. We're coming from two different perspectives. All you care about is being there in case something happens to her again after having the scare of your life. I'm seeing someone who is in desperate need of some rest and maybe even something to eat." She glanced at him as she drove. "I'm not sure if this is your first rodeo taking care of someone, but you're going to need your strength."

He didn't have the energy to reply, never mind think about what tomorrow would hold. They drove the rest of the way in silence. Pulling into the driveway, Cricket told him that he was to go upstairs for a shower while she put together something for him to eat.

By the time he had dried off, put on a t-shirt and a pair of track pants, and made his way back downstairs, every ounce of strength had drained from his body. Cricket sat at the kitchen table with two grilled cheese sandwiches, a container of potato salad, and two glasses of water.

"It's not much, but I didn't want to spend an hour cooking in case you wanted to go straight to bed."

"This is perfect. Just what the doctor ordered." He grinned.

"There's that smile. Hey, I can go if you want to wind down alone."

He shook his head and picked up a triangle of grilled cheese. "I like having you here. Want some?"

"Maybe just a bite of potato salad."

Realizing she hadn't eaten dinner either, he urged her to have something more. She resisted, saying that she didn't like eating this late because it upset her stomach.

Placing his plate in the dishwasher after inhaling his food, he thanked her again.

"I'd be happy to come back in the morning. I can go with you to the hospital, or I could get things set up down here to make Fiona more comfortable when she gets home. Whatever you need."

It occurred to him that Fiona might be less than thrilled to see Cricket walking into her hospital room, given the way she'd been acting. She may also consider it an intrusion of her privacy to have any of the people on this street making changes to her house, but he couldn't be in two places at once.

"It's going to be a while before she can get upstairs." He wavered. "I can always get what she needs once we're home."

"You could, but you'll probably make a lot of unnecessary trips up and down. I used to work in a hospital and can anticipate most of what should be down here. Cari would be willing to help, and Fiona might feel better knowing a stranger isn't rummaging through her house unattended."

He was relieved she understood. "Please don't take it personally. I trust you, but it would be good for her peace of mind to know Cari was here. I've been trying for years to get her to let me hire a cleaning woman, and she won't have it." He laughed. "One time I scheduled a maid to show up unexpectedly and she refused to open the door when she heard who it was."

"Sounds like Cari's uncle. It would take more than that to offend me." She walked over and wrapped her arms around him. "I'll see when Cari's available. Give me a call in the morning before you leave."

With a peck on his cheek, she let herself out. He watched her walk across the street, close the door behind her, and shut off the lights. Minutes later, he was upstairs, sound asleep.

At nine o'clock the following morning, Boris left for the hospital while Cricket and Cari set to work in Fiona's house. They tackled the bathroom first. Fiona was lucky to have a full bathroom with a walk-in shower on the main floor. Toiletries and towels were transferred from the master bath. Uncomfortable poking too much around her bedroom, they took a few books and magazines from her nightstand and moved them to the coffee table.

Cari looked around the room. "She's going to need clothes down there, but I'm hesitant to poke through her closet and drawers."

"Too bad she didn't have a basket of clean laundry we could've brought down."

"We're talking about Fiona. She never leaves things undone. Let's just wait until she gets home and ask her. She may prefer Boris to dig through her drawers."

Before leaving, they left a pile of extra blankets and pillows on the ottoman in the living room. Cricket locked up while Cari texted Boris asking him to let them know how things were going. He responded before they reached Cari's driveway, saying he expected they'd both be home this afternoon, and would they mind if he came by once he had Fiona settled in. Pia expected Cricket at the market, but she would be home by three thirty, so she and Cari agreed.

Cricket was thankful for the diversion of going to work. She didn't have an attachment of any kind to Fiona, but she worried about Boris. He'd been a ball of nerves this morning when he left. Stocking the shelves with fresh pies and various spreads, she tried to think ahead to her Christmas list. Now that she had a paycheck coming in, she'd be able to buy a few small things for the kids. She'd seen a buy one get one free sale for gloves and planned to pick some up this weekend. One pair for Ashling and one for Cari.

She racked her brain trying to think of a gift for Boris. Should she be getting him anything at all? What were the chances she'd ever see him again once he returned to New York? Still, she had a feeling he'd show up Christmas morning with a gift for her, and she wanted to be prepared.

Discharged with a list of services that include in home physical therapy and visiting nurses did little to assuage Boris's fear of being left alone to care for Fiona. The obvious time commitment concerned him, but the idea of tending to her more personal needs left him feeling even more uncomfortable. Fiona was an extremely refined lady. To have her grandson helping her in and out of the bathroom would be undignified. They both wanted to minimize that as much as possible.

At only ten past three, every time he heard a car drive by, he'd look out the window hoping Cricket had come home early. He got lucky ten minutes later when he looked out at the sound of a car door slamming and saw her walking into Cari's house. He knew that she probably needed a few minutes to do whatever it was that she did when she got home from work, but he didn't want to wait long and settled Fiona on her favorite couch with a snack and a cup of tea.

She snorted when he pulled out the TV tray. In her opinion, such things were severely lacking in class. He remembered the day his grandfather brought home a set of four and she'd banished them to the garage. Fortunately, she wasn't one to spend her free time cleaning garages.

Shrugging off his coat upon entering Cari's house, he began pacing and sharing his fears. This wasn't what he'd come over to do. His intention had been to graciously thank both of them for everything they'd done and to promptly get back to his grandmother. She wouldn't take kindly to being left alone for too long, having been home only a few hours. But once he got going, he couldn't stop. Cari jumped in with promises to help as much as she could and volunteered Cricket's and Ashling's assistance as well.

"Whatever you need, Boris, just say the word. Between the services the hospital put in place and the three of us as backup, you and Fiona are going to be fine."

"I'm not about to impose on you like that," he began.

Cari cut him off. "Don't be ridiculous. We can set up a schedule to make things more seamless for all of us." She turned to Cricket. "You know what our daily routines look like. Once Boris has spoken to all the home health care providers, you two should sit down and plan it out."

It was asking too much. He loved her dearly, but Fiona could be a tough pill to swallow. It wasn't going to be easy for Cricket and Cari. He should have adamantly refused their help, but overwhelmed in the moment, he assured them it would serve as a band aid to get him through the week. He had seven days until Christmas. During that time, he needed to firm up his offer and presentation while making arrangements for Fiona to begin once he returned to New York. He loathed the idea of leaving her in the care of strangers.

Seeing what had to be the fifth call today from Dean Stone, Boris apologized and excused himself to answer his phone. What was so urgent that it couldn't be handled in a text or an email? Not that he'd checked either today.

Cari and Cricket retreated to the kitchen to give him some privacy.

As luck would have it, Dean needed his help putting out a few small fires related to the apartment complex in Boston. A pipe had burst on the top floor and water was seeping through the ceiling into lower apartment units. Currently the closest in proximity, his partners asked him to make the hour drive over to meet a plumber and a contractor to assess the damage. They'd all come to an agreement to sell the units off as condominiums, and this new complication could have a major impact on their plans.

He glanced at his watch. If he left right now, he could be back in three hours. Maybe a little more. Sure, he had people lined up to help, but on such short notice?

"Penny for your thoughts."

He turned to see Cricket peeking in.

"Everything okay?" she asked.

"Not really. My partners want me to take a short road trip tonight."

"Tonight?"

He nodded and began to pace once again as he explained what had happened.

"Well, three hours isn't too bad. Do you want me to stay with Fiona while you go?"

Yes, of course he did. But, no, how could he ask that of her?

"The kids'll be in any minute. If Fiona can hang tight until I give them an early dinner, I'll come over soon."

"Are you sure? I know it's a big ask."

"You didn't ask. Besides, maybe Max will want to join us. He took a liking to your grandmother."

"The feeling was mutual," he said, wishing Fiona had taken a liking to Cricket as well.

"Go break the news. I won't be long."

With a ferocious hug and a firm kiss, he left and tried to not think of how this news would be received.

❄

Cricket silently berated herself while throwing together some pasta and a jar of sauce. Where were the kids? Maybe their bus was late. She hadn't had any other choice than to offer to stay with Fiona. She wasn't sure how much Boris had told Fiona about her over the past twenty-four hours, but for all she knew, Fiona thought they weren't seeing each other anymore.

How was she supposed to do that to him when he was so upset about what had happened to his grandmother? She didn't want to add one more source of stress to his life. Resolving to get on with it, she put the pasta in the refrigerator and left a note on the kitchen island for Ashling.

She braced herself walking through Fiona's front door. They'd be sure to get along about as well as two bees in a bonnet. The news blared from the T.V. Fiona looked up from her seat on the couch.

"Hello, Fiona," she greeted her brightly.

Fiona smirked. "Played my fall to your advantage, I see."

"I am really sorry about what happened to you. I mean that sincerely."

She grunted in response.

"Listen, I completely understand if you aren't comfortable having me here. I know that you don't trust me, and I understand that as well. You know Boris doesn't want to leave you alone just yet, but he was in a bind tonight." She stopped. That didn't come out right. "I mean, you are obviously far more important to Boris than his real estate deals, but I don't mind helping him out. I won't leave your sight. You can rest assured that I won't steal anything from you. But, if my presence really upsets you that much, I'll call and ask him to turn around and come home."

Cricket held her breath while Fiona remained silent for a few moments.

"Boris has been jumping through hoops trying to make sure I'm well cared for. The last thing I want to do is make things more difficult for him." She averted her gaze and smoothed her blanket. "If you're willing to come over from time to time, I can swallow my pride to spare him further inconvenience. However, and I'm sorry to say this, I would prefer it if you stayed in the same room with me."

"Done."

The remainder of the evening passed uneventfully. They didn't have much to say to each other unless Fiona asked for something. Cricket had expected her to be overly demanding, but nothing could have been further from the truth. Overall, things were peaceful, despite the tinge of awkwardness.

Finally, she decided to address the elephant in the room. "I want you to know that I haven't said anything to Boris yet. I had planned to talk to him, then you fell, and he was so upset, I just clammed up."

"I haven't said anything either. My feelings on the matter haven't changed in the least, mind you. But timing is important. He's had enough on his plate recently."

"What would you have me do?"

"What am I supposed to say to that, Cricket?" she asked, wide-eyed. "Here you are helping me in my time of need, Boris has been a wreck, and—" she paused. "This whole thing is short term. I don't expect to be in this predicament one second longer than necessary. Once I'm back on my feet, I do ask that you follow through and break things off with him. Maybe, in the meantime, try to not spend too much time together."

Yeah, that was easier said than done.

By the time Boris returned, Fiona had already fallen asleep for the night. Cricket joined Boris in the kitchen to work out a tentative schedule. She and Cari would rotate shifts until Fiona gained more independence. This should be interesting. Although Fiona couldn't physically get around, she remained as sharp as a tack and resented needing a glorified babysitter.

❄

After spending several hours at the community center the next morning, Cricket whipped up a quick lunch when she arrived home. Hearing Cari pull into the driveway, she made an extra turkey and cheese sandwich before sitting down.

Moments later, Cari joined her. "Tell me that plate on the counter is for me!"

"Sure is."

Cari picked up the sandwich and took an enormous bite.

"Mm!"

"Hungry?"

"Famished!" She took another bite and sat down at the table. "I was thinking, you could probably use an advance for gift shopping."

That was an understatement. Six days until Christmas, and she desperately needed gifts.

"I'd like to be polite and turn you down, but an advance is music to my ears. I'm going to see Fiona later, and would love to sneak in some shopping beforehand."

Cari pulled a wallet out of her pocketbook and counted out several twenties.

"This should help. I'm not going back out, so the car's yours."

"Thank you. I'm going to leave right now and start at All Goods. With any luck, it'll be a one stop shopping trip. I don't want to get back late and hold Boris up."

Less than thirty minutes later, Cricket walked into All Goods, pondering what department to hit first. The store was packed, as expected. On the way over, she had compiled a tentative gift list in her head. Running through it, she decided to head to the toy section first, followed by clothing, and finally food.

It was nearly impossible to pass through the aisles with all the carriages. By the time she emerged from the toy department with an indoor basketball hoop, clay, a building set, and the requested crayons she felt like she'd won first place in a triathlon. She breezed through every other part of the store afterwards and patted herself on the back for getting the worst out of the way first. After grabbing some clothes for both kids, then nail polish and a jewelry making kit for Ashling, she moved on to the grocery department to collect the ingredients for her homemade fudge and a pack of reusable red plastic containers.

Anxiety set in when she glanced at her watch. She'd need to get in line soon, but still didn't have anything for Boris other than the fudge. She walked slowly toward the front of the store for checkout, hoping an idea would come to her before she reached the lines. Scanning the aisles, a display of frames caught her eye. That was it! Why hadn't she thought of it before? Boris had loved her idea of gifting Fiona a frame of her favorite photographs. Countless pictures had been taken at the cook off. She'd ask Cari to print one that had all of them in it and frame it for him.

After a seemingly endless forty minutes standing in line, Cricket headed home with just enough time to drop off her purchases before relieving Boris.

Fiona's welcome proved slightly warmer than the previous day. They watched an episode of her favorite game show and were in stitches throwing out answers to the absurd questions asked by the host.

Declaring that there was nothing of value in her kitchen worth stealing, Fiona allowed Cricket to prepare a light snack. She stopped dead in her tracks before reaching the refrigerator. There on the door was a child's drawing of flowers and handwriting as familiar to her as her own. Quickly throwing some cookies on a plate and pouring a cup of tea, she took down the picture and put it on the serving tray.

"Fiona, I couldn't help but notice this picture hanging in your kitchen."

"Mm-hmm. Your little one brought that over after school yesterday."

"Max."

"Yes. Max. The older one was with him. What's her name? Ashley?"

"Ashling."

"That sounds about right, given her mother is named after an insect." She picked up her mug and inspected the contents, shrugged in approval and took a sip.

"They didn't mention it to me," Cricket mused more to herself than to Fiona.

"Oh? They were here again this morning. The little one likes to bring me something he's made and chatters away about his day. Ashling pokes through my old records," she said pointing toward an ancient looking console that opened up to a record player and storage.

"Does the record player still work?"

"It sure does. You know, that Ashling has quite the voice on her. She surprised me by knowing the words to all the old show tunes."

Cricket's mouth dropped open. "She sang for you?"

CHAPTER 19

"There's something about the old records that just brings out the joy in people," Fiona said, reaching for a cookie. "I'll be honest. I had my reservations about that one, but she's an old soul at heart. Surprisingly easy to chat with."

Were they talking about the same kid? Cricket knew that once upon a time her daughter could dazzle people. Between her beauty and ability to participate in a mature discussion far exceeding her years, she could charm the most uncongenial curmudgeon into a delightful conversationalist.

"I wish I had known they'd been stopping by. I know it's not easy for you to get to the door. If you'd prefer, I could tell them it's not a good idea to disturb you."

"You'll do no such thing!" She shook her head. "You know how I feel about...about...the whole thing. But whatever led you to St. Agnes's is through no fault of those children. They have been the brightest part of my week."

Cricket sat, stunned. "Okay. I mean, if you're okay with it."

This was a strange turn of events, but Cricket refused to allow herself to dwell on the unlikeliness of the situation and simply be grateful for it.

The energy between Fiona and Cricket had palpably changed. When Boris arrived home, he strained to process the sight before him. Cricket and Fiona sat talking companionably without realizing he had walked in.

"Greetings to you on this fine evening, my ladies!"

Fiona laughed out loud at that. "It might be a much better evening if my darling grandson would help me get this place decorated before Valentine's Day rolls around."

"You got me there, Fi."

With all the time he'd spent making sure her needs were met while simultaneously putting in the long hours his job required, they didn't even have a tree yet.

"Cricket is the Honeycomb Hills expert in the room at present. If she'd be kind enough to help me pick out a tree over at the farm, we should be able to turn this place into Christmas Land itself in a few hours."

Walking amongst the rows of trees in the brisk night air with music floating around them, Cricket told him how she finally understood what Cari had meant when she said winter was her favorite season on the farm.

"As someone who detests the cold, I actually get where she's coming from. There's almost a magical quality to this place."

Outwardly, he agreed. Inside, his stomach knotted at the thought of tearing all of this out. Next year at this time, this place would be nothing more than a construction site, if his partners had anything to say about it.

Pulling into the driveway, they saw Max and Ashling walking up the front steps to Fiona's house. They turned and waved at the sound of the car.

"Mrs. Glynn invited us over to help decorate!" Max hollered.

"Well, she must know you're the best people to get this tree ready for Santa's visit!" Boris yelled back.

Max jumped up and down on the top step clapping. "I am! I am!"

The four of them spent the evening putting up all of Fiona's decorations while she pointed around the room with suggestions. When every box had been emptied and returned to the attic, Boris felt his heart melt at the sight of Max drifting off to sleep with his head in Fiona's lap. It brought to mind vivid memories of how good she had been to him as a child.

"Looks like I might need to carry the little guy home tonight," he said, grinning at his grandmother.

She smiled back with a finger over her lips. He couldn't remember the last time he'd seen her look so happy and at peace. Cricket's kids had brought joy back into her home. Into her life. He silently asked himself how he'd be able to take all of this away from her.

When Cricket woke up Sunday morning, she didn't waste any time getting to work on her batches of fudge. The red containers would be filled, tied in a ribbon and given to Cari, Boris, Fiona, and Pia. Cari would likely deduce she'd be receiving a box after seeing Cricket making the treats all day, but at least the gloves would be a surprise.

Soon enough, the entire downstairs smelled like heaven on earth. After letting them each take a few squares, she had banished Max and Ashling to the living room so she wouldn't have to keep steering them away from the pans. Cari rounded the corner demanding answers.

"What magnificence are you creating in here this time?" She gasped, taking in the sight of the pans of fudge all over the island and kitchen table. "You have to be kidding me right now! It looks like a chocoholic's fantasy come true! I should know, being the queen of chocoholics anonymous!"

Cricket held up a pan. "Would you like to try some? Full warning though, you may ruin your breakfast."

"Who needs breakfast when they can have fudge?" She grabbed a square and took a bite. Her eyes bulged out of her head as she chewed slowly allowing the rich, gooey chocolate to melt in her mouth.

"Cricket! There are absolutely no words to describe how insanely good that was!" She reached for another piece. "It's an otherworldly experience eating this." As she finished swallowing, she grabbed Cricket by both arms. "You should be selling this. You *need* to be selling this!"

"It's just fudge. You can buy it anywhere."

"That," she said pointing at the pans, "is not just regular fudge. I've had fudge. I eat so much chocolate it's safe to say I'm an expert on the subject. It's the best freaking fudge I've ever had in my life."

Cricket rolled her eyes and smirked. "I appreciate the compliment."

"One more?"

"One more and no more."

She stopped as she reached for her third square.

"I'm having a thought. You should make a few more batches to sell at Honeycomb Market. People will go crazy!"

"You think?"

"I *know*. Do it. You could bring some over this afternoon and set yourself up a little table. Even put out samples. I'm telling you, once people try your fudge, they'll be buying pounds of it!"

Cricket looked around. She had enough here to set up a small display. With Christmas days away, she'd have plenty of time to make more for gifts.

"Are you serious?"

"Very. I'd recommend charging around nine dollars a pound."

"You need a cut for letting me sell it in your store."

"We can get into all that later. You're not going to sell enough in one day for it to make a difference. Let's talk details later."

"Deal!" Cricket felt like she was going to lift right off the floor. She dug under the counter to find a scale and set to work packaging up pounds of fudge. When the last package was wrapped, she figured she had the potential to make a small profit, even if she kept out a pound for samples. Not bad for a spur-of-the-moment venture.

"Oh, would you mind if Ashling comes with me to St. Agnes's this afternoon?" Cari then asked.

This gave Cricket pause. "Again?"

"She wanted to see the kids before Christmas break. She spends most of her time tutoring and doesn't think she'll be there much next week."

"Do you think it's a good idea?" She tilted her head in thought. "I can't put my finger on why, but the idea of it makes me uncomfortable."

"It's a hard place to visit. There aren't a lot of people breaking down the door offering their services. For some reason it appeals to her, so I haven't discouraged it."

"Well, it's fine for today. I'll make a point to discuss it more during her vacation. I guess I want to know why it's so important to her."

Cricket called ahead to let Pia know why she was coming in on her day off. Walking in with shopping bags in each hand, she beamed at the sight of an empty white table with a two-foot-tall chalkboard in front. The words scrawled in cursive read "Fudge by Cricket".

"Pia! Look what you did! It's adorable."

Pia scrambled over to relieve her of a few bags. "This is exciting. We've got every other delectable treat in this place. Can't imagine why no one's thought of fudge before."

They quickly emptied the contents from the bags onto the table and arranged the packages into a pyramid. To the left of the pyramid was a plate piled with small sample bites of fudge.

"I wish I could hang around and see people's reactions," Cricket sighed, "but I'm due at Fiona's soon."

"Call me when you get home, and I'll let you know how it's going."

"Will do," she said, giving her a quick hug and a thank you on her way out the door.

Boris had asked Cricket to stop by while he was out running errands and doing some last-minute Christmas shopping. Cari took the kids to the movies, so Cricket made some lunch to share with Fiona and thought they could find a movie on T.V. to watch while they ate. She did not expect to arrive and find Fiona with tears in her eyes.

Placing her bags on the floor, she moved to sit next to Fiona on the couch.

"What is it? Are you in pain?"

Fiona stared down at her hand while twisting the diamond ring on her finger. Finally, she removed the ring and held it up to Cricket.

"It still fits!" She gave a watery smile as a few tears slid over her cheek. She laughed and brushed at them with the heel of her palm.

"Is that your engagement ring?"

"I lost it years and years ago. I'd given up on ever finding it. Here, look. My husband, rest his soul, had our initials inscribed on the inside of the band."

"Where did you find it?" She blinked at the glittering stone. "How did you find it?"

"I didn't. It was Ashling. She brought over some muffins this morning and asked to listen to some music. She accidentally dropped one of the records and it slipped behind the console," she said, gesturing toward the record player. "When she pulled it out, she spotted the ring. It must have been under there this whole time!"

"It's gorgeous," Cricket breathed while holding it up to the light. The enormous diamond glinted in the sunlight shining through the windows.

"You don't need a trained eye to know it's valuable." Fiona placed a gentle hand on Cricket's arm. "I owe you an apology,

158

Cricket. I'm embarrassed by the things I've said to you. I just... I just jumped to conclusions. Your children have showed me how I've been wrong in every way. There is no way on this earth that they would be so wonderful without some sort of positive example from their mother." She then took both of Cricket's hands into her own. "Whatever you've been through, despite the struggles I'm sure you've had, you're clearly an excellent mother."

Cricket recognized her effort to apologize, but felt it was all wrong. "Fiona, I appreciate everything you're saying. But the truth is, an excellent mother wouldn't have landed in St. Agnes's. Not once, but twice."

"You have every right to tell an old lady to mind her own business, but I'm going to ask anyways. What happened?"

Cricket hesitated, then realized that nothing could be made worse than it already was, even if Fiona knew her history. She dove in, describing the series of events that occurred after Wally passed away and ended by sharing the poor decision she'd made at Shady Oaks.

"I made a mistake. I was wrong. But I promise you that I never intended to do something as awful as stealing from an elderly woman." She proceeded to relate every last detail of her life-altering error in judgement.

"Ultimately, it turned out to be the single biggest mistake of my life. The repercussions were enormous, and I'm still paying for it."

Fiona continued to fidget with her ring. Finally, she spoke. "I believe you."

After everything she had said to Cricket in the past, her words should not hold any significance. At all. Yet, her eyes stung with tears.

"You do?"

"Mm-hm. I can see how something like that could be misconstrued. I was recently in Helen's shoes. I felt like the staff went above and beyond for me during my own short hospital stay. And always with a smile on their faces, never once making me feel like I was a burden." She smiled at the memory. "I mean, I know it's their job. They signed up to take care of people. But you and I both know that not everyone goes about it the same way. Some people are burnt out and miserable going to work every day and others... Well, others are just different."

Cricket nodded. "True, but the same could be said for the patients."

"I had two favorites and, only just yesterday, insisted that Boris go over with a gift card for each of them. Neither refused it. Cash is a little different, and you should have refused, but I won't fault you for giving in. It was never my place to cast stones at your personal life," she said, shaking her head slowly. "I can honestly say that I wouldn't have made the same gesture, but I understand why Cari took you in. Especially with those children of yours."

"Thank you."

"It doesn't completely change the way I feel about you and Boris dating. It's nothing personal, I would have liked to see him start a relationship with a clean slate. No baggage, so to speak. But I'm not going to force your hand." She smiled, chagrined. "And, I can't deny the lot of you have grown on me. You do seem to make him happy, so we'll just let it play out organically and see where things land."

"That's fair," she conceded.

A middle ground had been reached. Fiona changed the subject to gripe about missing work, followed by reading until she eventually dozed off. Cricket decided to pick up some of the clutter around the room. By the time she finished, things were much more organized. Prescription information, appointments, home visits, and general mail had all been sorted into separate piles.

Walking to the tiny office nook in the corner of the room, she set everything down on the desk, but accidentally knocked over a small pile of paperwork. Trying to straighten them out, the word "Honeycomb" caught her eye. She looked at it a second time to be sure she had read it correctly. Sure enough, this stack of papers had something to do with Cari's farm.

Glancing over her shoulder, Cricket observed Fiona sufficiently sleeping. Quickly, she rifled through the top of the pile, knowing full well it was none of her business. From the looks of things, Boris's company had plans to purchase the farm and to turn the entire property into an upscale, outdoor shopping area. Did Cari know about this and hadn't said anything yet? That couldn't be true. The farm was too important to her. But there had been financial problems recently. Was Boris planning to take advantage of that?

Hearing a car door shut, she moved away from the desk as quickly as she could and slid into a rocking chair with a magazine as if she had been there all along. Fiona stirred as Boris entered the house holding a giant bakery box.

"Dessert for my two favorite ladies!" He set the bag from Sprinkles on the coffee table. "You know what this means? It means another trip to the gym tomorrow. I'm hoping my pretty work out buddy will accompany me."

Cricket needed to get out of there. She needed to go home and process what she'd just seen. Confusion crossed Boris's face when she mentioned helping Ashling with homework tonight and a busy day tomorrow. She knew he didn't believe her.

CHAPTER 20

B oris stood in the entryway staring at the door, wondering what just happened.

"Probably presumptuous of me to try and detain her any longer," he mused.

"Offer to take her out for a late dinner once Max is in bed," Fiona suggested. "He's still young, you know. She may not like spending so much time away from him while she waits on me hand and foot."

He bowed his head and sighed. It was easy to forget how little free time Cricket had on her hands.

He then jerked his head up, resolving to enjoy his grandmother's company. "More pastry for you and me," he said, opening the box and showing her the contents.

"Ooh," she squealed in a childlike voice. "Smell that frosting! They're obviously getting on just fine without me."

"I can assure you that you are very missed. Everyone was asking about your recovery."

"I'll start with a half moon cookie! Would you mind pouring me a glass of milk?"

"On it."

He set the box down on the TV tray. His appetite for

something sweet had disappeared, though. Something was wrong. Deciding to call her, he held his breath while the phone rang. She knew that he knew she was home, making it difficult for her to ignore the call. Just when he expected the voicemail to click on, she picked up.

"Hi."

"Hey, I was wondering if you'd be interested in a late dinner tonight."

It unnerved him that she didn't answer right away.

"What time?"

"I know you don't like eating too close to bedtime, but I also want to give you time to say goodnight to your kids. Is seven thirty too late?"

Again there was a lengthy pause.

"It's fine. I'll meet you outside."

He should have felt good hanging up. Cricket agreed to go to dinner with him. But something about her hesitation and flat tone of voice caused a pit to form in his stomach. Had she and Fiona had some sort of disagreement today? Had he done something to offend her that he wasn't even aware of? Maybe she had decided there was too much on her plate to be dating someone while simultaneously caring for that someone's grandmother. That would make sense. He braced himself for the possibility she'd be saying as much to him tonight.

The first thing Cricket needed to do was to find out what, if anything, Cari knew about Boris's plans. She ran through a series of conversation starters in her head in search of a natural way to bring up the subject. Failing miserably, she groaned and gave up. Fortunately, Cari provided an opening by barging out of her office during a phone call, insisting to the person on the other end of the line that she wasn't cut out for farming. She thrived on creating and marketing new products, not producing the ingredients for those products. Sitting on the top step and staring down into the foyer, Cricket glimpsed her swat away stray tears as she disconnected the call.

Praying Cari wouldn't view it as an invasion of privacy, she approached.

"I don't want to intrude, but is there anything I can do to help?"

"Yeah, next time I'm on the phone, make sure it's on a landline that can be slammed down."

Cari leaned forward with her head in her hands. Her shoulders shook with silent tears. Cricket moved to sit down next to her.

"Hey, whatever is going on, you'll get through it."

Cari sat up straight with hair disheveled and eyes wet with tears.

"I have a fortune dropped in my lap for no good reason and sit here crying about it. And I'm supposed to lean on you, of all people, for comfort?" She stood, incredulous. "Seriously, this whole thing is backward!"

"You have every right to feel overwhelmed now that you're wearing so many hats."

"Overwhelmed doesn't come close to how I feel," she said, walking down the stairs. "It's crazy because sometimes I love every second. But the rest of the time I'm frustrated and have no idea what I'm doing." She flung her arms up in the air as she paced. "It's exhilarating when things click into place. But there's no downtime. Ever. There's always something new to learn and a new mistake I've made because I didn't pay close enough attention to another detail that managed to escape me."

"Cut yourself some slack. Your life has been turned upside down. You'll get there."

"What if I don't want to get there?" Cari cried. "I never saw myself doing anything like this, but now I feel obligated. Like, if I don't make it work, I'm failing literally everyone who ever cared about me."

Cricket followed her into the living room.

"It's not just Uncle Otto or disappointing my mom, my failure will have arms that stretch into other people's lives. What happens to Lex and Pia if I call it quits? That was Lex on the phone just now. I can't tell if he wants to see me succeed for the sake of it or solely to save his job."

"It's probably a little bit of both."

"Right. I'm the one who isn't being fair."

Cricket didn't call attention to the fact that she'd be affected as well. She swallowed the cold fear creeping up her spine and asked Cari about her childhood dreams.

"If you didn't see yourself here, you must have had other plans for yourself."

Cari flitted a hand in the air, as if shooing away something unimportant. "I got a business degree and figured I'd end up working for a big, fancy corporation. Beyond that, I didn't look too far into the future and—" Placing hands on her hips with pursed lips, she stopped mid-sentence. "That's not entirely true. For years, until I decided to go the safe career route, I thought it would be wonderful to own a coffee shop. I'd sell pastries, sandwiches, and soups in a cozy gathering spot for the community. I'd even allow pets and sell dog treats."

She sounded so passionate; Cricket didn't have the heart to remind her that she loathed all things related to cooking.

"I know what you're thinking, Cricket!" She waggled a finger at her and perched on the edge of a nearby ottoman. "Try not to laugh. I've never shared this with anyone before. It was just a silly childhood dream."

"Did you enjoy cooking or baking when you were younger?"

"Oh, no!" Cari laughed. "I never intended to do any of the cooking, and I know that makes my fantasy sound even more ridiculous. I figured I'd just hire someone for that, and I could handle everything else. Doesn't matter now, anyways."

Surprised and touched that Cari would share something so personal, Cricket kept her opinions to herself. After all, far too many people never take the first step toward reaching seemingly unattainable goals. Did it really matter that Cari had been a naive teenager thinking that her lack of culinary skills wouldn't be an issue? In any event, Cricket had her answer. Cari didn't mention receiving an offer on her farm from Boris. So what were those plans and numbers she saw on the desk?

Ashling and Max interrupted them by bursting into the foyer from the family room.

"We brought Mrs. Glynn some muffins this morning and she said it's important to be at the next rehearsal for the Christmas Pageant," Ashling said in a rush. "It's too bad I wasn't here when solos were being handed out, because Mrs. Glynn says I absolutely would have gotten one. She would know because she volunteered there forever."

"Well, just put your best foot forward in the chorus this year and who knows what next year will bring," Cricket said.

"I'm going to be in the chorus too!" Max interjected, clasping his hands behind his back. He sounded so adorably serious, Cricket suppressed a giggle and folded her hands together in an effort to keep from wrapping him in a bear hug.

"Of course you are!" she said instead.

"I am going to try out for the school musical though," Ashling stated. "Auditions are tomorrow, and the cast list will be posted before Christmas."

Cricket couldn't recall the last time she'd seen her daughter so enthusiastic about anything. Solving the real estate puzzle would have to wait.

Never one to stew about something for long when upset, Cricket acknowledged that a wiser woman would allow things to percolate. To think things over. A less impulsive woman would bite her tongue until she'd had a chance to carefully plan out what she wanted to say and wait patiently for the right time to say it. She was not either of those things and had never been accused of being wise or methodical. After opting to meet Boris at The Seven

HOMEMAKERS' CHRISTMAS

Seas rather than have him pick her up, she spotted him at a table toward the back of the restaurant.

Boris had already heard that Ashling would be singing with the children's chorus at the pageant, since she had wasted no time in rushing over to share her news with Fiona. As much as Cricket would have loved to give in to the excitement, she took one large sip of the wine he'd ordered and got right to the point.

"Let me start by saying that I was not trying to snoop. Not in the least. But I accidentally knocked over some of your paperwork, and I know what you're planning."

He leaned forward with his elbows on the table and a genuine grin. "Enlighten me, what am I planning?"

"You want to buy Honeycomb Hills Farm right out from under Cari's nose," she said, trying to keep her voice down. "It's wrong! I don't know what ever made you think that she needs or wants to sell but let me assure you that she loves that place and isn't planning on going anywhere."

Taking a slow sip of his own wine, he nodded at her. "Thank you for letting me know." He picked up his menu, "Now that that's out of the way, what would you like for an appetizer? I was thinking the stuffed figs look good."

She shifted in her seat not sure what to say next. Cricket hadn't known what kind of a reaction to expect from him—anger, or maybe shock. But, not this.

"You're not wondering how I know?"

"I leave everything laying around the house, so I'm not surprised. Besides, I wasn't trying to hide anything."

The waiter appeared, pad and pen in hand, and Boris placed an order for the figs.

"I realize it's none of my business, but why haven't you said anything to me?"

He picked up his wine and swirled it without taking another sip. Red legs moved slowly down his glass.

"Buying Honeycomb Hills was the sole reason for me returning to Blue Cove. Honeycomb products have become a pretty big

167

name in the online shopping universe. One of my business partners heard about Otto's passing, knew I grew up here, and suggested I come out and make an offer." He shrugged. "Otto would never have sold. The farm was his entire life. When I heard that Cari had taken over, it seemed like a no brainer. It's common knowledge that she ran the online business and had never immersed herself in the actual farming aspect of things." He took a sip of wine and continued. "We came up with a proposal, an excellent one, and made the arrangements for me to make the trip."

The figs arrived and they each dug in. Cricket realized she hadn't eaten anything since lunch. Starving, she could have eaten the entire appetizer without his assistance. Her nerves had twisted in turmoil all day and thoughts of food never entered her mind.

"She didn't say anything about your offer to me. Again, not my business. But I'm living in her house and have become somewhat of a sounding board for her." Cricket didn't ask again why it had never come up during her conversations with him. That question rankled more than it should have.

"That's because our meeting never took place. I initially tried to get the lay of the land and get a feel for where her head was at. At first, it seemed like it would be an easy deal because she had handed the reins to Lex. Clearly, she didn't want to get her hands dirty out on the land itself. She seemed in over her head." He took another bite. "Then a series of events happened. I met you, Fiona fell, Cari started growing more hands-on with the farm while you worked at the store, and Pia's helping out with online orders. I started thinking maybe I'd missed my window of opportunity."

She rested her fork on the plate and clasped her hands in her lap.

"So what are you thinking now?"

"My partners are still pushing me to move forward, but it just doesn't feel right. I've been stalling them and hoping there's something else out here worth investing in."

He paused and rubbed his neck. She tried to decide if he was deep in thought or uncomfortable with her line of questioning.

"I gotta tell you though, few properties compare to Honeycomb Hills. If Cari continues to struggle with the entire estate, it may still be worth pursuing. I'd rather have her ear first since we are on friendly terms."

A waiter refilling their water glasses interrupted them. Boris thanked him and returned his attention to Cricket.

"I believe she'd rather sell to someone she knows. We could really make something spectacular there."

"It's already spectacular," she responded. And, just like that, her appetite disappeared again. "If you'll excuse me, I need to cut tonight short. It's been a long day." She stood up and left before giving him a chance to respond. Walking to the parking lot, relief flooded her at having had the forethought to borrow Cari's car. The last thing she would have wanted right now would be to be stuck in a car with him.

Stepping onto the front porch once she'd made it home, Cricket sat down as quietly as she could in one of the rockers. She could hear Cari's voice inside and wondered who she was talking to. Needing a minute to get herself together and decide what to do, she wondered if she should say something to Cari. The last thing she wanted was to stick her nose where it didn't belong. Maybe Cari would welcome an offer from Boris's company. She might resent the implication that Cricket somehow knew what was best for her. Worse, she might perceive Cricket as solely looking out for herself, since she'd be out on the streets again if the sale went through.

There was some truth to that, but Cricket also wanted to be a good friend and wasn't sure what that looked like right now. Resolving to give it more time, she went inside and kept the little information she had to herself for the time being.

As she opened the door, Cari came tearing into the foyer, breathless with excitement.

"I'm not one to say I told you so, but I told you so!"

"About what?"

"Pia called. She said your fudge flew off the table in the first hour. The first *hour*, Cricket!"

Cricket's heart skipped a beat. "I don't believe it."

"Believe it!" She bounced from toe to toe in a little dance. "And after that, she lost count of how many customers came in later asking for it. The news spread like wildfire."

"Sounds like I should make some more."

"A *lot* more. She told everyone that we'd be stocked again tomorrow morning. Care for a late-night trip to the supermarket? I would have gone myself, but I had no idea what to buy."

"No, I still have some ingredients left over." She headed for the kitchen. "I'll get a few batches out of it."

"I won't tell you what to do, but if it were me, I'd be making more than a few batches." She reached out and grasped Cricket's wrist with both of her hands. "If we can keep that table stocked through Christmas, you'll make a ton of money."

Cricket's heart began to race. She wasn't going to get much sleep tonight.

"Looks like we're going to have to talk details sooner than later."

"I've been thinking about it," Cari said, releasing her wrist. "You're not going to get rich over the next few days, being limited with how much you can reasonably produce in a short time frame. Just reimburse me for the cost of ingredients and packaging. If this looks like something you want to seriously pursue after Christmas, we'll talk more then. Sound good?"

"Better than good."

Cari tucked her arm through Cricket's and led her back toward the front door.

❄

Boris had steeled himself for that night's date, expecting the 'it's not you it's me' discussion. That might have been easier than

Cricket believing he had hatched a scheme to fleece Cari of her inheritance. Was he being honest saying he hadn't been trying to hide anything? It felt more like lying by omission. He suspected that was how everyone else would see it as well.

Sprawled on top of his bed, he still wore the same clothes he'd had on at dinner. With his eyes closed, the night's events flashed through his brain. He still couldn't fully understand why she'd gotten up and left so abruptly. Sure, Cari's her friend, but she couldn't proclaim to have any real attachment to the farm. If Cari wanted to get out from under it all, a good friend would be supportive. Cricket's reaction to his suggestion that it could be a good move for both him and Cari left him reeling.

Once again, he pondered the oddity of her sudden arrival in Blue Cove and spontaneous decision to move there permanently. It crossed his mind that her behavior tonight may tie back to the events that led her here. Their conversation was not over. He intended to pick it up where they left off when she unceremoniously abandoned him in the restaurant. That topped the list of the most embarrassing moments in his life. He could still feel how his ears had reddened when the waiter came over and he'd had to ask for the check.

He lay there, wishing that his mind would wind down and cease the monotonous circle of their disastrous dinner. They never even made it to the main course. He resigned himself to another night of mild insomnia. When was the last time he'd cared so much about someone's opinion of him? As a rule, he was a 'love me or leave me' kind of guy.

Boris tried to assume that mindset and failed. He opened his eyes with the realization that moving back to Blue Cove wouldn't have entered his mind for a woman whose feelings didn't matter to him. Everything about her mattered to him. Disagreements were a part of life, but he owed it to their relationship to hash it out and find a middle ground.

CHAPTER 21

S huffling into the kitchen, a yawn seized Cricket's entire body. She swept her hair up into a ponytail, resenting the fact that another night severely lacking in sleep had taken its toll. Cari sat at the kitchen table with her forehead resting on one hand. Her posture so still, Cricket wondered if she had dozed off.

"Are you okay?" she asked with hesitation.

Cari lifted her head to look up at Cricket. She used fingers to rake back the hair in her eyes. Shaking her head slowly, she groaned.

"Can I help in any way? You're making me nervous."

"Sorry. I'm nervous enough for the both of us." She covered her eyes with both hands for a moment and took a deep breath. Placing her hands in her lap, she raised her eyes. "Cricket, I literally have no idea what I'm doing. I never should have thought for one second that I could run this operation. I am not Uncle Otto. Farming is not coming naturally to me. I like numbers and food, not dirt, and most definitely not bees."

Cricket noted the frantic quality rising in her voice. "Leave them to Lex."

"It's my responsibility to be able to handle whatever the farm throws at me. That includes being able to ensure the hives are well cared for, but I have zero desire to be up close and personal with them." She slouched her shoulders and dropped her chin with a groan. "The thought of suiting up and disturbing the colonies while I extract their excess honey? Uh-uh. Not something I'd like to do in my spare time."

Cricket joined her at the table. "You're being too hard on yourself. Everyone experiences moments of self-doubt when they're trying something new or leaving their comfort zone."

"It's more than that. I can't give enough time to do everything well. There's been a major drop in online sales recently. At this rate, we'll be out of business in the blink of an eye."

"You're exaggerating," Cricket began.

"Maybe, but eventually…" She trailed off and fidgeted with her nails. "Otto would be so disappointed. He wanted this place to last for generations to come. Guess he picked the wrong person to make that happen." She stood up and smoothed her sweater. "I apologize for dumping my problems on you. That's the last thing you need."

"Things will look better when spring comes around." Cricket cringed at the naïveté evident in her voice. Too kind to point that out, Cari smiled and squeezed her shoulder on her way out of the kitchen.

Boris had resolved to ditch the whole thing and prepared to tell his partners as soon as they were all available to meet at the same time. That was until he came home from the gym, and Fiona nearly knocked herself off the sofa in a tizzy about Cari's state of mind.

"She's a wreck, I tell you! A wreck!"

'Why?"

"She's been running herself ragged trying to keep up with Otto's farm. She simply cannot do it any longer. You need to go over there and help her find a way out."

Fiona visibly puffed up in her determination to help Cari.

"She thinks she wants to put it up for sale but doesn't know where to begin. There are so many parts to this. It's not as easy as selling a house, as you well know."

"I do, but that's an enormous decision for her to make. I shouldn't be involved."

"Well someone has to look out for her. You know the business. You'd be a poor excuse for a friend to not step in on this."

His well-meaning grandmother had no idea what she was asking. From the sound of it, Cricket hadn't said anything about their conversation last night. If he approached her with his proposal now, would Cricket think even less of him?

"She's expecting you to call. So please, do that would you?" She grew perturbed that he wasn't moving fast enough.

"Yes, Fi. I'll even do better than that. I'll call to see if she's free and go see her in person."

Moments later, he put on his jacket and stepped outside, pulling the door closed behind him. From the top step, he could see Ashling sitting on Cari's porch. He couldn't imagine what would bring her outside in this mind numbing cold. He hurried across the street but approached her with apprehension when she hunched over with an elbow on one knee and her hand shielding her face.

"Everything okay?"

"Yup."

"I get the sense you're hiding your face from me."

"My mom's not home." She refused to remove her hand.

"Sorry to have missed her. I'm here to see Cari though."

"Go ahead inside."

"You know, it's hard to have a conversation with someone who won't look at you."

"We're not having a conversation." She averted her entire body away from him.

"We could though. Something is obviously upsetting you. If

you're trying to pretend otherwise, you're not doing a very good job of it."

Taking a risk, he walked up the steps, sat down next to her, and threw out his best guess. "School?"

"School."

"I've heard rumors that one of our neighbors hasn't been so friendly."

"That's an understatement."

Batting a thousand, he went with it. "Bernadette?"

"Bernadette."

"How's it going with the other kids in school?"

She relented and turned to face him, placing both hands in her lap to warm them. "Liz and Zane have been nice. But I have two classes with Bernadette. She sits behind me with her friends, and I can hear them saying stuff about me. I don't want to ask to move my seat because I don't want to tell the teacher why. It'll only make it worse."

"Sounds like it's going to take more than moving your seat to fix this."

"Oh, I know how to fix her. But that's not going to fly in Blue Cove. Bernadette is not my first rodeo. I've handled far worse than her. It's just…"

Boris waited for her to go on. He could only speculate on methods she might have previously used to stamp down a bully and wanted to know more.

"It's just that Cari has been nice enough to let us stay with her. I don't want to cause problems at school and disappoint her or make her regret her decision."

"I have an idea. Why don't you talk to Cari? Let her know what's going on. Tell her how you would have handled Bernadette in your old school and see if she has any better suggestions."

Ashling wrapped her arms around herself and hunched forward to keep warm. "Okay. It's worth a try."

"In the meantime, let's get inside and warm up."

Cari descended the stairs as they entered the house. Warmth

welcomed them in, but he frowned at the stress etched on his friend's face.

Cricket watched in awe all morning as customers quickly cleared her table of fudge once more. Her emotions swayed between thrilled and wondering if she'd ever get a full night's sleep again. If she started mixing as soon as she got home, maybe she could make enough that the display would last longer.

Her mind was also occupied with Cari's predicament. Cricket berated herself for not predicting that Cari would bare her soul to Fiona. If it had occurred to her, she would have stopped her rather than take a chance that she'd continue to ruminate on her fears with the grandmother of the wolf in sheep's clothing. But Cari had confided in Fiona. Not surprising, considering they'd all grown closer since Fiona came home from the hospital.

Of course Fiona had then shared her story with Boris. She was concerned for her friend and hoped he might have a solution. He had called soon after to schedule an appointment with Cari with a business proposition for her. She'd laughed at him, saying they were old friends and he should just come on over. Cricket had excused herself and headed over to the market, not wanting to be present for their meeting.

Returning from the market hours later, she found Cari sitting on the couch with a cup of tea looking over a folder of papers. The same one Cricket had spilled at Fiona's. Did Boris tell her about that?

Cari blinked up at her with a smile that failed to reach her eyes.

"I have what just might be the solution to all of my problems sitting right here in my lap."

"Then why the sad face?"

She shrugged unconvincingly. "I'm not sad."

"So, what is the solution?"

"Boris's company has made an offer to purchase Honeycomb

Hills and all that goes with it for a generous price. I have an opportunity here to just," she took a breath, "let it all go. I can take the money and do—do whatever I want."

"Is Boris going to make any changes to the farm?" she asked, even though she already knew the answer to that.

"He doesn't want a farm. He wants the land. I suppose that is the cause for a sad face."

Cricket walked over and joined her on the couch. "Please think this through. If what you want is this place and all that goes with it, not a bag full of get away money, promise me you'll give it a chance. There are so many people in place to help you." She rambled on, wanting to ease her own nerves. "I know for a fact that there are several employees who'd love you or Lex to give them the opportunity to do more. Just make sure you've tapped all of your resources before giving up."

"I can agree to that." Her voice lacked the conviction Cricket desperately needed to hear. Then Cari changed the subject.

"Hey, on another note, Boris was asking for you. Why wouldn't he just call you himself?"

Cricket hesitated, trying to formulate an answer. "He did. I just haven't had a chance to call him back."

He had called her several times since their disastrous dinner. Ashling fielded some of those calls and was demanding to know why Cricket wouldn't speak with him. When had she become so invested in their relationship?

With this new turn of events, Cricket truly didn't know what to say to him or how to feel. Was he taking advantage of the situation, or was he doing Cari a favor? In her heart, she believed he thought that the sale would benefit them both. She knew he was wrong. Sure, Cari might not enjoy all aspects of her business. Does anyone? Her love of the farm should not be dismissed so easily. The mission of bee preservation was practically rooted in her genetic makeup. If she sold, she would regret it terribly.

As much as Cricket worried about her friend, her greater concern was for her children. What would happen to them after the sale? Where would they go? She couldn't expect Cari to take all of them with her. Once Cari had herself a nice padded bank account, she could go anywhere in the world. Surely she wouldn't want a single mother and her two kids in tow. Cricket didn't dare speak her fears aloud, even when Ashling later confessed to overhearing their conversation.

Leave it to her daughter to be more concerned with what would become of the bee colonies than where they might end up. She barely heard a word Ashling said. Her mind was so consumed by a spinning reel of what if scenarios, the ringing phone barely registered. She picked it up once Ashling gave her a nudge.

Did someone just say that the roof at the community center had collapsed?

Yes, that was exactly what they said. Vera had called to let her know that due to the extensive weight of the season's snow, a large section of the community center's roof had caved in, damaging all the work that had been put in over the last few days. No, she shouldn't go over to assess the damage. People were not being allowed inside or even near the property. It would be impossible to use the space for the pageant.

Cari had wasted zero time in meeting with Boris. She'd thought it ridiculous that he'd mentioned looking at their calendars and had told him to come over right away. Gone was the frantic woman Fiona had described. In its place stood a somber woman with the weight of the world on her shoulders. Relaying a short summary of their conversation to Fiona later, he realized that he wasn't the one who brought up the possibility of him purchasing the farm. She had said it first in jest. That had been as good a time as any to tell her the truth.

"Then it's settled," she had said. "You buy it, and I'll start the next chapter of my life. Whatever that is."

He had brought the paperwork with him, but only highlighted

the major details in it. As he summarized their discussion for Fiona, vines of regret began to suffocate him.

"Was she thrilled?" asked Fiona.

"More like resigned. Like she was giving up."

"Oh." Fiona furrowed her eyebrows in concern. "Did she accept your offer?"

"I told her to think about it carefully. I'm in no rush for an answer."

His partners might disagree with that, but he found himself hoping that she would reject it. Lex was right. She just needed more time to come up to speed.

The telephone rang, and Fiona lifted one finger of interruption to signal she wanted to answer it. From the one-sided conversation and seeing additional worry crease her face, he knew something was wrong. Her hand trembled slightly as she rested the phone next to her.

Her mouth curved into a deep frown. "Well, that's just too bad."

"What is it?"

"The community center's roof collapsed. No Christmas pageant this year." She clasped her hands. "And, I was so looking forward to seeing Ashling and Max up on that stage."

"That's a shame. I'll take a drive over tomorrow and see if there's anything that can be done."

Nothing like adding some more 'wait and see' to their day. He shelved any and all ideas of sharing with her his plans for Cari's land for the moment.

It was never a great feeling to glance at an alarm clock and see 5:25 staring back after being in bed for barely more than two hours. Cricket had tucked in at ten past three and managed to fall asleep quickly. If only she had *stayed* asleep. Instead, she'd woken up to a still-dark sky outside her bedroom window. Since then, she'd avoided looking at her clock, knowing it would only make matters worse. Finally giving in, she saw no sense in continuing to pursue the sleep determined to elude her.

It tortured her to see how upset Ashling and Max were upon hearing the news of the cancelled Christmas pageant. This was the first time in a long time that they had been so looking forward to something. Despite Bernadette's antics, they had made new friends and begun to enjoy feeling like they were a part of a community. Now, in addition to the likely prospect of finding themselves back at St. Agnes's by Valentine's Day, they would also lose the opportunity to share in the joy of being a part of the pageant. She had spent what should have been her sleeping hours searching her brain in what felt like a futile effort to come up with a miraculous solution for both problems.

Genius had struck somewhere between 'all is lost' and 'maybe they could erect a stage on the lawn of the community center and ask the audience to wear boots while they stood in a few feet of snow during the performance'. It suddenly occurred to her that Honeycomb Hills Market might be an option. Sure, there wasn't any room in the store itself. But the warehouse attached was heated, large enough to hold at least one hundred people, and mostly empty. Decorations would be sparse, but better than nothing.

Pitching her idea to Cari did not go as smoothly as she had hoped. At first, she outright rejected the suggestion. That end of the building was a dump, as far as she was concerned. And what about the liability? She doubted that her insurance extended to such a large event.

"Not to further play up the downside of things, Cricket, but you could never in a million years get that place presentable in such a short time."

Max had been sitting quietly at the table eating his cereal. "What if everyone helps?"

"Max, honey, you would need absolutely everyone to pitch in, and this is just too busy a time of year to ask people to do that," Cari replied gently.

"How about this for an idea?" Cricket proposed. "You check on the insurance situation, and I'll see if anyone has a few hours to spare. There were so many people looking forward to this, it's worth a try." Cricket paused, wondering if she was asking too much. She had no right to push Cari on this matter or any other. "I'm sorry, Cari. Here I go jumping in and taking the liberty to make a decision like this for you. I'm way out of line. It's your place of business, and if you're not comfortable having the pageant there for any reason, I completely understand."

"You're not out of line," she said. "You and the kids have become invested in the performance. Of course you're passionate about it. I have to be honest though—it feels like an impossible venture."

"Yeah, it does," interjected Ashling. "Can't you find somewhere else to do it?"

"Adventures are supposed to feel impossible when they really aren't," Max piped in before shoveling another spoonful of cereal into his mouth, milk dribbling down his chin.

"You are correct, mister!" Cari laughed. "All right, Cricket, if you want to go for it, I'll do whatever I can to help. I'm always up for an adventure!"

Cricket suppressed the urge to sigh out loud in sheer relief. She needed to give her kids this. They deserved to create a joyful memory before returning to their old life. She chalked up Ashling's pessimism to fears of being disappointed again.

A few hours later, they found themselves in the warehouse, along with all the children and parents who had worked countless hours to prepare the community center. Most of them arrived with boxes of ornaments and decorations that had been stored in attics and basements, but never used. Others brought a variety of art supplies. Cleaning and painting had been going on for hours when Boris walked in with a tower of pizza boxes.

"Sorry I couldn't get here sooner. Hopefully, some sustenance will make up for it." He placed the stack on one of the buffet tables someone had been kind enough to lend. "There's more in the car. Drinks too. I'll be right back."

Cricket followed him outside.

"Let me grab some of those for you," she said, reaching for the soda bottles. "Thank you so much for doing this. I was just thinking to myself that people were probably getting hungry and would be leaving soon. Maybe with food they'll put in a few more hours before calling it quits."

"That's the plan!"

Cricket wondered if this act of kindness meant that she should apologize for the way their date ended the other night. A few pizzas, though a nice gesture, didn't change how she felt about him buying Honeycomb Hills. The thought terrified her.

"Fiona is currently basking in the attention of well-wishing friends, so I'm free for the rest of the afternoon. Just tell me what you need me to do and I'll do it."

What she needed was for him to find a new property to buy and to leave Cari and her farm alone. She pushed the thought aside. It wouldn't do her any good to waste energy focusing on that. Acceptance of whatever came and finding a way to cope with it were tasks for another day. In the meantime, Cricket intended to ride her small wave of success and spend every spare moment of free time over the next few days making as many pounds of fudge as was humanly possible for a single mother of two with a job and a warehouse that needed to be converted into a winter wonderland in two days.

As daunting as it all felt playing out in her head, she had to admit to herself that she thrived on the continuous buzz of having so much to do. The intense sense of purpose invigorated her with a burst of energy.

As expected, Cricket didn't welcome Boris's assistance with open arms. She broke out her best manners and politely assigned him several tasks.

He had to give her credit. Organizing this undertaking in such a short time was impressive. When he'd first heard about the plans for the warehouse, serious doubts had piled up in his mind. Now, looking around at all the people she'd gathered to help and the progress they'd already made, he believed she'd make it happen.

Pia and Lex appeared from the adjoining kitchen and waved him over.

"Someone's feeling the holiday spirit!" Pia called as he walked over. "Do you have any idea how much tinsel you're wearing?"

"Come on now, Pia," Boris laughed, "what's wrong with having a little tinsel in your hair?"

"A little? Hah!"

"Leave him alone," Lex chided. "It suits him! So hey, Cricket's something else tackling a project like this, huh?"

"Can't argue with that," Boris replied.

They wouldn't be in such good spirits if Cari had told them about his offer. He exhaled a sigh of relief.

"How's Fiona doing?" Pia asked. "I'd like to stop over when she's up to it."

"Oh, she's up to it. She's with a houseful of visitors right now and is savoring every minute of the attention."

"What are you doing for Christmas? Right now, it looks like it's just gonna be us. Our parents are leaving for Hawaii on Christmas Eve." Pia rolled her eyes. "Can you imagine spending the eve on an airplane? I guess the tickets were significantly cheaper."

"I'll bet! I think it's just me and Fiona this year," said Boris. "She's usually in Florida by now."

Lex lit up. "How about this—if Fiona isn't up to leaving the house yet, we can bring Christmas to you."

"She'd love that!"

Returning their focus to getting the pageant up and running, they agreed to finalize their holiday plans the following day. From

183

what was unsaid, Boris assumed that Cari had either not replied to Lex's dinner invitation or turned him down. He suspected it was the latter, knowing all too well how difficult it must be for her weighing a decision with such severe repercussions. It was fruitless to hope for her or Cricket to join them on Christmas Day.

Every muscle in her body ached. Between moving tables and chairs, painting, and not being able to remember if she'd even sat down today, Cricket felt ready to drop. It didn't help that she'd been running on only a few hours of sleep from the night before. Still, she'd volunteered to stay a bit longer if Cari would take the kids home with Tina.

They had made so much progress. It wasn't a beautifully finished room, but the rawness of the exposed wood and beams gave the space an old-world charm. She knew that they'd have everything ready before Christmas Eve. Boris continued to linger after almost everyone else had left. She assumed that he wanted to continue their discussion from the other night. Now that he'd presented Cari with an official offer, he probably wanted to know where they stood, given that he knew she didn't agree with his business plans. She did not have the slightest bit of energy to deal with that at the moment.

"Boris, I can't thank you enough for all of your help today," she began.

"No thanks necessary. I'll be here tomorrow too if you'll have me."

"The more hands the better. Go home and get a good night's rest."

He didn't make a move to leave. "I was hoping to maybe take you out for a drink first, if you're up to it."

"That's sweet, but I'm exhausted. I feel like I can barely string a sentence together." She tugged her cardigan forward for warmth.

"Maybe tomorrow. Tonight, I'm going to finish a few things here and then I'm going home and straight to bed."

"Anything I can help you with?"

"No, you go. It'll be nice to have the quiet and take stock of what we need to do tomorrow."

Everything she'd said was true. Once she'd convinced him to leave, Cricket sat down in one of the folding chairs that had been set up for the audience. She looked slowly around, taking in the incredible transformation. The once dusty cement floor had been cleaned and a red runner laid down the center of the room. Cobwebbed walls had been scrubbed and hung with an assortment of wintery posters and handmade artwork made by the younger children. They wouldn't have a stage, but an area had been cordoned off at the front of the room for the performance. Cari had donated a Christmas tree and several wreaths.

There was still work to be done, but they would be ready.

Something clanged to the floor in the adjoining kitchen, startling her. What could that be? She thought everyone had left for the night. Many of the boxes being stored in the warehouse had been dragged into the kitchen to keep them out of sight. Maybe they weren't balanced correctly, and one had tipped over. Standing up and deciding whether to take a look, she heard another noise.

Quietly pushing open the door with her heart thumping wildly, she turned on the light. Searching for something to grab if she needed to defend herself, she grabbed a broom, the only large object in sight. She held it in front of her as she took one hesitant step at a time toward the back corner of the room, while silently telling herself that an animal of some kind must have gotten stuck and was now terrified.

Peering over a heap of boxes, her breath caught in her throat. Her stomach seized. That was no animal.

CHAPTER 22

"Who are you?" Cricket demanded.

In front of her cowered a young woman and a little girl who looked about three years old at most.

"I'm sorry, we...we got lost...and somehow ended up in here," she stammered. "I can find my way out if we can just go now."

She didn't look much older than Ashling.

"I asked you a question. Who are you?"

"My name is Soleil. This is my daughter Rosie." At the sound of her name, Rosie turned away from Cricket, burying her face in the side of her mother's leg.

Looking past them, Cricket could see a makeshift camp on the floor with blankets, pillows, a half empty case of water, and an assortment of food packages.

"I can see that you didn't end up in here because you got lost. I'll put this thing down if you can tell me why you're here with all of this stuff. Just start at the beginning," she said gently leaning the broom against the haphazard pile of boxes that separated them.

"I don't even know where the beginning begins," she said, picking up Rosie. "We are trespassing, but we haven't taken anything or damaged anything. We didn't have anywhere else to go, and this really kind girl told us about this place and offered to help." With eyes cast downward, she stammered. "I should have said no, I just...I just didn't."

"What girl brought you here?"

"I don't want to get anyone in trouble," she responded wide eyed.

"No one's in trouble. I have a pretty good idea anyways. Is her name Ashling?" Cricket saw the flicker of recognition pass over Soleil's face. "Of course, it was Ashling. She's my daughter."

"Oh, I didn't realize."

"We're both going to be in trouble if anyone else finds you here." Even though she had nothing to do with this, Cari would be highly unlikely to believe that. She'd for sure think Cricket used this kitchen to help out friends from the shelter. This would be in direct violation of the blackout rule.

Soleil stood frozen in place, waiting for Cricket to tell her what would happen next. Looking again at Rosie, she couldn't help it. Her heart went out to them.

"Look, I'm really sorry. You are clearly going through a difficult time. But unfortunately, you can't stay here." Glancing again at everything on the floor, she asked, "If you were to leave right now, where would you go?"

"I don't know. I guess I'd try to head back to St. Agnes's."

"How did you meet Ashling?"

"She comes in quite a bit with Cari. Rosie took an instant liking to her. I think it had to do with her hair, she was fascinated with those curls."

"I'm sorry, I still don't understand why out of all the people staying there she'd single you out and tell you to come here. How is sleeping on a tile floor better than the beds at the shelter?"

"They've been out of beds for a while, which means using one of the mattresses spread across the basement floor. I was grateful for having a roof over our heads and got the chance to sit with the director, Eleanor Pace, to talk about how to get me a job and get us out of there." She swallowed and smoothed her daughter's hair. "When she called me in to her office, Rosie was past ready for a nap, so Ashling offered to sit with her. I guess she was appalled when she saw where we'd been sleeping."

"She's not known for having a filter. I hope she wasn't rude."

"She didn't mince words. Next thing I knew, she was pulling me aside and telling me she knew of a better place we could stay. She gave me the address and twenty dollars for transportation promising to meet us here that afternoon at four o'clock." Fingers raked through hair that hadn't seen a brush in days. "I don't even know why I trusted her. But, the conditions in that basement are subhuman! I know the staff does what they can, but there are just too many people down there..." She trailed off.

"Did you at least give Eleanor a chance?"

"I did. She thought my prospects would look brighter after the holidays are over, so I thanked Ashling and told her we'd wait it out. After she left, I found the money in my backpack with a note that said, 'I'll look for you tomorrow at four'. As luck would have it, that night it seemed everyone who came in was sick with one thing or another. Next morning, we hopped on the bus and came here."

"When was that?"

"Two days ago. She must have known I'd change my mind because I found books, blankets, water, and a bunch of snacks waiting for us."

Praying that she wouldn't regret her next words, Cricket caved. "You can stay here 'til tomorrow. I'll take you back to St. Agnes's in the morning. If they still don't have rooms with beds available, we can try some other shelters. Some of the larger ones may have more space or more options."

"You're sure?"

"I'm sure. But, absolutely no one, under any circumstances, can lay eyes on you. I'm taking a huge risk here."

"I understand. Thank you."

Uh, no. She did not understand. Not even the slightest bit. Cricket could lose everything if Cari found out. She wasn't supposed to be taking risks of any kind anymore.

It took everything she had to refrain from confronting Ashling immediately when she got home. She waited until Cari had headed to her own room for the night. Still, Cricket spoke barely above a whisper when she found her reading with her pen light instead of sleeping.

"I met some of your friends today," she began.

Ashling faced the wall, but Cricket saw her body freeze for just a moment.

"From school?" she asked without turning around.

"No, not from school. I believe their names were Soleil and Rosie."

Silence for a few moments. Finally, she put the book down and turned around.

"Please tell me you didn't kick them out…"

"I should have. It's our future on the line here."

"But you didn't?"

"I gave them the rest of the night and plan to take them back to St. Agnes's first thing in the morning."

"But, Mom—" she began.

"Don't even start. That was generous of me. I feel for them— you know I do! But you and Max are my responsibility. Not two strangers. We don't know anything about Soleil."

"We were three strangers to Cari, and she still wanted to help us."

"It's different Ash, and you know it. I'm not going to take advantage of Cari's kindness. We still have a long way to go—I have a long way to go toward getting on my feet. I don't have the means to help them the way she helped us."

Sitting down next to her, Cricket went on. "I love that your heart is big enough to want to try. Someday, I'd love to be able to help every family like ours. But, right now, I need to focus on just helping us."

"You're not mad at me?" Ashling asked with a small voice.

"No. I wish you'd talked to me first, because we are in a not so great situation now." Her eyes softened. "I can't be angry with you for wanting to help another person." Cricket rested a hand on her arm. "I promise that I will make sure we find her somewhere safe and comfortable to stay."

But, even as Cricket said it, she couldn't be sure she was telling the truth.

❄

Boris had just finished loading the dishwasher when his phone buzzed. Pulling it out of his back pocket, he said a silent prayer that the call wasn't about yet another issue with the Boston apartment complex. Relieved, he saw Cari's name.

"Hey Cari, what's up?"

"I hate to bother you, but could I ask a huge favor?"

"I'm in no position to say no after everything you've done for me and Fi these last few days."

"Here goes then. I know it's getting late, but would you mind going back to the warehouse? Cricket called earlier and said the sink in the kitchen over there isn't draining. I got busy with work and it slipped my mind."

"What is it with you two and sinks lately?"

"I wish I knew! Normally, I'd leave it 'til tomorrow, but Cricket's expecting another crowd early in the morning, so if you could get it resolved before then, I'd be forever grateful."

"Not a problem. There's still a set of keys somewhere around here. I can swing by now and give you a call in a bit."

"You are seriously the best!"

"I know," he said, disconnecting the call.

Pulling into the parking lot, he was surprised to see a few stragglers shopping for trees this close to Christmas. The biting cold wind whipped the exposed skin on his face as he climbed out of the car. With too much snow on the ground preventing him from walking around to the back entrance, he decided to take a shortcut through the market. Letting himself inside, he stomped off his boots as best he could before walking across the clean floor.

There wasn't much else he could do, but wet footprints trailed behind him.

The same key unlocked the door to the warehouse. Flicking on the light, he heard what sounded like boxes being dragged across the kitchen floor.

"Hello?" he called out.

Not receiving an answer, he walked toward the kitchen. From where he stood, he couldn't see light under the door. Mice maybe? But it had sounded too loud for that. Curiosity got the better of him, and he crept toward the kitchen entrance, stopping just outside it to listen once more. He could feel his adrenaline rising as he flipped the light switch up.

This time, he heard a voice. A child. Or maybe a cat.

"Is someone in here?" A heap of boxes stacked in the far corner caught his eye. If anyone was in there, that was where they'd be. No more tip toeing around. He stalked over and pulled down the top box.

A young woman tried to jump up from the floor as a little girl clung to her. "I'm sorry! We can go!"

Boris felt his eyes bulging out of his head as his mouth tried to form words. "What are you doing in here?"

"We... I..." As she stammered, the child began to cry. Picking her up, she tried again as the girl hid her face. "We didn't have anywhere else..." She stopped and tried to swallow. "Just please don't call the police. We'll leave. I swear I didn't take anything."

"This is breaking and entering." Incredulous, he pulled his phone from his back pocket.

"I know. It's just really cold outside and no one was here, so..." She trailed off, visibly shaking.

Cricket must have forgot to check the lock on the back door before she left. She probably didn't even think of it because no one was using it.

The woman standing before him looked a fright. Her hair was an oily mess, the coat she wore was ragged, and he could smell her from where he stood. Boris pressed a button and the screen on his phone lit up.

"Please!" Desperate, she stretched out an arm. "Please don't call the police. They'll take my daughter. I swear to you that we will never step foot in here again."

"I'm not calling the police. Yet. I'm calling the owner of this place to see what she wants to do."

Crawling into bed, Cricket's heart shattered into a million tiny pieces at the thought of sending those two young people back to the shelter. She resigned herself to the fact that there was nothing more she could do and ran through tomorrow's timetable in her head. Soleil would leave the warehouse before sunrise and walk to the end of the road unseen. Cricket planned to meet her at six o'clock, and they'd head into town without anyone knowing a thing about her stay.

Everything should have happened smoothly, if not for that ancient sink in the warehouse kitchen. Cricket had forgotten she'd called Cari about that earlier in the day, and unbeknownst to her, Cari had asked Boris to let himself in and take a look.

When Cricket heard Cari answer the phone, she briefly wondered who'd be calling so late. Then, overhearing Cari's side of the conversation through her bedroom door, Cricket figured out what had happened almost immediately. Cari told him to hang up and call the authorities as Cricket charged into the hall and frantically tried to get her attention.

"Hang on a minute, Boris," Cari said shortly. "What is it, Cricket? We have an emergency here."

"I know, just please don't call the police yet. Please. Give me a few minutes to explain first."

"Explain what?"

"They aren't dangerous. They're leaving tomorrow," she began.

Cari narrowed her eyes, her expression conveying an emerging understanding of the situation.

"Boris, don't call the police yet. I will be over in a few minutes." She hung up the phone and said, "You have exactly one minute to tell me what's going on here. Go."

Cricket took a deep breath before exhaling the flood of information. "They are from St. Agnes's. I don't know them, and I don't know why they're here. I only just found them myself and told them I'd be taking them back tomorrow morning. But please, Cari. They aren't dangerous."

"So, it's just coincidence that two people from St. Agnes's end up a half mile away on my property?"

From behind them came Ashling's voice. "It's Soleil and Rosie. I brought them there," she said.

Cricket hadn't gotten as far as conjuring up a story, but she never intended to throw Ashling under the bus.

Looking past Cricket, Cari's mouth dropped open. "You what? You don't even drive."

"I gave them the address and money to get here." Turning to look at Ashling, Cricket saw her tremble. "I'm so sorry, Cari, I just felt so bad for them. I felt bad for Rosie!" Tears welled up in her eyes.

"Where did you get the money?" Cricket dreaded the answer knowing she rarely had more than a few dollars on her. She'd notice if anything was missing from her wallet.

Ashling covered her face with her hands, overcome with choking sobs. "I'm sorry, Cari," she croaked. "You had asked me to hold your purse while I watched Rosie. We had never been downstairs, and it made me sick when I saw where they were sleeping. Not that it was okay to ignore all the other kids staying there, but the other kids aren't Rosie. The idea popped into my head, and there wasn't much time to overthink it. I promise to find a way to pay you back."

❄

"I need to get over there. We'll finish this conversation later."

Cricket wasn't sure if Cari wanted her company, but she followed her outside and hopped in the car anyways. An uncomfortable silence filled the space between them during the drive. Pulling up, she saw three figures waiting outside. Cricket braced herself for the fallout.

Cari's face softened at Rosie's genuine delight at her arrival. After explanations, Cari invited Soleil and Rosie back to her home for the night. She seemingly couldn't, in good conscience, leave a mother and her young child to sleep on a floor. Cricket asked Boris if he could take her back in a little bit. Nothing had been said about her connection to St. Agnes's other than the fact that Ashling had begun volunteering there with Cari. If she was ever going to tell him the truth, this was about as perfect of an opening that she'd ever be likely to get.

Cricket took what felt like a million deep breaths, praying her nerves would calm down. When it became apparent that wasn't going to happen, she dove in. "Boris, there's more to what happened here," she began. "I'm not really an old friend of Cari's." She pulled her scarf tighter around her neck. This was so much more difficult than she had ever imagined. "I met her at St. Agnes's."

"You were a volunteer too?" he asked, barely glancing at her as he rounded the car to get into the driver's seat.

"No. I was homeless."

He froze and looked at her over the roof of the car. Speechless.

"Please, let's get in the car, and I'll tell you the whole story." So she did.

When she finished, she said, "Now here we are, with Ashling taking a page out of Cari's kindness manual and trying to help someone else in need." She reached for his hand. "Boris, I can't tell you how sorry I am for keeping this from you."

"You've been lying to me for weeks. Just outright lying to me." He looked her in the eyes. "How could you not trust me? I get that in the beginning you wouldn't be quick to share, but once you got to know me? What did you think I'd do?"

"I had no idea how you'd react. It crossed my mind that you'd think I was taking advantage of Cari. If that happened, you might have convinced her to ask us to leave."

"You think so little of me?"

"No... I'm sorry..." she stammered.

He started the car and drove her home without another word.

CHAPTER 23

Reaching the porch, Cricket gave her back a good stretch and zipped her coat up as far as it would go. No need to go inside just yet to face the fire. It was a perfect winter night. The cool air breezed over her face as she gazed across the yard lit up by the night sky. The day's events worked through her mind as she perched on the edge of an icy rocker, staring at the ground. The creaking of the rocker echoed in the silence. She needed to find a way to deal with the questions that Cari would be hurling soon enough.

Dredging up the last of her nerve, she entered the house and followed the dimly lit path to the kitchen. Cari sat on a stool at the island with a bottle of wine and two glasses. She poured when Cricket walked in.

"I'm assuming you could use this right now."

"Where are Soleil and Rosie?"

"We stopped at the supermarket on the way here. I picked up milk, juice, the fixings for peanut butter and jelly sandwiches. They can raid the pantry tomorrow and take what they'd like. Right now, they are comfortably settled in the carriage house." She slid one glass toward Cricket. "I threw a bag of toiletries and bedding together and brought them over. We pulled the dusty sheets off the furniture. They're more gray than white now."

"Has to be better than a cold kitchen floor."

"Yeah."

"I'm surprised you didn't ask us to stay there instead of opening up your home."

"It didn't occur to me that first day. It was all so spontaneous, and Max was sick. Once you were here, it crossed my mind. But I like having people around, and you're easy to live with. Maybe you would have preferred the privacy, though."

"I can assure you, we are plenty happy."

Cricket pulled out a stool and took a sip from her glass. "I told Boris everything." She savored another sip of the warm chianti. "Now seemed as good a time as any."

"I suppose. You had to do it eventually." Cari turned the glass in her hands.

"I can't begin to tell you how sorry I am about all of this."

"You already apologized."

"It's not enough."

Cari's eyes flashed. "You should have come to me. Ashling should have gone to you, and you should have told me."

"I thought about it. I was so afraid that you'd be upset with Ashling and ask us to leave. I should have taken them back to St. Agnes's when I first found them."

Cari shook her head. "No, I didn't say that. You should have trusted me. Have I been such a tyrant that you honestly didn't believe I'd want to help?"

"No! Absolutely not!"

"Well, that's how it sounds…"

"I know it does. But, how could I ask more of you when you've already done so much?"

With hands trembling, she put down her glass.

"I didn't know what to do, but I knew I couldn't kick them to the curb and wanted more time to think things through. I needed a plan for them that would be of some help. Not just dumping them off to go sleep on a mattress on some basement floor."

"A dirty floor with no mattress was better?"

"She had her reasons for believing that. They wouldn't be asked to leave after breakfast to roam the cold streets in thin hoodies until dinner and then fight for another mattress at night." Cricket heard the tone of her voice grow heated.

"In all the years I've volunteered there, I've never seen the basement."

"The staff seems to genuinely regret sending people down there. But, during the winter, it can't always be helped. They won't leave mothers and children outside to freeze and starve. But conditions severely decline when they are inundated with large numbers of people coming in. So everyone's just grateful for being warm for the night." Cricket took another deep sip.

"I'm going over in the morning and asking for a full tour of the premises."

Cricket interrupted and blurted out her worst fear. "I understand if you want us to go back. I will tell the kids and get them up early."

"You didn't let me finish. Cricket..." she shook her head. "I know that it may not come naturally to you, but it's time to start trusting people. I do not want you to leave. In the future, I do want you to come to me with any—situations—that come up. Give me a chance before making assumptions." She tilted her head to one side and offered a small smile. "My grandmother always said, 'to assume makes an ass of u and me.'"

"Smart woman. I won't doubt you again. Or Boris, if he gives me the chance."

"I need you to stay here with Soleil and Rosie. I'm not ready to throw them to the wolves, but I'm also not comfortable leaving them alone in my house just yet. I know you'll want to get back to the warehouse but give me a few hours first. I'm sure Vera and Tess can steer the ship until you get there."

She tapped her glass with a tapered, red fingernail. "I didn't know you well when I asked you to stay, but the idea of sending Max back to the shelter sick as a dog was unfathomable. I just reacted."

"You took a chance on me. I swear to you that I never intended for you to even lay eyes on Soleil. You've done more than enough."

"Stop. It's not that I don't want to do more—I do. It's just that this isn't a homeless shelter," she said, circling her arm around her head. "This is my home. I can't take in everyone on the street. There has to be another way." Draining her glass, she stood. "Look, I don't want you to lose sleep over this. You are still welcome here. For however long I stay, anyways. I actually enjoy hearing everyone's voices and not being the only living thing in this house besides Arthur and Guinevere." She laughed at that. "I will be the one losing sleep tonight. I won't let Soleil and Rosie end up sleeping on a park bench, or even a mattress on a cellar floor. I just need some time to think about what comes next."

"Well, try to get some rest. Your conscience should be crystal clear." Cricket finished her wine as well. "And, Cari, thank you. Two little words seem insignificant, but there are no words on the face of this earth to sincerely convey my gratitude for all you've done."

With that, they both retired to their bedrooms. On some level, Cricket did feel better knowing that she hadn't ruined everything. But, like Cari, she knew it would not be easy drifting off to sleep with Soleil and Rosie in the back of her mind.

Boris couldn't bring himself to get out of the car and go inside. This must be what it felt like to go into a state of shock. And he thought he'd been keeping an explosive secret! For weeks Cricket had been lying, and she had the nerve to pass judgement on him. He knew for sure now: Lying by omission still constituted lying. It didn't feel good whether you were on the giving or receiving end of it.

He wondered if he had a right to feel betrayed. Cricket had some valid reasons for keeping him in the dark.

Cranking the heat higher, he saw an image of Rosie flash through his mind. Not her face, but the back of her head as she cried into her mother's neck, terrified. He was ashamed to admit it even to himself, but Soleil had repulsed him. She had passed filthy a long time ago. But to see a young child in a similar state shook him to his core. It crossed his mind that she might be better off if she was taken away from her mother, as Soleil had feared.

Leave it to Cari to invite them into her home. What in the world was she thinking? Okay, so they hadn't technically broken into Honeycomb Market, but it was still trespassing. Although notorious for being scatterbrained, Cari was generally considered to be an intelligent woman. This was the first time he could say she'd used poor judgement. One could argue that she already had Cricket and her kids living over there. What was two more? But who thought like that?

Frustrated, he laid his head back and closed his eyes. He needed to make a trip over to this St. Agnes's. Tomorrow.

Cricket awoke to the sound of voices outside in the driveway. Peering through the window, she could see Cari and Boris talking and then climbing into Cari's car. She guessed that they were headed for St. Agnes's.

She found Soleil and Rosie in the kitchen with a huge plate of bacon, eggs, and toast. A bowl of fruit salad sat invitingly as well.

"So Cari left you here to babysit us," Soleil said, smearing butter on a triangle of toast.

"It's not like—" she started.

Soleil looked up smiling. "It's okay, Cricket. I'm just teasing. Honestly, I can't believe that Cari left us here at all. I was floored when she said that she wanted us to stay while she sorted a few things out. Not that I know what she means, do you?"

"You don't know where she went?"

"Nope," she said as she handed a full plate to Rosie. "I didn't ask, and she didn't share. I'm grateful to be sitting here watching my daughter eat to her heart's content. You won't hear me complain while I wait things out until Cari is ready to talk to me." She filled two slices of toast with eggs and a piece of bacon and took an enormous bite, closing her eyes and sighing loudly. "Sorry," she mumbled, covering her mouth with one hand.

"Don't be! Once I get some coffee, you'll see me doing the same!"

After taking another bite and swallowing, Soleil put her egg sandwich down. "Did she tell *you* where she was going? I feel pretty sure it has something to do with me."

Cricket looked her over for a moment. She had clearly showered since arriving and wore what had to be a pair of Cari's jeans and a sweater. Her face scrubbed clean, hair combed, and teeth likely brushed. She looked lovely, almost happy, and most definitely afraid. The face of someone who felt like she had just stepped into a wonderful dream, and that the dream could end at any moment. She'd find herself waking up on a cold floor surrounded by strange faces. If it was meant to be a secret, then Cari should have said so last night.

"She went to St. Agnes's."

Soleil stopped chewing and covered her mouth again asking, "What? Why?"

"She's been volunteering over there for a long time, but she's never seen the actual living accommodations. So she wanted to go over and have a proper tour."

Cricket stuffed a forkful of eggs into her mouth as Soleil scooped some fruit onto Rosie's now empty plate.

"She is probably not prepared for what she's about to see."

"Oh no, she is not," Cricket agreed.

Boris had read articles; he'd seen news segments; he thought he knew what to expect when he got to the shelter. Walking in the front door, things didn't appear to be so terrible. To his left were a few offices, and the right side of the hallway opened to a large dining hall. He could see a Christmas tree standing in one corner. Eleanor emerged from her office at the sound of the door closing.

Cari greeted her first. "Good morning, Eleanor. I can't thank you enough for seeing us on such short notice."

"Not a problem. Though I would ask if we could keep it brief. This time of year is busy."

"So we've heard," said Boris.

Eleanor began by leading them into the dining hall and explaining that they sometimes served almost 100 people per day. The shelter was open strictly to women and children. Boys were only allowed through age fourteen. From there, she brought them to view the rooms where people slept. Legally, one standard room could accommodate six people using bunk beds, but they often exceeded that limit during the winter.

"Right now, we are significantly over capacity, with thirty mattresses set up in the basement. Unfortunately, they must come up here to use the bathroom. It's less than ideal, but it's warm."

"Could we see it?" asked Cari.

As they descended the stairs, Eleanor went on to explain their heavy dependence on donations. "At Christmas, there's always an influx of toys being dropped off. People forget there is a year-round need for things like deodorant, toilet paper, cleaning supplies. The everyday items most of us take for granted."

Boris absorbed everything she said until he landed on the basement floor. There wasn't an adequate word to describe it. Aside from the mattresses, the space was barren. Flat, fluorescent lights flickered above the gray walls.

"This room is usually home to mostly women at night. We try to put the ones with kids in rooms upstairs."

"But kids do have to sleep down here." This wasn't a question. Cari knew it to be a fact.

"They do sometimes. If a family arrives and the other rooms are overflowing, there isn't much choice."

"Please don't take this the wrong way," Cari began, "but isn't there something you could do to make it a little more welcoming?"

"At the expense of not feeding everyone? Not being able to provide clean bedding? You wouldn't believe how much is spent on detergent every week." She faced Cari. "Surely you've seen your expenses increase dramatically adding three people to your household."

Defensive, Cari replied, "They've added more to my home than expenses."

"I'm not questioning your decision to take them in. But facts are facts."

"Cricket is working now and contributing. What she can't cover is made up for in other ways. She keeps the house spotless and does all of the cooking."

Eleanor pressed her lips into a small smile. "I know I seem about as soft as sandpaper. I've probably been working in this field too long. I am sincerely happy for her, if it's working out."

Boris observed Cari's face. Her grim expression subtly brightened. Another one of those original ideas must have popped into her head. She kept it to herself, but he felt certain she was up to something as they thanked Eleanor for her time and left. Neither of them said much on the way home, lost in their thoughts about Cricket and Soleil.

"Imagine being a kid and that's where you get to spend your Christmas."

That statement dropped him back into the present with a thud. "Speaking of where to spend Christmas, did you ever get back to Lex?"

"About what?"

"He said he'd asked you to spend the holiday with him and you never gave him a straight answer."

"Of course I did. I told him we'd talk about it later, figuring he and Pia could come to my house. With everything going on, I haven't had time to touch base about the details."

Boris shook his head. Leave it to those two to speak in tongues to each other. "He took that to mean you'd think about it and get back to him."

"Oh, no."

"Oh, yes. Just call him as soon as you get in. The poor guy's been mending a broken heart needlessly."

"You're exaggerating," she laughed.

"I'm not. He's head over heels and thinks you want nothing to do with him." He stopped, second guessing himself. "Actually, if you're not interested you should let him know."

Cari laughed. "I've been interested in Lex since I was twelve years old and he wouldn't give me the time of day. Now I'm supposed to believe he has romantic intentions? Not that I haven't wondered."

"Wonder no more. You two should get things out in the open." He turned on to their street. "As for Christmas, he and Pia are joining me and Fiona. Looks like you won't have to travel far if you'd like to spend the holiday with him."

"Are you inviting Cricket? Her mom is supposed to be joining us."

"I was planning on it." But who knew what she'd say?

CHAPTER 24

By ten o'clock, Cari and Boris had not returned. Rosie proved herself a force to be reckoned with. Did all children who have yet to reach three possess such a clear and vast vocabulary? They didn't, as far as Cricket knew, but Rosie did. She motored around with authority showing them everything she loved most about the farmhouse, which consisted of everything she could see and touch. She gave out hugs each time she became excited about something, which was often, to say the least. With tight curls, enormous brown eyes, and lashes straight out of a mascara ad, she was a living ray of sunshine.

"Is she this friendly to everyone?" Cricket asked, after receiving the umpteenth bear hug to her knees.

"Oh, yeah!" Soleil laughed. "She loves just about everyone she meets. It's endearing, but I hope she tones it down when she gets older. How am I ever going to teach that one to stay away from strangers?"

It wasn't her place to ask, but the question tumbled out of her mouth anyways. "What brought you to St. Agnes's?"

Soleil's mouth twitched and despite her youthful face, a line formed between her eyebrows. "Let me start by saying I've never touched drugs. We weren't living well, but we were living with my mom and getting by. I worked at a daycare center that allowed me to bring Rosie." She sunk onto the couch and pulled Rosie onto her lap. "When my mom was diagnosed with cancer, I tried to take care of her and Rosie while working full time. It got to be too much. The daycare center was sympathetic, but they needed someone more reliable. By the time my mom passed, we were flat broke."

"I'm sorry you've been through all that. Have you told Cari anything about it?"

"She had asked one time a while back. It's probably the only reason I'm sitting here right now."

Another glance at the clock and Cricket's anxiety began to rise. She wanted to get her fudge over to the market soon. She could walk the half mile with her bags. It wouldn't be the worst thing in the world. But she couldn't leave Soleil and Rosie there alone. With few viable options to choose from, she called Vera and asked if she'd mind driving them over.

Hanging up the phone, she awkwardly asked Soleil to say as little as possible during the ride and to just go along with whatever she said. Her stomach churned at the thought of what might come out of her own mouth on the fly. If the truth got out, the neighbors would be banging on the door wanting answers. They might be willing to donate toys to the needy, but she didn't see them readily accepting a homeless shelter on their street.

She stuck mittens, a hat, and a coat on Rosie that may have been bigger than the child herself and found a jacket of Cari's for Soleil to borrow. Fortunately, Vera still had an old car seat in her garage for Rosie. Better than that, she didn't ask any questions about Soleil after being introduced. All topics of conversation revolved around the pageant.

Exhaling dramatically after arranging her display, Cricket suggested they walk the short distance to the farm's playground while Vera poked around the store. Now that they didn't have to hide, Rosie could enjoy herself like any other kid on the property. Despite the icy temperatures, she rode down the spiral slide at least fifteen times. Cricket thought they'd never get her off the spinning wheel. The child's laugh rang out in a beautiful song. This was the first time she'd seen Soleil genuinely smile, and she thanked the heavens above for the sunglasses that hid tears threatening to spill over. It took an effort to remind herself that Soleil was not some stray puppy she could take care of.

They arrived back to the house frozen solid but beaming ear to ear. The car was in the driveway. Cricket didn't know what to expect walking in. It certainly wasn't a tearful hug from Cari, but she clung to her as if someone had died. Over her shoulder, she spied Boris sitting on the couch with his elbows resting on his thighs and his head down.

"Is something wrong?" Cricket asked, growing concerned at the sight of them.

Pulling back and gripping her by the arms, Cari squinted for a moment as if meeting her for the very first time. "Everything is wrong with that place, Cricket! I never knew." She shook her head and pulled one hand away to swipe at tears. "I'm so sorry, but I never knew."

"What happened?"

The sight of such inadequate living conditions was eye-opening for them. To know that countless families crammed into a dank space with nothing more than a mattress on the floor to sleep on chilled them. Cari was determined to find a way to make St. Agnes's a more comfortable place for families who need emergency assistance. The current director had a limited amount of financial resources and donations to work with. Through fundraisers and her own money, she planned to restore the house. Yes, crowding would still be an issue at times, but the people staying there would be provided with a clean place to sleep. No vermin. No mold. No cockroaches. Additional walls would be built to provide some privacy for families.

Boris crossed the room toward them. "What happened was we saw where Soleil and Rosie had been sleeping. Them and countless other women and children." He began pacing. "For crying out loud Cricket! Is that how you lived before you came here?"

Out of the corner of her eye, she saw Soleil's jaw drop. She could feel her eyes boring into her and didn't dare to meet her gaze. Until this moment, she had no idea why Cricket lived in Cari's house. Before she could conjure up a response, Boris's arms were around her. His embrace so tight, she could hardly breathe. She wasn't sure if the tears that sprung to her eyes were those of pain or sorrow. He pulled away and grasped the back of her head with both hands.

"I get why you didn't say anything. I won't pretend to understand what you've been through just because I walked through those rooms over there today. Can I tell you what I do know? I know that you are a good person. A wonderful, beautiful person and I have no right to judge the choices you've made to take care of your family." He kissed her hard, conveying that the necessary apology was his to make. Through the fog of the moment, she heard Cari speaking to Soleil.

"I'm sure you're pretty confused right now."

"Well, you'd be pretty right."

Cricket pulled away to find Soleil gaping at all of them.

"But you know what? It's okay. Your business is not my business. So, I'll just go tidy up over at the carriage house."

She started to head for her coat, but Cricket pulled away from Boris and stepped in front of her. "It's fine. I'd like to explain, and you'd probably like to hear what I have to say. It all revolves around how you ended up here in the first place."

By the time she'd finished, Soleil turned toward Cari. "What you did for them is...is...I don't know how to describe it. But I know this place isn't a homeless shelter. I'm ready to go wherever there's a bed. I'll figure things out eventually." Her eyes scanned each face in the room. "I had a really good meeting with Ms. Pace right before I met Ashling. I'll give her a chance, and I'm sure she'll help me find a job." She looked at Cari. "Despite the sleeping conditions right now, the people there are decent. They're doing the best they can with what they have. That's true for the volunteers too."

"I'm sorry, Soleil," Cari said steering her out of the room, "but you're wrong. Everyone can always do better. It's time I did better, and I have a plan to do just that."

What was she talking about? Cricket attempted to guess at where Cari might be headed, in addition to trying to wrap her head around what Boris had said. She wanted him to understand why she hadn't told him the truth, not feel like he needed to save her.

Once they were alone, Cricket frantically searched her brain for the right words. She didn't turn at the sound of Boris's footsteps and felt tears sting the back of her eyes as his hands gently fell on her shoulders and his forehead rested on the back of her neck.

"I had planned to bring this up a while ago, but then everything happened…"

"Bring what up?"

"If you're not doing anything Christmas Day, everyone's coming to Fiona's for dinner."

"Who's everyone?"

"Pia and Lex. Cari, if you say yes. That's a story that'll make you laugh." She heard the smile creep into his voice. "Cari's been assuming this whole time that he and Pia would be coming over here. But he's been nursing a broken heart thinking she didn't want to spend the holiday with him at all. Classic case of miscommunication."

Under other circumstances, Cricket would have found this funny and asked how it had happened. As it was, she just said, "I'm glad they worked it out."

"So, are you in? Cari won't come unless you do."

His hands slid down her arms.

"Sure. We'll all be there."

She swallowed the lump that had formed in her throat and pinched the bridge of her nose to prevent any tears from escaping.

Her voice barely above a whisper when she spoke, "I've got to get going."

Realizing she would be unable to get more words out without spinning around and falling into his arms, she left the room. He'd be leaving in three days. What was the point in allowing herself to start down a road that would lead to nothing more than a dead end?

Fiona looked up as Boris came through the front door. It was late afternoon, and only a hint of sun remained in the sky.

"Someone got a jump start on the day. Where were you off to so early?"

"I hope I didn't wake you."

"You left the house quietly enough. But it's impossible to sleep in the morning down here once the sun is up."

"Did Tina check in on you?"

"Oh, yeah! She brought that gorgeous baby with her too. I didn't keep her long, though, I've been doing fine fending for myself."

That was true, but she still moved unsteadily, and he didn't want her putting herself at risk for another fall. He felt more at peace knowing she had additional eyes on her during the day.

She stared at him. "You don't look good."

He sighed, unzipped his jacket, and walked the rest of the way into the living room.

"I've just experienced quite the revelation, to say the least." She waited patiently for him to go on while he collected his thoughts. "Last night, I accidentally stumbled into learning about Cricket's past."

Fiona froze. He could tell from the look on her face that she already knew the truth.

"It won't be new news to you will it? How did you find out?"

She leaned forward to place her mug on the coffee table. "It was the day of the cookie swap. Eleanor came late and saw Cricket leaving with you. She recognized her right away."

"She knew her?"

"She'd just taken a position at the homeless shelter and had recently sat down to discuss job opportunities and housing options with her. She lingered after everyone else left and asked me how I knew Cricket. You should have seen her reaction when I told her how the three of them had just moved into Cari's. That's when the whole story came out."

"Sounds kind of unprofessional for her to air someone's dirty laundry like that."

"I can't blame her. She thought there was some sort of scam going on." She reached for her mug again, wanting to busy her hands.

"You never said one word about it to me."

"Don't be angry," she pleaded. "Cricket was supposed to break things off with you. As soon as I'd learned the truth, I went to see her and told her you were going to hear about it one way or the other, and it would be better coming from her. I honestly believe she had every intention of following through, but then I fell. You had that meeting over in Boston my first night home. When she came over, she admitted she hadn't gone through with it. Boris, you were a basket case! I had to agree with her that it would be best to wait. And now, well, I'm really very sorry." Her eyes cast down. When she looked up, he softened at the sorrow on her face. "You know I'd never do anything to hurt you. I'm glad she was honest with you."

"Not by choice," he said feeling the hurt rise up to his throat. By the time he finished telling her the series of events that had taken place since last night, her eyes shone glassy with unshed tears. She inhaled and tilted her head back to look at the ceiling. Regaining her composure, she returned his gaze.

"She must be absolutely devastated."

"Her and me both."

"Yes, but imagine how humiliating it must have been for her to tell you under those circumstances."

"She could have had a little more faith in me."

"Something tells me trust may not come easy to her." She reached for his hand and grasped it firmly. "If you had asked me about this not too long ago, I would have told you to cut your losses and move on. I would have been wrong. She has a good heart. You don't know how harsh I was to her. But she still showed up in my time of need. In the short time I've gotten to know her and her kids, I've seen a woman who exudes both strength and kindness." Her face crumpled filled with the emotions she could no longer control. Her voice caught as she tried to speak. "A—a mother who has managed to raise two shining stars despite having *every* obstacle thrown at her. Yes, she cares for you. But, you're off to the big city in a matter of days. It would be foolish of her to bare her soul to you."

"I'd been thinking of moving back here."

She gasped. "Have you told her?"

"No," he admitted, "I was afraid she'd think I'm moving too fast."

"Sometimes strong feelings hit hard and fast. Not much you can do to prevent it."

"Now what?" he asked, jamming thumbs through his belt loops and rocking back on his heels.

"Has everything changed so much?"

"Not on my part. I can't say the same for her. I don't know if it's like you said and she figures it's better to part ways now because I'm supposed to be leaving, or if she's angry with me for being upset with her. For being judgmental."

"Sounds to me like you two need to talk. If you want to be with her as much as I think you do, you don't have much time to waste."

He looked toward the front door at what sounded like running footsteps on the stairs. "Who could that be?"

Pulling open the door, he found a glass pan covered in tinfoil and spotted Bernadette halfway down the street. She ignored him when he called after her. Confused, he picked up the pan and went back inside.

"What's that?"

"Looks like a casserole from Tess. Her daughter was running down the street toward home."

"Hmph. She can be an odd one. Probably too bashful to say hello."

Perhaps, but the behavior unsettled Boris. Had she overheard their conversation?

CHAPTER 25

The rollercoaster ride of Ashling's school experience took another dip. 'Stormy' was the word that entered Cricket's mind when her daughter came charging into the warehouse. Like her mother, she wasn't one to keep things bottled up inside.

"I am so done dealing with that girl. It's taken every ounce of self-control I have to not tell her off!"

"What happened?" Cricket braced herself. Her daughter was not someone who allowed herself to be pushed around.

"The cast list came out today for Bye Bye Birdie, and I'm playing Kim."

Cricket grinned. "That's fantastic! Congratulations!"

"Thanks. That's the first time I've heard those words all day. Bernadette spent the entire day telling everyone that I was chosen because the drama coach felt sorry for me being the new girl. She has everyone saying they scraped the bottom of the barrel this year when casting. The few friends I've made, except Liz and Zane, don't want to have anything to do with me now. They are all threatening to boycott the production!"

"They're jealous Ash, you know that. I know it's not easy, and I don't want to diminish your feelings about it. But could we maybe shelve it for a few days? We'll just focus on tomorrow's show and then move on to the next one."

"Easier said than done, once she starts spreading her poison around here," Ashling said bitterly.

"You're strong, Ashling. You'll get through this."

"I don't think my strategy for dealing with girls like Bernadette would be appreciated in this town." She chewed on a fingernail. "Boris said I should talk to Cari."

"He did?"

"Yeah. I want to be careful not to do anything that she wouldn't like."

Cricket agreed that might not be a bad idea. The real question was, when had Ashling started confiding in Boris?

She watched her daughter march off to join the rest of the chorus. Cricket hated to see her struggle, but it didn't make sense to give it too much attention, knowing they probably wouldn't be here for Bye Bye Birdie anyways.

Just as Cricket began to wonder about dinner, Cari entered with a flourish and strode straight toward her. She had dropped off Soleil and Rosie hours before and had not been seen since. Now, in a state of near euphoria, she pulled Cricket into the kitchen and announced that she wanted to buy St. Agnes's. Restoration efforts would start immediately after the sale was finalized. She would use the money from the sale of the farm.

Cricket didn't know whether to laugh or cry at the news. Of course, she'd love to see things improve at the shelter, but not at the expense of her family being ousted from their new home. It sickened her how selfish that thought made her feel. Cari practically danced her way back into the flurry of activity in the warehouse.

Alone for the first time all day, she paused to process everything that was happening. Her moment of pensive solitude was short lived, as Ashling came barreling in and burst into tears. A torrent of words mixed in with sobs, but Cari couldn't understand a word she said.

She closed the gap between them in three steps and held her tightly hoping to reduce the trembling. "Let's just breathe. Focus on your breath before you tell me what's going on."

Once she had regained some control, the tears turned to searing anger.

"She is a horrible, horrible human being!"

"Bernadette again?"

She scrubbed at her eyes and took a deep breath. "She knows."

"Knows?"

"Somehow, she found out that we were staying at St. Agnes's."

Panic set in. "Did she say something to you?"

"No. I knew something was up because some of the other kids in the chorus were acting weird toward me when I got here. When Liz and Zane came in, they told me Bernadette had texted it to her friends after school and it spread. Mom, everyone knows."

Cricket's heart sank. "It's going to be okay. We're just going to have to find a way to deal with the fallout." The words tasted bitter on her tongue. She said them only to put Ashling at ease. The whole town knowing her business wasn't the problem. But Cari had been insistent that they keep their history a secret. Their future here already teetered on a cliff. This turn of events might push it over the edge.

"I don't want to go back out there."

Liz poked her head through the doorway. "Can we come in?"

Ashling spun around at her voice. "I guess."

Zane followed his sister in, but Liz spoke first. "We wanted to say that we're really sorry Bernadette did this to you. She's the one who's going to end up looking bad."

Ashling didn't respond, so Cricket spoke for her. "Thank you for saying that."

"We don't care where you lived before Blue Cove," Zane said.

Liz gave a half smile. "He's right. Nothing has changed."

"Everything has changed!" Ashling insisted. "I've got to go back out there with everyone staring and whispering about me. They're not even trying to hide it." At Liz's hurt expression,

Ashling walked over and hugged her tightly. "I'm glad I have you guys."

Cricket suggested they leave early and led the way as they reentered the warehouse. She avoided eye contact on her way to collect Max and exited the building with both of her children. Once outside, she scanned the parking lot, unsure what to do. They were supposed to leave with Vera, but the thought of that churned her insides. Spotting Lex hopping into his truck, she shouted to him and started jogging.

"I'm sorry to bother you, but is there any chance you could give us a lift?" She was out of breath. "Our ride fell through."

"Not a problem. Hop in."

Lex didn't give any hint that he'd heard the truth about them yet. Quiet on the ride home, she realized it didn't matter anymore. Right now, she needed to talk to Cari.

When Fiona told Boris about Cari's plans, he felt like he'd had the wind knocked out of him. He'd left Fiona alone for less than an hour to run some errands, and Cari had come by while he was out. Her excitement must have been contagious, because Fiona was bursting with the news. Taking the top prize in the category of impulsivity, Cari had decided to use the money from the sale of the farm to purchase St. Agnes's. She wanted to overhaul the property.

New to the real estate game, she didn't realize that selling Honeycomb Hills wasn't a prerequisite to that goal. There had to be enough equity in the farm to purchase St. Agnes's ten times over and make the necessary renovations. He wanted to know what she planned to do after that. He called and asked how soon he could come over.

Minutes later, he knocked on her door.

"Mind sitting on the porch?" he asked her once she opened the door.

"Sure. Let me grab a jacket."

"So talk," she said, stepping outside and zipping up. "Something must be really nagging at you."

He looked at Cari. "I want you to reject my offer."

She looked shocked. "What? Why?"

"You feel like you need to sell if you're going to buy St. Agnes's, but you're wrong."

"I'm not. I need the money for renovations, and I need the time to set things up properly."

"You don't. If you reject my offer, I will help you decipher Otto's maze of financials. He wasn't great at keeping things organized and asked me to straighten things out a few times, so I'm familiar with what's there."

"It's a disaster. I've been spinning in circles trying to sift through it."

"Once we do that, I'll help you to negotiate the purchase and kick off the renovation. You're going to have to be careful, because you don't want to send those women and children into the street while the work is going on."

"How do you plan to do this when you're back in New York?"

It was a good question. He'd never been more certain of an answer. "I'm not going back."

If possible, she looked even more shocked. "I do need to sit down."

She sat while he began to pace. "I'm not comfortable being so far away from Fiona. She took care of me when I most needed it. Now, it's my turn. Selling her home out from under her is not the answer. You've brought life back to this neighborhood. Spending time with you, and Cricket, and the kids has revitalized her."

"What about your corporation? Your partners?" she blurted out.

"I'm going to ask them to buy me out. This might sound like a snap decision, but it's something I've been thinking about for a long time."

Speechless, Cari stared at him.

"I thought you were happy."

"I was happiest there when I was flipping houses. The big deals we do now come with their own brand of excitement. But there's something fulfilling about beautifying neighborhoods and creating something people fall in love with." He stopped and turned to face her. "No one's falling head over heels for shopping centers. Especially when a large percentage of shopping takes place online these days."

"I can understand your perspective. But, there's still the problem of me running the farm into the ground."

"That's a dramatic statement if I've ever heard one. Cari, you haven't even given it a year. You don't have to do it all alone. You have a team of people at your disposal. Start delegating."

She didn't look completely convinced, but there was a spark of hope in her eyes.

"What are your plans after St. Agnes's is up to snuff?"

"I don't have a degree in social work, so I suppose it'd be another learning curve. Honestly, I think Eleanor Pace is capable of doing an excellent job given the appropriate resources. My ultimate goal is to help the women find long term, stable employment."

"Do you have any positions to offer at the farm?"

She began to shake her head, then stopped abruptly. "I might be going overboard here, but I have an idea."

Leave it to Cari to take one idea and blow it into a million more. He listened as she shared her childhood dream of owning a cafe. Thinking aloud, she wondered if it would be possible to convert the warehouse. It already had a kitchen where they prepared donuts, pies, muffins, and cider amongst other baked goods. What would stop her from adding a few coats of paint, some tables and chairs, and a touch of charm? Waitstaff and counter help could be hired from St. Agnes's.

Before he had a chance to respond, their conversation was interrupted by Lex's truck pulling in the driveway with Cricket and the kids inside. He stood, seeing the expression on Cricket's face as she climbed down.

"Everything okay?" he asked.

"I need to talk to Cari," Cricket stated.

"Should I leave?"

"I suppose it doesn't matter at this point. Let's go inside though. It's freezing out here."

Ashling brought Max into the kitchen for a snack, leaving them to talk privately in the living room. Cricket spoke quickly. Her voice trembled. Boris reeled, furious when she'd finished.

"I knew Bernadette was up to something. She left a casserole on Fiona's porch after school but never knocked. I heard her footsteps and saw her running down the street. She must have overheard our conversation."

Cricket's eyes blazed with unshed tears. "I'm so sorry, Cari. I knew you wanted us to keep our history under wraps. The whole neighborhood will probably be storming at your door by morning over the decrease in their home values."

"Did you think I was protecting myself by hiding how you came to live here?" Cari asked, incredulous. "I couldn't care less what other people think. You should know me better than that by now. I wanted you and the kids to have a fresh start without some stigma attached to you."

They jumped as the doorbell rang. Lex rose in a state of quiet confusion and opened the door to Vera, Tess, and Bernadette. They didn't wait for an invitation and walked past him into the living room.

Tess's face, creased in concern, said, "I want to apologize for my daughter's behavior today and to..."

Bernadette interrupted, "I want to apologize too. When I left Mrs. Glynn's, I should have kept what I'd heard to myself. I didn't give it too much thought and texted two of my friends. Not to be mean. I mean, I know I can be mean. But, in this case I was stunned. My friends must have felt the same way and the whole thing took on a life of its own."

She spoke quickly in a shaking voice, giving Boris the impression she was being honest. He might have done the same thing at her age. Heck, at this point the town was probably filled with grown adults discussing Cricket's personal life not intending ill will, but out of curiosity and concern.

"I don't want her making excuses," Tess insisted. "It was broadcasted because of an error in my daughter's judgement. I want you to know that we are still your friends. We love having you for a neighbor and hope this catastrophe doesn't change that."

Boris glanced at Cricket. It would take time before things returned to normal for her. "It might help if you spoke directly to Ashling," Cricket said finally.

"I'm here," came a firm voice from the entrance to the room. Her stance rigid and her face revealed nothing.

Bernadette shifted from one foot to the other chewing on a nail. After an uncomfortable silence, she stuffed her hands in her coat pockets and walked toward Ashling.

"I'm sorry about what happened today."

"What about the other days?" Ashling asked.

"The other days were about me being jealous."

"Of me?" Ashling was incredulous.

"Yeah, you. You're pretty, you have great hair, then you turned out to be smart too. I should have been nicer." Her voice broke for a moment. "But I swear that I didn't tell my friends about St. Agnes's to be cruel. I was trying to wrap my head around it, and then all of a sudden everyone was talking about it."

"It's okay. People have been pretty nice after hearing the truth."

"It was your truth to tell, not mine."

"It can't be undone, so let's just move forward."

Boris stared at Ashling, marveling at the strength and forgiveness Cricket had instilled in her daughter.

❄

Although that first night she had adamantly insisted she'd make other arrangements for Soleil, Cari didn't breathe another word of it after what became known as "the tour." Christmas Eve morning, it was evident that some online shopping had taken place, as several boxes arrived in the mail.

Cricket needed to take kids to the warehouse an hour before showtime. Vera picked them up on her way over with Liz and Zane. Tess made room for Soleil and Rosie in her car. When they arrived, Cricket paused to stand at the back of the room alone, taking in the scene before her.

The people of Blue Cove were miracle workers. This place was stunning. The dreary cement walls were covered in children's artwork. Twinkling lights drip-dropped across the ceiling. Some of the volunteers painted elaborate murals depicting wintery scenes. A red carpet had been rolled out in the center aisle. A massive Christmas tree towered at the front of the room with empty, but beautifully wrapped boxes spread underneath.

"Rumor has it you were the mastermind behind all this," came a voice behind her. Her mother's voice.

She spun around. "Mom! What are you doing here?"

"Well if that's not a warm welcome then I don't know what is," she said with a half grin.

"Of course you're welcome," Cricket said, throwing her arms around her. Leaning back, she clasped her mother's arms. Tears sprung to her eyes as the enormity of how much she'd missed her mother these past weeks hit her. "I just... How did you know?"

"Ashling called me. She knows how much I love that voice of hers and said I had to be here."

A million questions raced through Cricket's head. How much had Ashling said? Did her mother know the whole story? This was turning into quite the week of bringing secrets out into the open.

"You're wondering what she told me."

Releasing her mother, Cricket tucked her hair behind her ears. "I tried calling you a few times."

"And, I knew something was going on from your messages. I was beginning to worry."

"I'm sorry."

"You could have come to me for help."

"I wasn't about to drop three mouths on your doorstep to feed when I know you're barely making ends meet."

"We would have figured it out. You're not alone in this world."

Cricket swallowed the lump forming in her throat.

"Ashling told me you're staying with a woman named Cari."

"She's wonderful. It's a long story, and I promise to tell you every detail after the show."

"I'm going to hold you to it," her mom said, with another half smile.

Taking their seats in the main hall, Cricket's nerves rattled. Boris and Cari arrived just as the lights were dimming and mouthed hellos. They had both disappeared this afternoon and she'd been wondering what they'd been up to. Her mother looked Boris up and down appraisingly.

"Mm-hm. Does handsome have a name?" she whispered. Cricket rolled her eyes.

Once the curtains opened, she let go of her worries and began to allow herself to enjoy the show. Max, adorable during his song, puffed out his little chest with determination. As Ashling's group walked onto the stage, Cricket forgot to breathe for a moment. Tears sprung to her eyes as her daughter's pure voice poured over the audience. She flushed with pride, not for the first time, at her daughter's fearless spirit.

The spotlight fell on Bernadette. She froze. Even from a distance, the terror registered in her face stilled the audience. Suddenly Ashling stood beside her singing the first few notes. With a nod and squeeze of the hand, she gently prodded Bernadette into joining her. At first, she sang so softly that only Ashling's voice filled the room. Visibly taking a deep breath, her fear seemed to lift as they walked to the center of the stage still holding hands, and both of their voices soared beautifully. As their song came to an end, confetti resembling snow began to fall onto the stage area as all the participants came together for one final song.

A celebration followed at the opposite end of the warehouse. Typically, the room lacked décor, with its gray walls and tables and chairs stacked here and there. Tonight, it glittered, resplendent with lights, a tree, and tables ringed in holly.

"Sorry we were late," Cari said, taking a seat at Cricket's table.

"You made it," she replied with a grin. "That's all that matters."

Boris sat down beside Cricket. "The kids did great. What a voice on Ashling!"

"She doesn't get it from me," Cricket laughed. Then she placed a hand on her mother's arm. "I'd like to introduce you to someone. This is my mom, Cassie. Mom, these are my friends Cari and Boris."

"Your mom!" gasped Cari. "I'm so happy to meet you!"

"Pleasure's mine," she smiled, stretching her arm out to shake hands.

"Ashling and Max must be over the moon that you came to see them!"

"They will be, if they ever make their way over here. Too busy with fans at the moment," her mom laughed, looking pointedly toward a large group of kids.

"Mom, this is Soleil and her adorable daughter Rosie," Cricket added as Soleil joined them and pulled Rosie into her lap.

Cricket stiffened as Nadine also sat down with them. "Wonderful show," she said. "I have to admit, this room is unrecognizable. I didn't think you'd pull it off."

Unsure whether to take her words as a compliment or criticism, Cricket smiled at her and changed the subject directing her gaze toward Boris and Cari. "So, where'd you two disappear to today?"

They looked at each other.

"You tell her, Boris," said Cari with a mischievous grin.

"We spent the afternoon meeting with Cari's lawyer. I can't say he loved us for taking up his time Christmas Eve, but he didn't have the heart to say no when he heard what we were thinking."

"And, what was that?" Cricket asked.

"Cari had a formal offer drawn up to purchase St. Agnes's," Boris said with a grin. "It helps that I've spent so many years in real estate and had some decent templates to start with. Everything moved fairly quickly, and they accepted her offer!"

CHAPTER 26

Speechless, Cricket stared at them. Finding her voice, she asked, "What happens next?"

Cari jumped in, bursting at the seams. "Well, due to the cold weather, there is only so much that can be done on the exterior of St. Agnes's. I'm going to host a New Year's Eve gala to raise funds for the improvements needed on the property. You are well aware that it's crying for a total renovation from basement to attic. Fortunately, this meant a drastically low purchase price for us."

"The rooms at St. Agnes's will be refreshed with paint, furniture, and bedding right away. We'll install accordion walls in the basement and move in bunk beds." Boris grimaced. "Room capacity will decrease slightly but being able to close spaces will allow for some small amount of privacy. We're also adding a much-needed commercial bathroom."

Cricket tried to squash the voice of negativity creeping in, but the whole endeavor sounded impractical.

"What happens if you run out of money?" she asked Cari. "You might be well off, but it would be impossible for you to feed hundreds of people indefinitely. And what about you? Aren't there things you want for yourself? Trips you want to take?"

"Of course, but you should know by now that I'm not into

couture or cars or—or whatever. I didn't earn this money anyways. And I think that as long as I tend to his bees, Uncle Otto would be happy with what I'm doing." She paused to wave at Tina across the room. "Do you know he almost never spent money on himself? Other than good food and the occasional nice bottle of wine, he didn't treat himself. When I looked through his past finances, I found he gave insane amounts to charities."

Cassie smiled. "Must be a genetic trait—generosity."

"I'm not seeking a charitable label. What I want is to convey to people in need that they have a right to be treated like human beings regardless of the season." Cari briefly directed her attention to Nadine. "This isn't merely about giving people a place to stay the night. I know St. Agnes's tries to help the women find jobs, but I'm going to take it one step further. Do you remember my cafe fantasy?"

Cricket nodded. Where was this headed?

"St. Agnes's is round one. The Honeycomb Hills Cafe is round two."

"What?" Cricket's head spun. Was Cari planning to manage the farm and St. Agnes's?

"I'm going to help the women, and they are going to help me."

Cricket's head was reeling. "Cari, I am just not following you. How do you expect to run Honeycomb Hills Farm with all of these other things spinning in the air?"

Boris leaned forward steepling his chin on his fingertips. "Well, miracle of miracles—would you believe it all comes down to my grandmother?"

He explained Fiona had been slowing down prior to her fall. That was the straw that broke the camel's back. She decided to retire from her lengthy career at Sprinkles. She adored her work, but felt the hours were too long at this stage of her life. Cari had been checking in on her as had become part of their routine, and she'd happened to mention it in conversation. Cari hadn't thought much of it at the time, other than to see her friend closing a thirty-two-year chapter of her life spent working in a bakery. It wasn't until she'd lain soaking in her tub with a rare quiet mind that the thought came to her.

Fiona didn't want to retire completely but felt like she didn't have any other choice. Cari had never stopped envisioning herself running a cafe, but believed it impossible given her other responsibilities, not to mention lack of restaurant experience. If Fiona would be willing to serve in a consultant role, Cari just might be able to make this happen. Her farmer's market already had a commercial kitchen where they made pies, jams, and salsa. Yet a vast amount of space stood unused. Only fear of the unknown prevented her from expanding it into a cafe serving breakfast and lunch. She'd love to add on a small patio outside for additional seating.

Overall, it wouldn't require a huge financial investment, because the bones were already there. The women at St. Agnes's would be hired as part time employees until they saved enough money to find permanent housing. It was near impossible to apply for a job without listing a home address. This would allow the women to gain experience and references.

Cari always saw the world through those rose-colored glasses of hers, but she wasn't delusional or stupid. She understood it wouldn't be a walk in the park for many predictable and unforeseen reasons, but it would be worth it. Maybe nothing would change for a percentage of the women, but she was confident the cycle could be broken for some. Sometimes people just needed a lift.

Ever the list maker, she pulled up the notepad on her phone. It outlined a model showing that the income generated from the café would cover salaries and all things related to keeping the lights on and the doors open. Unlike most small business owners, she wouldn't need to take a salary. For this to work, employees would adhere to the same budget she'd laid out for Cricket. Their savings accounts wouldn't be touched until they were ready to leave the shelter.

Cari's next step entailed setting up a nonprofit organization.

She recognized her desperate need of assistance and wouldn't be shy asking for it. Her days of feeling like the whole world rested on her shoulders were long gone.

"My goal is to have everything up and running with inspections signed off by the end of summer. What better month to hold the grand opening of the Honeycomb Hills Cafe than September? It launches the busiest season for the farm."

Cricket knew she was right. "What can I do to help?"

"You've already done more than you know. Cricket's fudge has given me serious inspiration," she explained to the rest of the group. "Think about this. If a woman staying at St. Agnes's has a talent that she's passionate about, such as jewelry making, she can present her product to me and potentially put it up for sale either at the market or the café, under the Honeycomb brand."

Cari acknowledged that she'd have a limited number of positions to fill at the new cafe, and an abundance of women eager to work there. She already dreaded the thought of turning some away and admitted needing more time to figure that out. The idea for women to make and sell things of their own helped to bridge that gap, at least.

Despite previous misgivings, Cricket found herself loving the entire idea. "Cari, I am so glad that you're not giving up on the farm just yet. You are the smartest woman I know—have ever known. You can do this."

"Then you better prepare yourself for me to start delegating some stuff in your direction!" she laughed.

"Bring it! I'd love to be involved."

"I'll talk to Lex tomorrow about who he thinks is ready for more responsibility."

Max appeared behind Cari with his little face pinched in deep thought. "One of the kids in my class said her mom is a homemaker." He smiled with full dimples piercing his pudgy cheeks. "I want to be a homemaker like you guys when I grow up."

"Oh, honey," she laughed ruffling his hair. "We're not homemakers. A homemaker is someone who…"

Cassie finished for her, "makes a home." She beamed at her grandson. "You two might not be prancing around the house in an apron over a house dress circa 1950. But you have clearly created something special for Ashling and Max."

Soleil's eyes glittered. "You create hope."

The car ride home was a flurry of excitement. Ashling had accepted Bernadette's apology last night, but no one would have expected the generosity of spirit she'd shown at the pageant.

"I am so proud of you for so many reasons," Cricket said, looking over her shoulder into the backseat.

"Don't make it a big deal," Ashling mumbled, blushing. "The show must go on, and all that. I couldn't let her flounder up there and ruin the whole performance."

"It was more than that and you know it," Cricket insisted. "After the show, you girls gave me the impression there might be a friendship in the making."

"Mom, it wasn't this huge thing. She thanked me for helping her out on stage, apologized again, and then we started talking about winter break. We'll probably hang out or something."

Cricket turned around and smiled unseen in the front seat. Ashling could deny it all she wanted, but her actions tonight had significantly impacted her relationship with Bernadette.

"Oh, something kinda huge did happen though."

"What was that?"

"Zane invited me to a movie the day after Christmas. Can I go?"

Cricket stifled the urge to giggle, hearing the excited tremor in Ashling's voice.

"Just the two of you?"

"Liz and her friend Joel are going too."

Cricket wasn't ready for this phase of motherhood, but reassured herself with the fact that at least they weren't driving themselves anywhere yet. "It's fine. Let me know the details before then." Out of the corner of her eye, she could see Cari failing miserably at trying to hide her smile.

When they arrived home, the kids were still consumed with the thrill of the successful pageant and the idea of Ashling going on her first date. Add to that the fact it was Christmas Eve and their levels of euphoria soared sky high. Cricket still had a smile on her face after getting them to bed.

Cari stopped her in the hallway. "I'm about to make that smile even wider. Join me in my office for a minute?"

The laptop on her desk opened to a spreadsheet. "Christmas came early for you," she said, handing her a check.

Cricket had to look closer to be sure she was correctly reading the amount. Cari grinned from ear to ear.

"Every last piece of your fudge has been sold. And might I add that Pia said the phone has been ringing off the hook with people calling to see if it's been restocked? Looks like you might be on your way to starting a little business for yourself."

"Do you think sales will go down after the holiday?"

"Maybe, but we have customers coming in year-round. Fudge isn't a seasonal product. Don't forget, our online store is growing. There's no reason we can't ship fudge. We might be having that talk about splitting profits sooner rather than later. You're also going to have to think about setting up a new schedule. Working all day and all night is not sustainable."

Cricket agreed with that sentiment after running on empty too many consecutive days. Going to bed at a decent hour tonight was Christmas gift enough for her.

At almost ten thirty, Cricket started up the stairs to her bedroom after checking the locks when she heard a light knock at the door. She nearly jumped out of her skin. Peeking through a window, she saw Boris on the porch. He spoke first as she pulled open the door.

"I know I'm here without calling first, and I know it's late. I never would have rung the bell and woken everyone, but I'd also never sleep tonight if I didn't come over and at least try to see if you were still up. The light was on, so..."

"Give me your coat, we can sit in the library where it's quiet."

Sitting down on the rich, brown leather couch, Cricket looked at him expectantly. After a few moments, Boris moved to join her.

"I'm just going to get straight to the point. I was wrong to get upset with you when I learned the truth." He ran a hand through his hair and leaned forward, resting his elbows on his thighs. "There's no other way to say it. I am very sorry."

"Thank you. I'm sorry too. I should have told you the truth."

"You had some valid reasons not to. I'm also here to tell you that I'm moving back to Blue Cove."

Her heart skipped a beat, but she tried to hide it. "Fiona must be thrilled."

"Fiona isn't the only reason for the move."

"Will you open a branch of Glynn, Stone, and West here?"

"I've asked my partners to buy me out. The plan is to launch a smaller company here. I'm not meant to sit behind a desk."

"I'm really happy for you." Her voice was even, but her pulse raced at record speed.

"It gets better. Cari has already agreed to hire me for the shelter renovation and to build the cafe. I've got to get started right after Christmas, but I've already tapped a few people I used to work with, and they're on board."

A sliver of worry ran through Cricket. What would this mean for her? For them? Cari had given her an opportunity to change her life. She wasn't going to waste it. She refused to risk becoming dependent on anyone other than herself ever again and knew better than anyone that there are no guarantees.

Cynical? Maybe. Practical? Definitely. She had two goals. First, help her children to grow into responsible adults. And second, build a career for herself to be able to stand on her own two feet and provide for her family. She wasn't sure she had enough energy for a third goal. Relationships require work.

"That's great." She feigned a yawn. "I should get to bed. Max will have us up before the sun."

She could see he wasn't ready to end the conversation, his eyes told her everything she needed to know. He didn't press her to stay, but as she said good-bye at the door, her stomach lurched with sorrow at the hurt and confusion registering in his expression.

CHAPTER 27

Max's squeals had everyone up at the first sign of daylight. Cricket smiled at the memory of him tearing open the gifts in a joyful blur. He had worn himself out and currently lay sound asleep under the tree, with his head resting on the three-foot plush Tyrannosaurus rex Cari had not so carefully hidden behind the lower branches.

Ashling had already opened her jewelry kit and was hard at work in the kitchen creating her first necklace. Rosie slept on Soleil's chest, and Cari lounged on the recliner.

"This might be the most fun I've ever had on Christmas morning," Cari said happily.

Cricket raised an eyebrow. "Even as a kid?"

"You forget that my childhood wasn't a glamorous one." She sat up, closing the footrest. "This morning, my heart is full."

"You only have yourself to thank. We could have been waking up today on bunk beds at St. Agnes's."

"Worse," interrupted Soleil in a whisper. "We could have been waking up on mattresses on the floor of that musty basement if we hadn't been lucky enough to have some of Cari's fairy dust sprinkled on us."

"What do you say we spread some of it around?" Cari looked

234

back and forth between them. "I'm sure they could use some extra hands serving dinner over at the shelter. They're eating at noon and we don't have to be at Fiona's until four. I was going to go on my own, but the more the merrier. Ashling has become quite the dedicated volunteer lately. She reminds me at least once a day to let her know if I'm going."

Cricket stood. "I'm in."

Soleil wavered.

Cari guessed at what the problem might be. "If Rosie doesn't last, one of us can drive you back here."

"That works. It's just—I've been putting off bringing this up. I think it's because I'm afraid of the answer, but at the same time I can't stand the not knowing. We can't stay here forever. What happens next?"

Cari crossed her legs and leaned forward. "I'm not going to get up some morning and decide it's time for you to go. That said, it's not practical for me to make a habit of having random people move into my house."

"Of course not," Soleil agreed.

"Give me some time to think it over. I promise that you and Rosie won't have to worry about sleeping in a basement or on a kitchen floor again. We'll work together to find a solution." She pursed her lips. "I'm sorry. That's still not the closure you're looking for."

"No. But I'm going to choose to see it as the new beginning that I didn't expect to receive."

Cari tried to call ahead to let Eleanor know they'd be coming in but didn't leave a message when the voicemail kicked on. When the bunch of them stepped into the dining hall, Eleanor's head jerked up with an initial expression of dread at having more mouths to feed. Recognizing Cari, she came rushing over.

"We'd like to help out however we can," Cari greeted her.

"I don't know what to say. This is a wonderful surprise. Cricket, Soleil," she said nodding at each of them. "It's nice to see you again."

"Thank you, Eleanor, for doing what you could to make us comfortable while we were here," Cricket said sincerely.

Eleanor shifted her eyes toward Soleil. "I try. Sometimes, I know that's not enough."

"You didn't turn us away the night we arrived. At that moment, it was more than enough." She gestured to the line snaking around the room. "You might want to start doling out our jobs."

Hours later, after they'd had time to go home, change their clothes, and squeeze in an extra nap for Max and Rosie, they found themselves in Fiona's living room surrounded by food, music, and laughs. Nadine's greeting would never be considered warm, but she tried to be pleasant. Pia perched next to Cassie to spill all the details about Cricket's new business venture. Cricket watched Nadine listen in with interest spreading over her face until Boris interrupted her delight in that moment, inviting her onto the back deck for some privacy. He held a gift behind his back.

"You're not very subtle you know," Cricket giggled, pulling a gift from her pocketbook.

"You open mine first," he insisted as they exchanged presents.

Tearing off the paper, her jaw dropped. In her hands was the exact same picture she had printed for him. The only difference was the frame.

"It's perfect! Open yours."

As the wrapping paper fell, he laughed out loud. "I could have asked for nothing more!"

"Nothing?" she asked with a tilt of her chin.

"I have everything I never knew I wanted," he said bending his head to kiss her.

Cricket's life up to that moment flashed through her brain. Here was this sweet, caring man ready to share his wonderful world with her. She suspected he loved her and jerked away at the flash of that revelation.

"I'm so sorry, Boris. It would be so easy for me to fall into your arms and let you take care of me forever." She was afraid to step back because he might never pull her toward him again, but she did it anyways. "I haven't become what I'm going to be yet. That has to come first, or it will never happen." She took a deep breath. "It's not a 'never.' It's an 'until.' I haven't done much right in my life. But this I'm going to do right. It would break my heart to let you go," she paused, her voice cracking. "If you can live with this situation, I'd love for us to continue on as is. But, if you need more, I can understand and respect that. If you need to move on and find someone else who can give you what you're looking for, I care enough about your happiness to accept that." A few tears escaped, and it was all she could do to not totally fall apart as Boris stood there, staring.

"You have to know that Fiona and my job aren't the only reasons for me moving back here."

She knew what was coming but wasn't sure she wanted to hear it. Placing a hand tentatively on his arm, "Boris, you can't base this decision on me. Please take me out of the equation altogether." Yes, she had missed Boris the past few days, but she also found that there was more than enough to occupy her time. She cared for him, but it was important to not lose sight of her goal.

"Are you saying you don't want to see me anymore?"

"No, I'm saying that I'm not in a position to make promises to anyone other than my children. I have been given the ultimate gift of an opportunity to rebuild my life and to ensure a real future for Ashling and Max. To make the most of that opportunity, I need to focus on achieving my own goals first." She grabbed both of his hands.

"It's only fair to let you know that you cannot come first in my life right now. Not first, not second, or even third. I've already been down the road of married life with a family, and I'm not in a rush to do it again right now. Maybe someday, but at the moment I have other plans." She attempted a watery smile. "You are young and handsome, with everything to offer someone. If you want a wife and babies in your near future, I understand if you need to move on."

He took her face in his hands and kissed her. She could feel more tears filling up behind her eyes.

"Cricket Williams, I'm not going anywhere. I don't care where I fall on your list, as long as I'm on it."

At that moment, all hope was lost of holding back the tears as she returned his kiss.

Don't miss out on your next favorite book!
Join the Satin Romance mailing list
www.satinromance.com/mail.html

THANK YOU FOR READING

Did you enjoy this book?

We invite you to leave a review at your favorite book site, such as Goodreads, Amazon, Barnes & Noble, etc.

DID YOU KNOW THAT LEAVING A REVIEW...

- Helps other readers find books they may enjoy.
- Gives you a chance to let your voice be heard.
- Gives authors recognition for their hard work.
- Doesn't have to be long. A sentence or two about why you liked the book will do.

ABOUT THE AUTHOR

Jill Piscitello is a teacher with a passion for writing and an avid fan of multiple literary genres. Although she divides her reading hours among several books at a time, a lighthearted story offering an escape from the real world can always be found on her nightstand.

A native of New England, Jill lives with her family and three well-loved cats. When not planning lessons or reading and writing, she can be found spending time with her family, traveling, and going on light hikes. Jill loves to try out new restaurants, but if truth be told, she will order a chicken Caesar salad wrap whenever possible.

www.jillpiscitello.com

 twitter.com/Piscj18
 instagram.com/jillpiscitellobooks

Made in the USA
Coppell, TX
22 January 2021